BOOK TWO

THE FAE REALM SERIES

CATHLIN SHAHRIARY

**Exile**
**by Cathlin Shahriary**

Cover design by Indie Solutions by Murphy Rae
Formatting by Alyssa Garcia at Uplifting Designs

*To Callie,*
*Because you asked for more*

# EXILE

# CHAPTER 1

## Conall

**IT'S BEEN** 7 *days, 8 hours, and 23 Fae minutes since I last saw her beautiful face, since I last gazed into her gorgeous violet eyes, my beautiful Ianthe...not that I am counting or anything.* Conall sighed as thoughts of her swirled through his mind. He had tried countless times to reach her in the dream realm, but just like the first time he had returned to Fae after meeting her, he'd found it to be impossible. Conall recalled that Ianthe was able to visit with her aunt in her dreams while she stayed at the palace in Fae, but he suspected it was only due to their shared bloodline, or perhaps the fact that human minds were easier to manipulate than those of the Fae. Perhaps her powers weren't strong enough to breach the realms yet, although it was always difficult to tell with half Fae. Ianthe's powers might continue to develop, or this could be a permanent limitation. His every thought seemed to center on her, and he missed her as if a portion of his own heart was gone.

The truth of that statement struck a chord deep within him: a portion of his heart was gone.

He had given it to her.

He surmised she must worry about him and the way things had ended. He'd tried to send word to her with Alfie, his old tutor and confidant, before he left. He stole away the morning of his departure to speak with Alfie in private, and Alfie assured him he would do his best to get his message to Ianthe. He was the only one Conall trusted. Conall wished King Corydon hadn't sent him on a mission so quickly so he could've told Ianthe what was going on and shown her he was okay. He guessed he had Casimir to thank for that. Stupid, foolish Casimir. Apparently, after their confrontation in the woods, Casimir had gone on a rage-filled rampage, picking fights with anyone within reach, including some Seelie soldiers, and now Conall was the one who had to smooth things over. Hopefully, after this mission, he could request leave. He yearned to return to his beloved every day, and he worried she might doubt his love the longer he stayed away.

Conall shook his head, trying to dislodge his thoughts of Ianthe and instead refocus on his mission. His company, which included several of his most loyal soldiers and the king's advisor, Drummond, was moments away from crossing the Seelie border, and he needed to be on high alert. He knew that even though they came to discuss peace, Casimir's actions would have put the Seelie on edge. "All right lads, be on the lookout for any Seelies. Even though we've come to negotiate peace, that does not mean they will be peaceful in the beginning. Only defensive maneuvers allowed." At that comment, a couple of the soldiers groaned, but he pressed on. "We do not want to exacerbate the situation into a full-blown war. Avoid physical confrontation if at all possible." Drummond gave his nod of approval, and

Conall waited for the men to meet his eyes, acknowledging his orders. He would not have anyone under his command make the situation ahead of them any more difficult. After a short pause, they all bowed their heads or nodded to acknowledge what he'd said.

He pulled his horse to the front of the company and trotted farther down the dirt road, crossing into Seelie territory. He knew it wouldn't be long until they encountered someone. He just hoped whoever they met had been informed of his mission and would not attack or provoke his men. While he was the first in command, he was no king, and his men were Unseelie soldiers who thrived on violence with every bone in their body. The men progressed deeper into Seelie territory, heading through the woods toward the Seelie king's castle. A snap to Conall's left brought him up short. He yanked on the reins of his horse and raised his hand to halt his men. Several swords were drawn within a heartbeat as they paused to see what was to come next. Within moments, Seelie soldiers stepped into the sunlight to Conall's left, followed by others inching forward to his right. Without even realizing it, his men had been surrounded.

"Greetings, warriors. I have been sent by King Corydon to discuss peace with King Lachlan. We do not wish for a confrontation on our journey." Conall spoke calmly and with authority.

One Seelie warrior brought his horse through the encroaching circle of soldiers. His steed was black as night, matching the hair upon his head, which shone against his deeply tanned skin and amber eyes. He looked as deadly as the aura that surrounded him. Had Conall not known he was Seelie, he would have sworn the knight craved the fight in front of him, but most Seelie were peaceful people. The soldiers parted ways, allowing the dark warrior to pass, an action that reinforced Conall's belief in his authority over the soldiers.

"No confrontation, you say?" The warrior scoffed, his cocky voice interrupting the silence that had fallen among the men. "Maybe you should have told that to Casimir before he slaughtered my brother." The Seelie surrounding Conall's company drew their swords as the tension grew among the warriors from both parties.

# CHAPTER 2

## Ianthe

**I**ANTHE SIGHED AS she climbed out of her car in the school parking lot. *Thank God I only have one more year of this place. The rumors about me have most likely multiplied since the last time anyone from school saw me was when I was at the house party the night Casimir attacked me. Who knows what they have said about me since then? I'm sure the words 'crazy' and 'loser' were thrown around.* Her fingers gripped the car door tightly as thoughts swirled within her, causing a growing unease. She glanced down at her wrist and smiled. It seemed to be a new habit. Instead of snapping her elastic, all she had to do was glance down and see Conall's leather tie wrapped around her wrist. Even though all of his calming essence had been used up, it still gave her strength. It was a reminder of what she had already overcome and of those who believed in her.

*Man, do I miss him.* She wondered what was keeping

him away. She hoped he hadn't decided she wasn't worth the trouble, but she would have been lying if she said the thought hadn't crossed her mind—any girl is bound to have insecurities after not seeing her guy for a while. She knew something had to be keeping him from her, or he would have made it back to her before she left Aunt Grace's place where she had spent the remainder of her summer. *Maybe King Corydon forbade him from seeing me. I hope Casimir took my threat seriously and isn't causing problems for him.* So many questions, so many what-ifs and maybes. There were many nights when she couldn't sleep because of all the thoughts bouncing around her head. She knew from experience this train of thought would only make her depressed, so she pulled herself back into the moment at hand—the first day of school.

Ianthe traced her fingers across the smooth leather once more before grabbing her backpack and closing the car door. She trudged toward the building, ignoring the stares and whispers already happening around her. As she climbed the steps to her high school, she glanced to her right and noticed a familiar tiny brunette with overly bronzed skin wearing gold, strappy, wedged sandals and a rather short, pink lace skirt. "What are you looking at, freak?" Aubrey's acidic voice cut through Ianthe's thoughts as her gaze reached Aubrey's low-cut white tank. A flash of a memory flickered through her head—sleepovers and shopping trips with Aubrey, giggling and gushing about guys. *She used to worship the ground I walked on, calling me for every little piece of advice.* It seemed like a lifetime ago, not just the previous year.

"Oh my god, is she still on drugs?" Beth, the school's resident queen Barbie and mean girl, fake whispered to Aubrey. Ianthe supposed she had paused longer than she thought. She tore her gaze from her ex-friends, focused on the day ahead, and tried her best to ignore the stares as she stepped through the door.

She had decided to start going by her first name that year. She knew most people would probably still call her Lola, and she would probably still answer to it. However, after the summer, she felt like a new person, and she was hoping her name would help people realize she wasn't the same girl she had been before. Since most of her teachers were new, she simply wouldn't correct them when they used their roster and called out Ianthe instead of Lola, like she had in the past. The students, on the other hand, would take some time. She grabbed her schedule from her bag and located her locker as the first bell rang and the hall flooded with students. She took a moment to observe her surroundings. It seemed surreal to be back after everything she had been through the previous months. Hell, she wasn't even fully human, something she was attempting to come to terms with.

To go with the new self, she had a new look. Since the reason behind the dark hair was to piss off her father—unsuccessfully, she might add—she decided to do something that would make her happy. She had the dye stripped from her pale blonde locks and exchanged the blue streaks for a vibrant lavender. She smiled, remembering how Conall loved her blue streaks. He'd probably be surprised, but she knew a little thing like hair color wouldn't change how he felt. Her pale blonde, almost white hair was lighter than her mother's golden blonde, but she knew she looked more like her mom with it. Of course, she still loved a bit of color, a touch of rebellion, and the purple was a silent reminder of the violet flowers Conall used to leave for her. The combination complimented her violet eyes perfectly, but she also knew it might cause the gossip mill to go into overdrive.

She glanced down the hallway, noticing a new girl a few lockers down from her. The girl had wavy, fiery red hair and a unique style all her own. Her nails were painted a myriad of colors and patterns unique to each finger. It looked like a rainbow explosion, but somehow it worked for her. She wore frayed skinny jeans with teal Converse, a Star Wars t-shirt, and a worn, black, leather jacket. She was gorgeous in an unexpected way, a fact that several boys had already noticed. Bryce, star soccer player and conceited douche from Ianthe's former circle, groped the girl's backside as he walked by. He turned around and winked at the redhead with a cocky smile as he said, "Love me some fresh meat."

The girl spun on him, smiled coyly, and Ianthe sighed. She had higher hopes for the new girl. She had hoped someone else would see through the popular crowd's bullshit. She watched as the fiery redhead strutted up to Bryce, running a hand up his muscular arm. Bryce's smile grew, but it only took a second for the girl's knee to reach his groin and his groaning to echo down the hall. The guys around him immediately stepped back, and a few reached down as if to block her attack. "Touch me again, asshole, and I will cut it off," the girl spat out before flipping her hair and returning to her locker. Ianthe's booming laughter bounced off the walls. The new girl was officially her hero. Bryce continued to writhe on the floor, holding his junk and moaning while the guys stepped forward to help him up.

"Crazy bitch," he hissed before catching sight of Ianthe laughing at his misfortune. "What are you laughing at, Lola?" He aimed his anger her way.

She chuckled. "Oh, just a pathetic loser getting exactly what he deserves. Karma's a bitch, ain't it?" She grinned before closing her locker and walking toward the fiery redhead. "Can I just say you are my hero?" The girl smiled politely at her. "No, seriously, I've wanted to do that for ages. I'm Ianthe, by the way," she said, holding out her hand. She drew out each syllable as she said her name (eye-AN-thee) so the new girl could grasp the proper pronunciation.

"Callie," the girl replied as she shook the proffered hand. "Ianthe, huh? That's a unique name."

"Yep, it's Greek for 'violet flower'." She smiled, remembering Grace's explanation of her name.

"Oh, like your eyes," Callie observed.

She looked into Callie's hazel eyes. "Exactly. I used to go by Lola, my middle name, but this year I decided it was time for a change."

"I like it." Callie looked her up and down. "Fits you a lot better than Lola. So, Ianthe, do you know how to get to Ms. Wolf's English class?" She held her schedule out for Ianthe to see.

"Yep, just follow me."

Callie linked their arms together, a comforting gesture, and Ianthe knew immediately that she had made a friend, perhaps the first true friend since Conall and Alfie.

# CHAPTER 3

*Conall*

AS MUCH AS Conall didn't want a fight, this guy was trying hard to start one. "I am sorry for your loss, but Casimir is not with us. King Corydon will make sure you get the retribution you seek. We merely wish to negotiate a peace treaty with your king. If you do not allow us to pass, you will force my hand," Conall stated, fingering his own weapon at his side. He had yet to draw it, refusing to be intimidated by the Seelie knight in front of him.

A figure loomed in the distance, approaching with great speed. "Evin, let them pass!" yelled a man Conall quickly recognized as Torin, the Seelie king's first in command.

"But, Father, they are Unseelie. Their future leader murdered Reid," Evin growled, looking toward the imposing figure who had now breached their circle.

"I understand, son. You seek retribution for your loss. I

do too, but this is not the way and you know it." Then Torin turned his attention to Conall. "My apologies, Conall.
Evin is still training in his position and has a lot to learn."
Torin's eyes glared with meaning toward his son. "Please,
follow me, and I will lead you to the king. He's awaiting
your arrival."

Conall had dealt with Torin many times in past negotiations and had always found him to be a very logical and
serious man. "Thank you, Torin," he answered, nodding
for his men to accompany him behind Torin's lead. Evin
growled again and yanked his horse to the left, racing off
toward an unknown location.

"I swear that one will turn all my hair grey before
long." Torin sighed under his breath while the rest of the
Seelie warriors fell in line behind the Unseelie.

The men rode for the entire day before they were able
to see the Seelie castle looming in the distance. Most of
Conall's company kept their distance from the Seelie soldiers, not wanting to converse with them. Drummond and
Conall shared meals with Torin during the ride, maintain-
ing polite conversation and attempting to garner favor with
him before their meeting with Lachlan. Conall always
found that if you had the respect of people right below the
king, the king himself would be more likely to respect you.
Perhaps this was one more reason why he was so good
at negotiations. During the remainder of their journey, he
didn't see any sign of Evin, so he assumed the man must
have returned home.

When they reached the castle, they dismounted their
steeds. Conall's soldiers were directed to care for the horses while Conall, two of his men, and Drummond entered
the castle. They were led to the throne room where they
would complete negotiations with the king. There was a
small table set below the dais where the throne resided,

and King Lachlan remained seated in his throne as if the whole idea of negotiating peace tired him.

Conall approached the table and bowed before him. "Greetings, King Lachlan. King Corydon sent us to formally apologize for Prince Casimir's actions. I do hope we can reach an agreement and avoid a war." The king motioned with his hand for them to sit, so Conall sat at the table and Drummond took the place to his right, while the two soldiers stood behind them.

King Lachlan remained seated as he sighed and turned his attention toward Conall. "I grow weary of these conversations, Conall. I thought we had reached an understanding the last time you were here." He raised his eyebrow to see if Conall recalled their previous negotiation and terms.

Conall rose from his seat. This was the part of the job he hated the most. This was why he often considered leaving Ianthe alone for good, because she deserved better than the monster he had become for King Corydon. In one smooth motion he drew his sword from its scabbard and raised it in front of him as he pivoted toward his own soldier. He forced his peaceful aura to encompass the warrior as he thrust the sword directly into the man's heart and whispered the words, "Thank you for your service, warrior. Godspeed." He then withdrew his blade, knowing it had been an instantaneous and relatively painless death, and turned back toward the king. "Prince Casimir's blood debt has been paid—a life for a life, as was agreed upon at our last meeting." He wiped the blade of his sword against his brown leather pants before returning it to its sheath then reclaimed his seat without glancing toward Drummond or the other soldier. He knew the judgment and disdain he would see upon their expressions. He couldn't process the guilt or the pain that came with taking a life, not there, right in front of an enemy. He had to look as cold as ice, as cold as King Corydon himself. It was his duty and what he had been raised to do.

# CHAPTER 4

## *Ianthe*

**T**HE **FIRST DAY** of school passed quickly. Ianthe only had two classes with Callie—Spanish and calculus—but she was beyond relieved to discover they both had calculus for fourth period so they shared the same lunch break. They ate outside, enjoying the weather before it got too cold to do so. Over lunch, she and Callie discovered they liked the same music, shared a love of the Winchester and Salvatore brothers, and both had a secret passion for getting lost in a good book. It was nice to have a friend she could truly be herself around—well, her human self, at least. No way could she to let Callie see the other half of her; no one could know about that.

After lunch, she had the unfortunate experience of being assigned a seat in physics directly in front of Bryce. She sighed, sitting down at her desk. She could already tell it was going to be a long semester. The overdose of Abercrombie cologne wafting from him almost made her gag, and the only thing worse would have been sitting next to Aubrey or Beth. Of course, at that exact moment, the buxom blonde Barbie decided to make a tardy entrance.

Ianthe sighed. She couldn't help the disappointment that washed over her. It hadn't always been this way, and sometimes it was hard to ignore what used to be. Beth had been her closest confidant when they were younger, their friendship only strengthening when they got to high school and were taken in by the popular crowd. Of course, she had been too blind to see it was popularity that had attracted Beth to her all along, so the minute she fell from grace, Beth was the first to start rumors and never failed to torture her in person. Come to think of it, Beth seemed to enjoy her misery so much it wouldn't surprise her if she turned out to be part Unseelie.

She smiled at that thought as Beth sat in the seat to the right of Bryce (and thankfully not the one next to her). *After facing a room full of Unseelie Fae at my bacchanalia and battling with Casimir, facing off with Bryce and Beth doesn't seem all that bad.* Besides, she had a secret weapon, even though she didn't particularly relish the idea of using her Mara magic on unsuspecting humans, no matter how much they deserved it.

"Ugh, what is she so happy about? If I were a loser like her, I wouldn't have a reason to smile. In fact, I would just overdose and end it all." Beth's overly loud whispers interrupted her thoughts.

"Maybe she got some play from the new redhead. Batting for the girls' team would definitely explain why she wasn't affected by my charm," Bryce replied, rubbing his knuckles against his navy polo.

Ianthe snorted at the reminder of Callie's assault on Bryce that morning and turned around in her seat. She smirked at both of them before narrowing her focus on Bryce. "Really Bryce? If that were the reason women at this school were 'immune to your charms', more than half of the female population would be lesbians. Pretty sure the reason is just you." The shock on both their faces was priceless. They probably assumed she would withdraw from their insults or ignore them like the old Lola would have. Nothing had prepared them for this new version of her—the real her.

She turned back around in her seat as the teacher began his lecture. A smile graced her lips. She knew Conall would have been proud to see her standing up for herself. *And who are they to try to put me down? I am a freaking princess, after all. I don't have to take their crap anymore.*

# CHAPTER 5

*Conall*

**A**FTER THE GREETING in the throne room, King Lachlan had a servant show Conall, Drummond, and their remaining soldiers to the guest quarters. The Fae believed it was bad luck to conduct business in the same room with a dead body, so further discussion would have to wait for the body to be removed and the hall to be cleaned. Dinner would be brought to their rooms, and the peace negotiations would commence the next day since the blood debt had been paid. He would discover what the Seelie would further require to smooth over Casimir's mistakes. He was grateful for the reprieve from the scrutiny of others and to be left alone in his room with his thoughts. If Casimir were there himself, Conall would be sorely tempted to use his blood to pay the debt. He still wasn't exactly sure what had transpired between Casimir and Ianthe while he was injured, but Casimir was not happy. *What will I do when Casimir inherits the Un-*

*seelie throne? He certainly won't want me as his first in command,* Conall wondered.

It wasn't the first time his thoughts had wandered toward the future. He hadn't mulled over such things in the past. He had never doubted his place in this life until he met Ianthe. He used to feel honored to serve as the king's first in command. He knew his place in the world and his direction in life. Things were safe and predictable, but now... now everything had changed. It had changed the moment he'd set eyes on her at her aunt's house. Even then, he had bent the rules for her, sneaking into her room at night to wake her from those horrible nightmares. Of course, he always snuck back out before she realized he had been there, but he couldn't help himself; he never could when it came to her. He didn't know exactly what it was that drew him to her, but it was a powerful force.

He couldn't wait until these negotiations were done and he could sneak away to see her again. He had suspicions that part of the reason he was on this mission was because Corydon didn't want him going after her. He knew she had been exiled, but his life in the Fae realm didn't seem to matter much anymore. He could fit into the human world if it meant being with her. He was half human after all.

He dreaded what would happen if she discovered what it truly meant to serve as the king's first in command. When she last stayed in the castle, she was naïve about many things, including what his position entailed. She was either too stubborn to admit she was naïve, or she really didn't want to know the truth, because she never questioned him beyond his vague explanations. He knew she wouldn't approve of what he did. It was one thing to slay men in battle, another to slaughter an innocent soldier from your own ranks as he had just done. Although, being Unseelie, he was sure the soldier wasn't entirely innocent, but he'd certainly had nothing to do with the crime committed. Guilt settled into his belly like a brick. He'd always felt a twinge of regret paying a blood debt, but nothing like this. He didn't think he would last much longer in this role if he wanted to be the sort of man who could be worthy of Ianthe.

*Oh, sweet Ianthe, I miss you so much.* He removed the elastic band holding back his hair and smiled, remembering how it had once graced her wrist. He used to hate the thing and the way she kept snapping it to hurt herself. He still didn't quite understand why she did that, but he was glad to have something of hers. He wondered if she still wore his leather strap around her wrist. The magic would be long gone, but it would mean she still cared for him. He ran his fingers through his hair. *Gods, I need to get away and see her. This constant doubt and silence is driving me insane. Loving her may just be the death of me.*

A knock interrupted his thoughts and a servant stepped inside with his dinner. Had it been a time before Ianthe, he might have been tempted by her. She had a lithe figure and wavy golden hair pinned back on her head. Her sapphire eyes glittered and she smiled flirtatiously. "Your dinner, sir." She bowed, although it was unnecessary, and Conall worried she might topple out of her dress. It wasn't unusual for Seelie girls to flirt with him; some of them were drawn to the bad boy image of the Unseelie. He wasn't sure if they knew of his half-human heritage and just didn't care, or perhaps to them it made the forbidden fruit that much sweeter.

"Thank you…" He trailed off as he did not know her name.

"Arabella," she said as she blushed. He expected her to leave with the thanks, but she lingered. "Perhaps you would like some company with your meal," she suggested, licking her lips. In the past, he might have taken her up on her offer. In fact, the last time he had visited, he'd enjoyed the evening with a Seelie noble's daughter, Bronwen. She was a delicate thing with curves in all the right places and soft chestnut ringlets. She was drawn to him like a moth to the flame. He hoped he would not run into her on this visit, since they had not parted on good terms. She thought a night in his bed meant a permanent place in his life, when that was not the case.

Arabella's eyes shone with hope at Conall's silence. "No thank you, Arabella. I'm quite fine on my own." Her face fell with the rejection, and she quickly left the room. He sighed. The only company he craved at that moment was a certain violet-eyed princess. He ate his meal and got ready for bed. As he did every night, he centered his thoughts on Ianthe just in case she might find a way to cross the realms. Just in case…

# CHAPTER 6

*Ianthe*

**THE REST OF** Ianthe's day passed rather uneventfully, including Spanish class with Callie.
*I'm not sure when I might need to use Spanish.
It would probably be better for me if they offered a course
in ancient Fae languages.* She chuckled at her own joke.
Callie was right about one thing: they fit together like they
were sisters separated at birth. Before leaving school, they
put each other's numbers into their cellphones, and she
won a place in Callie's heart by promising to stop by Starbucks on her way to school the next morning to grab them
both a morning pick-me-up for their second day.

She pulled her car up to an empty house. It would be a
few hours before her dad arrived home. It was still a little
weird knowing he wasn't her biological father, but honestly when she compared the two, she would choose him over
Corydon any day. She decided to get her homework out of
the way. Yes, apparently some teachers do believe in giv-

ing homework on the first day of class. With it being her senior year, it seemed everything the teachers did was in order to prepare the students for college and the real world.

An hour and a half later, with her homework completed, she decided to watch some Netflix in order to reward herself. She scrolled through her queue and decided a mini *Buffy* marathon would be enough to cheer any girl up. *Who doesn't love David Boreanaz and James Marsters, AKA Angel and Spike? Both of them are quintessential bad boys with hearts of gold.*

Several episodes later, she decided to cook dinner. One of the things she'd brought back from Aunt Grace's house along with her broken heart was a book full of recipes Grace had written for her while she was being held captive at the Unseelie palace. Her aunt had included recipes they had made together that summer, recipes Grace's mother had passed down to her and, of course, Ianthe's mother's favorite recipes. Ianthe made it her goal to make dinner at least once a week from Grace's book. It would make her think of her aunt and the good times they'd shared that summer. Tonight she had planned on the pasta marinara with fresh basil that Grace had made on her first night at the cottage.

At seven o'clock she decided she had waited for her father long enough and ate the dinner she had spent an hour preparing alone. *I don't know why I expected him to come home or at least call.* She missed the family meals she had shared with Aunt Grace, but this was the way things always were with her dad. After her meal, she wrapped up a plate for him, set it in the microwave, packed up the rest of the leftovers, and put a sticky note on the fridge telling her dad where he could find his dinner. She headed upstairs to her room. Their house was ostentatiously large for just the two of them, but it was all about her dad's image. Sometimes it felt a little creepy being in such a large house alone, but she knew they had a state-of-the-art security system and that helped ease some of her paranoia.

Once she got to her room, she sat down at her desk, booted up her laptop, and video chatted with Aunt Grace. In a spark of genius, she had set up a video chat app on Grace's computer before she left so they didn't always have to depend on dreams to see each other. After a few rings, Aunt Grace's beautifully wrinkled face appeared on her screen with a grin that stretched from ear to ear. Ianthe couldn't help but smile in return.

"Aunt Grace! I miss you!" she gushed before the woman could even speak.

"I miss you too, sweetheart. How was your first day of school?" Grace asked. She filled her aunt in on her day and her classes, including her new bestie, Callie. "I'm so glad you were able to make a friend so quickly. It makes me happy to see you moving on," Grace commented.

"Moving on?" Her smile vanished at the idea.

Aunt Grace realized her mistake. "Well, dear, I know you may not want to hear it, but it's probably for the best. I know how much you cared for Conall, but with you now being exiled from the Fae realm, you know it can't work." Grace was the voice of reason, but that didn't mean Ianthe wanted to hear it.

"I love him, Aunt Grace. We'll figure it out. I'm sure Corydon is just keeping him busy," she tried to argue, but even as the words left her lips, she realized how lame the excuse sounded. "Have you heard anything from your contact on the other side?" She desperately hoped for any news of him, no matter how insignificant, every time they spoke.

Aunt Grace offered a sad smile of condolence. "Yes,

23

I spoke to Enora yesterday." Enora was a Fae healer Aunt Grace worked with from time to time. Sometimes Enora needed some of Grace's poultices or knowledge of plants when her Fae healing magic wasn't enough. In exchange, she gave Grace some of her own healing salves, and they had built a sort of a friendship over the years. "Are you sure you want to hear this?" Grace paused.

"Of course!" she practically yelled to the laptop screen. She couldn't help it. She hadn't heard or seen anything about him since Alfie's last visit to the cottage, and she was desperate to hear anything where he was involved.

"Well, apparently, shortly after you left, Casimir got into an altercation with some Seelie soldiers outside of a tavern on the border. He killed one of the men, so the king sent Conall to negotiate peace with the Seelie to prevent Casimir's actions from starting a war." Aunt Grace studied Ianthe's face closely through the computer screen, the relief spreading across her features apparent.

She sighed. "So, he has been busy. That's why he hasn't come to see me."

"Darling, I want you to be careful. I know you have feelings for him, but he is still Fae, and an Unseelie at that," Grace cautioned.

"So am I!" The words burst from her lips before she could stop them. "I mean, we're both half Unseelie. It doesn't mean he's bad. He's wonderful, Aunt Grace. I wish you had the chance to meet him. If you did, you would see exactly what I'm talking about."

"I bet I would, sweetheart, but I still want you to be careful." She opened her mouth to argue again but her great-aunt shook her head and held her hand up to the camera. "While he may be a great guy, he's still quite a bit older than you are. You're still so young, and you don't understand the Fae as well as I do yet." Grace quickly changed the topic away from Conall, sensing an argument looming on the horizon. "Now, you may not believe this, but I have a feeling about this thing with Casimir, and it isn't a good one. From what Enora has told me, he is furious, and he is the kind of Fae who holds a grudge. I don't think he's finished with you yet." Grace held her hand up again as Ianthe started to argue that she had taken care of Casimir. "I know you think you have, darling, but he is extremely dangerous. Just be on the lookout and stay alert. Promise me."

"I promise," she said as she sighed. *I can't understand why Grace is so worried. In my last encounter with Casimir, I made sure he'd take my message seriously.* "I know you mean well, Aunt Grace, and I appreciate that you love and worry about me."

"Lord knows someone needs to," Grace mumbled under her breath. "Is your father home yet?" Ianthe shook her head no. "Have you finished your homework?" She asked the question in a very mom-like manner that made Ianthe smile.

"Yes, ma'am."

"Good. I love you. Go get some rest, darling. Please, ask your father to call me so we can discuss Thanksgiving, okay?"

"Will do. Love you too, Aunt Grace."

"And no dream visits tonight—I want you to get a full night's rest now that you're back in school. We can save those for the weekend. Now, good night and sweet dreams."

"Good night," she replied, waving goodbye to Grace's smiling face on the screen until she ended the call. She would miss their dream visits, but she would respect

Grace's decision to not have them during the week.

Glancing at the clock, she noticed it was later than she realized. She quickly changed into her pajamas, washed her face, and brushed her teeth then picked up one of the Fae books she had brought back with her from Grace's house. Grace said since they had belonged to Ayanna, Ianthe's mother, she should feel free to take any of them home with her. The one she held in her hands was best described as an encyclopedia of the different types of Fae based on folklore. It included the races of Fae, their origins, and the powers they were speculated to have along with other creatures commonly encountered in the Fae realm. She had already looked up Incubus, Succubus, and Mara—the three she was most familiar with. She had also discovered that Killian, an Unseelie noble's son she had met at court, was a Lampir (lamp-eer), a vampire-like Fae that feeds on human blood and induces lust (*no surprise there*). Killian's father, Lord Dante, was a Skepseis (skip-sees) who could read minds and feed on memories, strangely enough.

She had been skipping around to different letters over the last few days, trying to read at least a letter's worth every night, but you would not believe how many different kinds of Fae there were. Of course, she had no way to know how accurate the information was, but the ones she was familiar with seemed pretty spot on, so she assumed it was a decent resource.

She crawled into bed and read all the entries under the letter C until she was fighting to stay awake. She put the book down, flipped off her reading light, and centered her thoughts on Conall as she did every night, just in case.

# CHAPTER 7

*Conall*

ONALL WAS WOKEN from his slumber by a knock on the door, and light streamed into his room from the window as the door creaked open. Arabella stepped inside with a sly smile. "Good morning, Sir Conall. His Majesty requests your presence at breakfast."

"Of course. Thank you, Arabella." Her cheeks flushed pink with his words as she lingered in the doorway. "I will be there shortly." He waved his hand to dismiss her. She curtsied and smoothed her hands down her curves as she rose. *Some girls just don't get it when a guy isn't interested.* He was sure with her beauty, she probably wasn't used to being turned down.

As soon as she closed the door, he rose from the bed and dressed. He packed his satchel and found the rest of his men in their rooms. He gave them orders to prepare the horses and be ready to leave at a moment's notice in case the negotiations did not go well or King Lachlan decided to dismiss them. Conall made sure two of the soldiers would join him and Drummond at the negotiations before Arabella found him once again to lead their group to the Great Hall. He sighed at her eagerness and attentiveness. *Apparently there is no deterring this one.* He tried to act cold and callous toward her, hoping she would take the hint, but it only seemed to spur her on. Thankfully, their walk was a short one.

Breakfast went well. Lachlan seemed to be appeased with the blood debt settlement and uneager for a war, but he advised Conall to warn King Corydon that in the future he would not be so forgiving and kind. One more infraction against the Seelie people and there would be serious consequences to pay. Conall was grateful everything went smoothly and the Seelie king was more reasonable than his own. He had a feeling had their positions been reversed, Corydon would have retaliated. He and Drummond thanked King Lachlan for his hospitality and headed out of the palace toward the horses.

Just as they were exiting through the main hall, Bronwen stepped through the door behind her father. *Of course. Things were just too easy for me this morning.* Conall sighed internally. She lingered behind as her father wandered toward the throne room in search of the king. He had to admit she was beautiful, which was what had drawn him to her in the first place, but she was nothing compared to Ianthe. It was as if Ianthe were a goddess and all other women paled in comparison to her, and it was more than just her outer beauty. She was so thoughtful and kind that it radiated out of her, increasing her appeal a hundred times over.

Just thinking about her made him smile, and unfortunately it was poorly timed. Bronwen lit up, mistaking his smile for happiness at the sight of her. He quickly let it fall from his face.

"Greetings, Conall. I was hoping to see you on this visit." She placed her hand on his arm and began caressing his skin.

Conall tugged his arm out of her reach. "Greetings, Lady Bronwen. We were just leaving."

Her brow pulled down and her smile morphed into a frown. "I'm sorry to hear that. I was hoping we would get to spend some time together." She stepped closer to him, trying to rub against his side, but he stepped back. *Time to put an end to this.*

"I apologize if I led you on the last time I saw you, Bronwen," Conall started as her frown deepened. "I enjoyed our time together, but that's all it was—one night, no more. I've met someone since then and am no longer available. I-I hope you understand," he stammered. He never did well with female confrontation. Thankfully, before Bronwen, the other women he had been with were just looking for a night of fun as well.

He could see the pain in her eyes, but she quickly recovered and put on an air of indifference. "Of course, Conall." She smiled, but her eyes narrowed. "I hope you understand that you were lucky to have a chance with a Seelie noble like myself. I was only curious what it would be like to be with a half Fae anyway. I wish you well with your 'someone'." She spat the last word as if it left a bad taste in her mouth, and he could tell by the malicious glint in her eye that this was not the last time he would have to deal with her. In some ways it made him glad that Ianthe was exiled and would never get to meet Bronwen.

He let her have the last word and joined his men outside. They had prepped the horses well, so it took him very little time to mount his steed and lead them out of the court walls. As they were exiting the town, a midnight stallion came galloping from the east. They came to a halt and each of his men placed their hands on their weapons, ready to draw if necessary. As the horse and rider drew closer, Conall saw it was Evin, the Seelie they had met on our way in.

Evin held his hands up in a nonthreatening gesture as he neared and called out, "Conall, if I may have a word, please." He pulled up a small distance from their group and Conall approached him. He could see that Evin had no visible weapon on him, but he was not about to let his guard down. Evin spoke softly, not wanting to be overheard by the rest of the Unseelie. "Will you please pass along a message for me?"

"I'll do what I can, depending on who the message is for."

"Tell Casimir I do not consider his blood debt paid. My brother was one of the best. I fully intend to find something Casimir loves and take it from him just as he took my brother from my family. I will avenge Reid's death if it is the last thing I do," Evin threatened.

Conall felt sorry for Evin, he really did. He remembered Reid, who'd had the same bronze skin and dark hair as his brother. He had seen Reid training with Torin during his last visit. "I am truly sorry for your loss, Evin. I know you may not believe it, but I respect your father greatly and it saddens me to know Casimir stole his son, your brother's life. I will pass along your message, but I don't know what good it will do. Casimir is a sadistic son of a bitch and I can't think of one thing he cares about other than himself and the throne." He understood Evin's pain and need for revenge, so he decided to be honest with him. "There are many, myself included, who would like nothing more than to see Casimir suffer, but he is the heir to the Unseelie throne, and any threats you make now may come back to haunt you later." Conall offered the same words of advice Alfie had given him when he found out Casimir was betrothed to Ianthe.

"I understand, but my message remains the same," Evin replied, and Conall nodded his head in acknowledgement. "Thank you, Conall. My father has great respect for you as well. He was the one who told me to talk to you. I wish you a safe journey." With that, Evin turned his horse and galloped away. Conall rejoined his men and they started their journey home.

# CHAPTER 8

*Ianthe*

HE FIRST MONTH of school passed before she knew it. Every day she spent more time with Callie and they found more they had in common. They both had a secret love for T.V. shows like *The Vampire Diaries*, *Firefly*, and *Dr. Who*. They expanded each other's musical horizons by sharing playlists of their favorite songs, and they hung out together on the weekends, going out to lunch, the movies, and thrift store shopping, or just talking. She still video chatted with Aunt Grace at least once a week and visited her via dreams on the weekends. She hadn't seen any sign of Casimir, but she did glimpse an unfamiliar Fae from time to time. They usually didn't let her get too close before slinking off, knowing somehow that she was not someone to be messed with.

She didn't see her dad a whole lot, but that wasn't new. He didn't drag her to any of his functions and when he had something at the house, she usually stayed the night at

Callie's place to avoid any unpleasant confrontations. She thought about Conall constantly. The nights at home were the worst. She wanted nothing more than to see him in her dreams, but it never happened. She began to wonder if she would ever see him again. She didn't want to lose faith in him, but it was hard. She doubted herself and whether she was good enough for him. Maybe he had found someone prettier, like a full-blooded Fae. Maybe he had found someone he could stay in the Fae realm with. Self-doubt was the worst, and it was starting to eat away at her confidence.

One night she finally broke down and told Callie about Conall. Of course she left out anything Fae, explaining that he was a summer fling with whom she had hoped to continue a long-distance relationship. She said he didn't currently have access to technology and Callie was sympathetic, but she was also slightly suspicious of the story. *Who wouldn't be in this day and age? I mean, we all have cameras on our phones and social media accounts and video chat at our fingertips, but I have no evidence that Conall actually exists other than my words and memories.* Her thoughts depressed her. Thankfully, Callie didn't push the subject upon seeing how Ianthe's mood had shifted.

She told Callie everything she could about herself. She shared her history of drug use and rehab. Callie shared the gossip she had heard, but said she never believed rumors. Callie told Ianthe about her life in Arizona, before she moved. Apparently, Callie's parents were going through a bad divorce after her mom caught her dad having an affair, so her mom had decided to make a fresh start by moving her and her little brother, Sean, to their grandmother's house. Callie was a drama geek through and through, complete with an amazing singing voice, and she could play the guitar. She even met Aunt Grace on video chat one night, and she was Ianthe's piece of sanity in the sea of crazy that had become her life.

On a Monday in early October, Callie went to Ianthe's place after school. She had been giddy all day, but very tight-lipped about the reason. The minute the girls walked through the door, Ianthe began her interrogation. "So, are you going to tell me what has you on cloud nine today?"

They tossed their backpacks on the living room floor before heading to the kitchen for a soda and snack. Callie's smile was now a dreamy wide-mouthed grin as she hopped up on the kitchen island while Ianthe grabbed a soda for each of them.

"Wait, wait, let me guess—is it a guy?" Callie giggled in response and Ianthe slid the beverage across the island toward her. She grabbed a package of popcorn from the cabinet and stuck it in the microwave, tapped the popcorn button, and then spun back around, determined to make Callie tell her what was making her so bubbly. "Spill already!"

"Okay, okay. I met a guy this weekend. Oh my god, Thee! He is so hot! Like, I'm talking Ian Somerhalder hot!"

Ianthe giggled, knowing he had to look really good if Callie was comparing him to her beloved Damon from *The Vampire Diaries*.

"So where did you meet?" she asked as the smell of buttered popcorn filled the kitchen.

"I was sitting on the patio at Starbucks enjoying a latte and composing a song in my journal. Apparently he had been sitting a few tables behind me and could hear me singing and strumming, working through the song. He came over and sat down across from me and introduced himself just like that."

The microwave beeped and Ianthe retrieved their snack, dumping it into a bowl for the two of them to share. Callie grabbed their drinks and they headed into the living room, plopping down on the sofa. Ianthe placed the bowl of popcorn between them.

"So…" she prompted, getting Callie back on track.

"So, his name is Reid. He has jet black hair that's the same style as Stefan Salvatore only little longer on top, and some yummy, scruffy facial hair…like five o'clock shadow hot." Callie used her hands to show exactly where his hair fell. "I think he might be Native American. His skin is like a deep caramel and his eyes are like chocolate swirled with butterscotch. I just want to eat him up!"

They both giggled and snacked on popcorn.

Callie's happiness was contagious as she continued. "He was just so darn cute. He said he thought my music was beautiful and I had the voice of an angel. He recently moved here too and hadn't really met anyone close to his age yet. I swear we stayed at Starbucks talking for hours, and he offered to buy me lunch if I showed him around a bit, so we grabbed some food and walked around the square. It was perfect…magical almost." Callie sighed so dreamily that Ianthe couldn't hold in her squeal. She almost knocked over the entire bowl of popcorn hugging her with excitement.

"I'm so happy for you! When do I get to meet him? As your best friend, I have a right to threaten him with bodily harm if he dares to hurt you."

"Well, I was thinking we could hang out all together this weekend, go bowling or something."

"Perfect! I'm in. I can't wait to see this hunk who has stolen your heart." They both smiled before deciding they should probably get started on their homework.

Once homework was done, Callie packed up her stuff so Ianthe could drive her home for dinner. They were walking to the car and Ianthe was searching her purse for her keys when Callie's elbow collided with her stomach. "Hot runner at nine o'clock," she whispered conspiratorially.

Ianthe glanced up to see a shirtless Adonis jogging their way. He had short, curly, sandy blond hair and abs that made a girl's hands itch to trace the hard planes. It was like a six pack and then some. He looked about their age, but she had never seen him in her neighborhood before.

"Good evening ladies," he said, slowing as he approached, probably because they were staring at him like fish with their mouths hanging open.

"Hello there," Callie flirted. "Did you just move in here or have I been blind every other time I came over?" Ianthe rolled her eyes and saw him smirk in return.

He stopped in front of them. "I just moved in, about five houses down." He jerked his thumb over his shoulder toward the direction he'd come from, but they couldn't really see his house from her driveway since they were just on the other side of a hill. She tried not to notice the fine sheen of sweat glistening on his chiseled chest. He stuck out his hand. "I'm Kyle."

"Callie." She grasped his hand in a firm handshake. When she released him, he turned his attention toward Ianthe.

"And you are…" he prompted. Ianthe glanced up into his green blue eyes. She'd never seen a combination quite like it before. Callie's elbow poked her side again, waking her from the trance his eyes had put her in.

She stuck out her hand. "Ianthe." Instead of shaking her hand like he had with Callie, he grabbed it and brought it to his lips, placing a kiss across her knuckles. She swore

Callie practically swooned next to her. She, however, had the most bizarre reaction. *I should be swooning too—I mean, he looks like a Greek god—but instead his lips feels wrong against my skin*, she thought. Her stomach turned and she fought to not yank her fingers from his grasp. She didn't want to seem rude, but something was off. She smiled weakly, trying to cover up her slip, and politely removed her hand once he released it.

He flashed a wolfish grin. Had she not known better, she might have considered he was Fae, but his eyes didn't glow and she didn't see any hint of pointed ears or sharp teeth. In fact, his smile was movie star perfect.

"Well ladies," he said, his voice interrupting her thoughts, "I should continue on my run. Perhaps I will see you around?" His voice was husky and hopeful at the same time. His light blue and green eyes flashed with something familiar she couldn't quite place, causing chills to run down her spine.

Callie's voice broke through the awkward silence since Ianthe had apparently forgotten how to respond. "Oh, I certainly hope so."

Kyle gave a slight wave before turning around and continuing down the street on his run.

"Oh my god! Was he not totally delish?! I wanted to rub my hands all over his yummy abs. I swear his smile made my panties drop."

Ianthe laughed at Callie's words. Leave it to her to say out loud what most girls only mused in their heads.

"We're definitely spending more time at your place if I have the chance of seeing him running shirtless again," Callie added as she sat down on the passenger seat of Ianthe's white Nissan Leaf.

Ianthe knew most people would have preferred the Lexus, but she decided her new self was environmentally responsible, so she traded in her Lexus for a Leaf. She climbed into the driver's seat and started the car to take Callie home.

Callie put her hand on Ianthe's arm and squealed in delight. "I know! Ooo, this is perfect! You should totally ask Kyle on a date. We could double this weekend!" Callie was obviously excited at the prospect, but Ianthe didn't know how to tell her that for some bizarre reason, Kyle gave her the creeps.

She could tell her expression gave her away by the way Callie's eyes narrowed slightly as she said, "I know you're not over Conall, but we're young. We have our whole lives ahead of us to settle down and get serious. Right now, we should be out there having fun. Maybe Kyle can help you get over Conall." Callie's concern was sincere. Ianthe knew how much she hated to see her pine away for a guy who hadn't contacted her in several months, but Callie didn't know the whole story. She could never know.

"We'll see," she acquiesced. Callie squealed again, bouncing in her seat and turning the radio up to do a celebratory dance. Ianthe didn't know how she would get Callie to let go of her idea of a double date, but there was no way she could be in Kyle's presence for that long. Just the thought of a date with him turned her stomach sour.

# CHAPTER 9

## *Ianthe*

**IANTHE HAD HOPED** Callie would have forgotten about Kyle and the double date, but she was sorely mistaken. Callie seemed even more obsessed with the idea the next morning at school.

"So, I talked to Reid last night and he is totally in for the double date this weekend. I can't wait! This is going to be so much fun. Can you believe our luck? Both of us finding hot new guys around the same time?!"

Callie's words only increased the unease growing inside Ianthe. Somehow, this seemed more than pure coincidence or luck. She went from careless to high alert with Aunt Grace's words about Casimir holding a grudge echoing through her mind. Perhaps that night she would pay him a little visit. It wouldn't take long to figure out if he was in her world or back in Fae.

Her day passed rather uneventfully with Callie gushing about Reid and planning their double date during every minute they had together. She didn't have it in her to tell Callie she had no intention of asking Kyle out. She'd let her down eventually, but Callie was having too much fun with the fantasy. Callie made school easier to bear, but it didn't stop the whispers, the rumors, the glares, and the insults in the hallway between classes. Ianthe had made enough enemies to last a lifetime, and they all seemed to be enjoying watching her suffer. She tried not to let them get to her, but sometimes it was hard, especially in physics with Bryce and Beth constantly trying to provoke her. She was glad for the day to end.

A moment after she had pulled meatloaf from the oven, she heard the garage door open. *Dad must be home early.* She went ahead and set the table and was just finishing when her father came in and set down his briefcase.

"Something smells wonderful," he called out.

"It's meatloaf, one of Aunt Grace's recipes," she replied, bringing the meatloaf, green beans, and mashed potatoes to the table for them to eat. Her dad entered the dining room and took a seat at the table. Anyone looking in one of their windows would have seen a nice family meal, but they wouldn't hear the awkward, strained silence that hung around as they ate.

Her father seemed to be in a good mood as he attempted to start conversation. "The food is delicious, Lola. Thank you."

"You're welcome," she politely replied, thinking that might be the extent of their conversation for the evening.

"So, how is school going?"

"Fine."

"Have you started any college applications yet?"

"No."

"Did you finish your homework?"

"Yes."

"What are your plans for this weekend?"

*"Not sure yet." This must be what the Spanish Inquisition felt like. She wasn't sure why he was curious all of a sudden, or if he was just trying to be a dad. Perhaps someone at work asked about me and he needs something to tell people.*

"Geez, Lola, I'm trying here," his voice growled, silverware clattering onto his plate.

"I know, Dad. I'm just not sure why. Why the sudden interest?" she asked honestly.

He sighed and ran his hands through his hair in a familiar frustrated motion. She tended to frustrate him easily. "Can't a dad simply be interested in his daughter and her life?"

"He could, but we both know that's not the kind of dad you are." She hadn't meant the words to come out so sharp and accusatory, but she couldn't take them back once they were said. She picked up her napkin and started twisting it in her hands.

"People change, Lola. Hell, you're proof of that."

"What's that supposed to mean?"

"I don't know who you are anymore. I don't know who you're hanging out with and it...well, it worries me."

"You've met Callie, Dad. You know who I'm hanging out with."

*"She seems like a nice girl, but you've come so far in your recovery I'd hate to see you fall off the wagon." Ah, so that's what this is about. I know Callie has her own unique fashion sense and a wild, loud personality, but that doesn't mean she is into drugs. Hell, Callie doesn't even drink at parties. If anything, my friends from before, when I was Lola, were the ones who got me into partying and drugs. Of course, she would have a hard time convincing her father of this.*

"Callie doesn't do drugs, Dad. She doesn't even drink," she explained, her eyes narrowing as his eyebrows rose in disbelief. "But thanks for the vote of confidence." She picked up her plate to leave the table, glaring at him.

His eyes softened, but she was too angry to feel any sympathy for him. She turned away and took her plate into the kitchen, leaving him to clean up the rest of their meal. She stomped upstairs and spent an hour or so surfing the web before calling it a night.

As she lay in bed trying to fall asleep, she remembered that she needed to confirm or deny her earlier unease by checking on Casimir. So, instead of focusing her mind on Conall, as she had every other night, she kept the image of Casimir's ice blue eyes and spiky blond hair in her mind. She was probably just being paranoid about the whole thing, and if her dream turned up nothing then she would know Casimir was still in the Fae realm like Conall.

*Ianthe opened her eyes to find herself sitting on Aunt Grace's porch. It was the perfect night with a full moon casting a bright glow on the clearing. A breeze ruffled through her hair and she sat for a few minutes gathering*

*her thoughts, her purpose, and her courage. Just because she had faced Casimir once and won, that didn't mean she was eager to do it again. She didn't know if she would've been so brave the first time had she not seen him almost kill Conall. Fury had fueled her actions that night and she had unlocked a part of herself she hoped to never see again. She stood and sauntered into the clearing, nearing the edge of the woods. If he didn't show up soon, she would know for sure that Casimir was back in Fae.*

*The snap of a twig to her left brought her head swinging in that direction as a familiar form approached from the woods.*

*"Well, this is a treat." His voice raised goose bumps down her arms. "To what do I owe this honor, Lady Ianthe?"*

*"Cut the bullshit, Casimir. What are you doing in my world? Did you not take my warning seriously?" Before she could blink he was standing right in front of her. Those same icy blue eyes that had haunted her nightmares for months were looking her over from head to toe as if she was his favorite flavor of ice cream.*

*He took a step closer, trying to intimidate her, but she stood firmly in place. "Oh, I remember your warning, little one." He leaned forward, invading her personal space, and drew in a deep breath as if to inhale her scent. She could taste bile building in the back of her throat. "It was delicious. You have such darkness trapped inside of you, begging to be let out." He brought a finger up to her left cheek and traced it down her jaw in an intimate gesture.*

*She knocked his hand away and took a step back. "You don't know what you're talking about."*

*"Oh, I don't?" He feigned disbelief, quirking his right eyebrow. "I was there, Ianthe. I saw your desire." He start-*

43

ed circling her slowly. *She could feel his breath against her throat as he leaned in toward her ear. "I saw how it pleased you to cut me, how much you enjoyed inflicting pain." His tongue snuck out and traced the shell of her ear. She wanted to shove him away but his words froze her in place. She had enjoyed enjoying cutting him. The Unseelie part of her had been excited by being in control and causing pain. It was the greatest high she'd ever experienced and more addictive than any drug. It was something she didn't want to admit to anyone, not even herself.*

*"I did not," she whispered, but her voice cracked, betraying her self-doubt.*

*Casimir's hand landed on her stomach, tracing around to her hip and back as he stepped behind her. "Oh, but you did. I could see it in your eyes, the Unseelie princess finally letting go. I can free you, little one. You can hurt me any time you please." His husky voice came from behind her as his hand grazed from her waist down to her left hand, which was clenched against her side. He uncurled her fingers and slid the handle of a blade into her palm.*

*Her fingers grasped the blade despite her revulsion at the idea of feeding off anyone's pain. How had she let things get so out of control? She was a Mara, dammit. This was her realm. She forcefully thrust her right elbow back into Casimir's gut. He groaned in pain, or moaned in pleasure; she couldn't tell for sure. Oh sweet baby Jesus, what is wrong with me? She quickly put space between the two of them and spun around to face him. Switching hands, she held the knife in front of her defensively, ready to strike if he approached.*

*Casimir smiled as he straightened. He moved toward her again, like a cat toying with its prey. "Does Conall know what secretly thrills you or am I the only one?"*

*His words infuriated her and without thinking, she slashed the knife in his direction. She expected him to dodge it, but instead he stood in place as the blade sliced through his forearm. He drew in a sharp breath and moaned. What the hell? A pleasant heat crept through her body seeing the red blood drip down his forearm toward his fingers. He opened his eyes. She had never seen them glow so brightly. What's wrong with me? I shouldn't be enjoying this—neither of us should.*

"There she is. I was wondering what I'd have to do to get her to come out and play." *He smile widened as he reached down with his left hand and wiped some of the blood from his right arm. He brought his bloodied fingers to his lips and licked them clean then smirked at her seductively. Her stomach rolled and she fought back the vomit that was crawling up her throat.*

"Stop it!" *she yelled as she stepped back, putting some distance between them. How could I hurt someone who seemed to get off on the pain? This is so messed up.* "Leave me alone for good, or else."

"Or else what, little one?" *He licked the blood stain from his lips.* "I enjoy it when you hurt me. Besides, I don't see your boyfriend here to save you. Where is he, Ianthe? Why isn't Conall here with you?"

*Casimir had struck a nerve, and he knew it the minute she let the heartache seep into her features. She quickly tried to school her expression, but it was too late.* "He left you," *he stated, slowly approaching her once again.*

"He did not. King Corydon has kept him busy fixing your mistakes." *She tried to justify Conall's absence but the excuse seemed weak even to her own ears. She dropped her arms to her sides.*

"If you were mine, little one, I would never leave you."

*He reached his hand up to cup her face and his expression appeared apologetic, almost tender, until she brought the blade up between them.*

*"I will never be yours, Casimir," she sneered. As the words rang around them, his adoring expression shifted to rage. She slammed the blade into his stomach and he staggered back, roaring in fury. He yanked the blade from his stomach and flung it on the grass.*

*"Is that the best you can do?" He spat blood onto the dirt. Since this was her dream, she was done letting him have control. She imagined a large, metal, barred cage around him, and it materialized instantly. He placed his hands on the bars and growled.*

*"We're done here. You will stay away from me, or I will find a way to make you pay. I promise you that," she warned before walking away.*

*"One day you won't be able to contain your Unseelie side anymore. She will demand to be fed. Don't expect me to take you back so easily when she does." His voice echoed through the night air behind her as she tried to shake off his words. She would never let her Unseelie desires free. She would always have a choice, and she would always choose love over causing pain.*

# CHAPTER 10

*Ianthe*

S HE AWOKE WITH a start. The sheets were tangled under her, and her pajamas were soaked with sweat. *What the hell was that? What is wrong with me?* She glanced at the clock. It was only about half an hour before her alarm was set to go off for school, so she saw no point in trying to go back to sleep.

*She took a scalding hot shower and scrubbed herself raw, trying to erase the feel of Casimir from her skin. Her mind raced, replaying every minute of her dream while she scrubbed. Where is Conall? Maybe he can tell me what is going on since he's half Unseelie too…but what would he think of me if I told him? I can't imagine such darkness living inside him. He's so good. Would he understand what I'm going through or would he turn me away because of it? The doubt raged through her head.*

One thing was for sure: Casimir was in the human realm. It was the only way she would have been able to pull him into her dream. *What is he doing here?* She would need to be on high alert until she could figure out what was going on. She finished getting ready for school with plenty of time to spare, so she decided to grab breakfast on the way. She texted Callie saying she was making a Starbucks run. She already knew Callie's order by heart, but she wanted to give her a heads up so she wouldn't worry about breakfast if she was running late.

The line for the drive-through was insanely long so Ianthe parked the car to head inside and order. Luckily, the line inside was only a few people deep. She was checking her phone to see if Callie had texted back when she heard the barista's voice call, "Kyle!" *Shit. Just my luck.* She saw him step up to the counter and grab a steaming hot cup. He was in his running clothes again, but this time he wore a navy blue shirt that clung to his sculpted muscles. She saw the moment he spotted her. His blue-green eyes, like bits of the sea, glinted with recognition as he smiled widely. She guessed she had been staring because the girl at the counter interrupted her thoughts, asking, "What can I get you today?"

She gave her order and stepped over to wait. Kyle was standing by the pickup counter, sipping his coffee, and staring at her. "Ianthe," he greeted, "what a nice surprise to see you here."

"Just grabbing breakfast before school." She shrugged like it was no big deal. "Do you go to school?"

*"Yeah, I'm taking classes at the community college right now,"* he replied. *Ah, an older guy. Damn, that will only make Callie that much more interested in getting him to go out with me. Too bad Callie didn't meet Kyle before she met Reid.*

*"Cool." Wow, my conversational skills are superb this*

*morning. Oh well, it's not like I wanted to impress Kyle anyway. She berated herself while an oblivious Kyle beamed.*

"Did you sleep okay last night?"

She frowned at his question; she didn't think she looked that bad this morning. Sure, there were slightly dark circles under her eyes, but she had covered them up with a little concealer before she left.

He must have caught her expression. "You aren't very talkative this morning. I thought maybe you had a rough night and were tired," he explained.

"Oh. I'm not really a morning person," she replied.

"That's good to know. Here I hoped you were up so late thinking about me that you didn't get enough sleep," he flirted.

*Well that's a little cocky. Kind of a turn-off actually.* "You wish," she mumbled under her breath just as the barista called her name. She grabbed her order and turned back toward Kyle. "Well, I have to go or I'll be late. I'll see you around."

"You certainly will." He smiled, but this time it felt predatory instead of flirty.

She gave him a tight-lipped smile in return and headed out to her car where she sat for a moment, trying to shake the unease he had stirred in her. Finally she glanced around before pulling out. There was a guy in a grey hoodie standing at the edge of the parking lot watching her. What disturbed her more than the fact that he was staring was that his eyes were a striking shade of amber, and they were definitely glowing. She quickly pulled the car out of the lot and zoomed toward the school.

When she arrived, Callie practically pounced on her in the hallway. "You're the...best! I love...you so...much,"

Callie cooed around bites of her blueberry scone. Her current ensemble included torn black skinny jeans, hot pink flats, and a white David Bowie t-shirt topped with her worn leather jacket. Her fiery red hair was in its usual wavy mass of disarray that somehow ended up looking like styled beach waves. Ianthe loved Callie's carefree style.

"Oh, you're just using me for food and caffeine, is that it?" she joked.

"Not the food—it's all about your hot body and those mesmerizing violet eyes." Callie batted her eyelashes coyly, and Ianthe burst out laughing. "Speaking of hot bodies, have you seen Kyle since the other night?"

Ianthe hadn't expected her to jump in so quickly about Kyle. Callie was one determined woman on a mission. She sighed. "Yes. I saw him this morning."

"What?! And you're just now telling me this? How'd it go? Did you ask him if he was free for Friday night?" Callie drilled until she tore her eyes away from her last bite of scone and glanced at Ianthe's face. "You didn't."

"Come on, Cal, you know how I am in the mornings. He caught me off guard this morning. I was like a zombie."

"Well, I wasn't going to say anything, but you do kind of look like shit," Callie teased.

"Oh, ha ha, you're so hilarious."

"So if you didn't ask him about Friday, did you at least talk to him?"

"Yes." She bit her lip nervously, not wanting to reveal the information she had gleaned. She knew Callie would be even more gung-ho about the whole double date thing if she found out he was in college. Thankfully, she was saved by the bell, but she knew she wouldn't be able to avoid Callie's interrogation forever. "There's the bell. I'll tell you later." She closed her locker and rushed off to first period.

"Girl, you better!" Callie called out, her voice trailing down the hall behind her.

It took until lunch for Ianthe to crack. Of course Callie took the news just as she had expected and squealed so loudly that they drew the eyes of several surrounding tables. "This is awesome! A college boy." Callie waggled her eyebrows.

"Which just makes me even more wary. I mean, what could he want from a high school girl?" Ianthe retorted. "Wait, don't answer that. I know what he would want from a high school girl, and he isn't going to get *that* from me."

"Come on, Thee. One date won't kill you," Callie pleaded. "Don't tell me you're still holding out hope for Conall." Ianthe's face fell at the mention of his name and her chest ached. "Oh hell, girl. You've got it bad. I know it's tough, but trust me on this—you have to move on. You haven't heard from him since when...July, right?" Ianthe nodded. "It's time to test the waters with someone new."

"I don't know." She knew Callie thought she was crazy to still be pining for Conall, but Callie didn't know what they had shared and how time worked differently where he was. Callie didn't understand, and Ianthe couldn't blame her because she couldn't exactly tell her, could she? *Nope, Callie would drop me like a hot potato and join the rest of the school thinking I have bought a one-way ticket to Crazyville.*

Callie's eyes softened with sympathy and she bit her lip, worried she may have overstepped. She was just concerned about her friend. "Okay, how about you meet Reid today? I was going to meet up with him for some froyo after school anyway, so you can just join us. Hmmm, come to think of it, maybe he has some hot friends, because if they look anything like him..." Callie whistled.

Ianthe had to give it to the girl—she was determined, and she knew it came from a place of love, of wanting her friend to be happy. "Yeah, that sounds great. Are you sure Reid won't mind? I've been dying to meet the guy who has stolen my BFF's heart but I don't want to impose." Callie's cheeks stained crimson. "Oh, look, he's got my little Callie blushing," she teased.

"Shut up!" Callie punched Ianthe's shoulder lightly before they picked up their trash and threw it away so they could get to class on time.

The rest of the day passed quickly. Ianthe was a little nervous about meeting Reid, but she figured it was just her residual paranoia over the whole Casimir thing. Surely he was a good guy if Callie was interested in him. Callie was so excited, she was practically bouncing on her heels as they climbed into Ianthe's car. Ianthe grabbed her sunglasses from the console before pulling out of the parking lot.

"Did you tell Reid you were bringing me?" she asked curiously.

Callie smirked. "Nope. This will be a pop quiz—how will the boy deal with the introduction to the BFF?"

Ianthe chuckled. Callie had once explained her pop quiz theory at one of their sleepovers. Callie believed you learn the most about people by how they react to being thrown out of their comfort zone. Callie had done this to Ianthe countless times, but she had a feeling this may be the first test for Reid. *I sure hope he passes.*

They pulled up to Yogurt Land and Callie barely waited until Ianthe had the car stopped before jumping out. "Come on, slowpoke!"

"Well, someone is excited," Ianthe said sarcastically. She rolled her eyes, though she knew Callie couldn't see them behind her shades.

"Hell yes I am! You would be too if you were meeting up with the hottest guy on Earth. Oh, wait, that could be you on Friday night if you just ask Kyle out," Callie goaded, and Ianthe stuck her tongue out in reply.

The bell chimed as Callie pushed open the door and squealed. She ran forward, throwing herself into the arms of a guy a few tables from the door, almost knocking him over. "Well, hello to you too," he murmured into Callie's hair, his voice deep.

"I brought a surprise," Callie said, stepping back so he could see Ianthe. The second Ianthe saw him, she froze. He was gorgeous, just like Callie had said, with caramel-colored skin, jet black hair that was perfectly styled, and sharp, well-defined features, but that wasn't what made her freeze. It was his eyes—glowing amber eyes to be exact, and she knew his smile would reveal sharp pointed teeth.

Reid was Fae.

# CHAPTER II

## Conall

**A**FTER CROSSING THE castle gates, Conall dismounted from his white stallion and passed his reins to the stable hand. Corydon would want a debriefing on their visit with King Lachlan, and then hopefully he would be free to contact his Ianthe in person. He couldn't bear to be away from her any longer. Because no one had seen Casimir since his fight with the Seelie, Conall could only assume he might be stalking her. Casimir was not one to take rejection kindly, and Conall had a feeling that even though she thought she had taken care of things, it was only the beginning. Casimir would not give up so easily.

Drummond and Conall met King Corydon in the throne room. "Greetings, Your Majesty." Conall bowed, as did Drummond.

"Conall, Drummond, how did things go with the Seelie?" their king inquired.

"Well..." Drummond replied, looking rather uncomfortable and unwilling to elaborate.

"Unfortunately, Casimir's actions required a blood debt to be paid. We return one soldier short, milord," Conall explained with a tight-lipped expression so as not to grimace with the reminder that he had taken that young man's life.

"Very well," Corydon stated, looking at his fingernails, completely unfazed that he had lost one of his men.

"King Lachlan wanted me to notify you that if Casimir oversteps his boundaries again, he will be forced to deal with him personally, regardless of the fact that Casimir is the Unseelie heir," Conall continued. "He also demanded that any future blood debt caused by Casimir be raised— two of our men for any one that Casimir kills." Conall took a breath, knowing this would not please the Unseelie king at all.

Corydon slammed his hand on the armrest of his throne. "That arrogant ass thinks his men are worth two of mine," he growled. Things were going about as well as expected.

"Sire," Drummond squeaked. "Is Lachlan's condition really worth starting a war over?"

"Gather the other advisors immediately. We need to deal with this," Corydon yelled in reply, rising from his throne, and Drummond nodded then quickly exited the room to rouse the rest of the council members. "What happened to your negotiating skills, Conall? Have you gone soft?" The king eyed Conall suspiciously.

"Sir, the boy Casimir killed was Torin's eldest son, not just a peasant. Had it been a lesser Fae, I believe the blood debt would have been sufficient without the added conditions. Casimir's choice of an opponent was unfortunate," Conall explained.

"I see. That does complicate things." Corydon's anger cooled a smidge upon the news.

"Perhaps if Casimir was given more of a leadership role here at the palace it might help center his energy and appease Lachlan long enough for him to forget the transgression and return to our previous agreement," Conall suggested cautiously.

Corydon's eyes narrowed. "You're not one of my advisors, Conall. When I want your advice, I will ask for it. You're lucky to still retain your position after your recent actions. I understand that you were defending my daughter, but as her betrothed, Casimir had a right to pursue her. You're walking a very, very fine line," Corydon warned.

*Shit, I've overstepped my bounds.* Conall knew he was walking a fine line. He had been since the moment he laid eyes on Ianthe, and he wasn't quite ready to cross it just yet. He needed to make sure he could control the consequences before he crossed that line, for her sake.

"My apologies, milord." He bowed, turning his eyes toward the floor in submission. "Is there anything else you need of me?"

"No. You may retire to your quarters, but do not stray. Once I reach a decision, I will want you here to enforce it." *In other words, no visiting the human realm and no chance of sneaking away to Ianthe.*

The ache in Conall's chest grew, but he knew better than to reveal his discomfort. "As you wish, Your Majesty." He bowed once more before he left.

He walked to the stables and found Rain, his horse, waiting for him. "Well, old boy, I was hoping we could pay a visit to a beautiful lady, but I guess we'll have to wait." Rain huffed, and Conall stroked his muzzle fondly before mounting. "Let's go home," he whispered in Rain's ear, knowing he knew the way and would take him there without any guidance.

# CHAPTER 12

## Ianthe

**S**HIT.

*Reid is Fae.*

*What the hell am I supposed to do now? Does he know who I am? He probably does if he is Unseelie. At least I've changed my hair color—that might help, and thank God I still have my sunglasses on or my eyes would be a dead giveaway. Ianthe's mind raced.*

Reid stuck his hand out in front of him. "Hey, I'm Reid. You must be Ianthe." His voice definitely carried the accent she had begun to associate with Fae, a unique blend of Gaelic and Old English. She hesitated a moment too long before shaking his hand.

Callie looked at her curiously. "You okay, hun? You look a little pale," she commented.

"Uh, yeah, sorry. I like your accent. Where's it from?" she asked, reaching out to return his handshake.

"A little bit of everywhere. We moved around Europe a lot when I was younger," he replied vaguely, and she nodded her head as if that explained it all. *Seems like Mr. Fae has thought through his cover.*

"Froyo?" Ianthe grinned nervously. Suddenly she wasn't so hungry. How was she going to get Callie out of this situation? She seemed to really like him. *Is Reid controlling Callie in some way? Just what kind of Fae is he?*

She must have been spacing out in front of the frozen yogurt machine because Callie nudged her. "You sure you're okay, Thee?" Ianthe snapped out of her thoughts at the sound of Callie's nickname for her.

"Yep, just tired," she lied as she turned her attention to filling her cup with cake batter flavored frozen yogurt and toppings. When she returned to the table, Callie was snuggled up against Reid's side, smiling at him in adoration as he raised his spoon to her lips for a bite of his frozen yogurt. Ianthe's thoughts collided. She had no clue how to stop Callie from seeing Reid. She couldn't just tell her the truth—Callie would never believe her—but if she made something up, Callie might be able to tell she was lying. She unconsciously sighed out loud, drawing Callie's concern and focus to her.

Crap. I am completely blowing this. Snap out of it, Ianthe. *She gave herself an internal pep talk.* You can do this. Just remember pageant Lola and play your part. Maybe I can get Reid to slip up or find something to use against him. *"So, Reid, tell me about yourself. I mean, I've heard some about you from Callie, of course, but I'm curious—what brought you to town?" She realized she was rambling.* Not a great start.

Reid wasn't at all fazed, as if he had rehearsed his story many times. "Well, my brother recently died, so I decided a change in scenery was in order."

Callie frowned in sympathy and squeezed her arm around him to comfort him, showing they had tackled this tough topic before. For some reason his words rang with partial truth. He must have lost his brother recently. *How hard is it to kill a Fae?* she wondered. She knew they aged more slowly and that some of them had healing magic, but what would it take to kill one? A knife to the heart? A bullet? How different were they from humans? And where did that leave her? She had actually never considered those questions. Thankfully he took her silence as her listening and continued with his story while she pondered her own mortality.

"Luckily, I met this beautiful creature." *Interesting choice of words*, she thought as he hugged Callie closer to his side. "It seems like fate brought me here." He paused, perhaps waiting for a response from Ianthe, but she didn't give one. She focused on her yogurt, and he pressed on. "So, I hear we're having a double date on Friday?"

"Yep, as soon as Ianthe can get off her butt and ask Kyle out, we'll be all set," Callie commented, shooting Ianthe daggers, indicating that she meant business.

She sighed, knowing Callie wasn't going to let it go any time soon. "Fine, I give in. I'll ask him if I see him. It's not like I have his number or even his last name to Google him," She replied, hoping that would satisfy Callie. She took a couple bites of her yogurt and then directed her next question at Callie, hoping her answer would be a yes. "So, do you need to study for the Spanish test? I was going to cram tonight if you want to join me."

"*Perfecto!*" Callie exclaimed. They finished their treats while Callie tried to keep the small talk going between Reid and Ianthe. He seemed to be rather interested in her, asking about her hobbies and preferences—simple questions that sounded like the casual interest of meeting someone new but raised red flags and put her on the defensive. She wondered if he noticed the tension in her body or if she was keeping it under control. She fingered Conall's leather tie around her wrist. Oh, how she wished for some of his magical calm right now. Unfortunately, the movement brought Reid's attention to the strap and his eyes narrowed slightly.

"Where did you get that?" he asked, pointing to the leather bracelet.

"Oh, um, a friend gave it to me," she replied vaguely. Callie knew the story and probably didn't want to kill the mood by mentioning Conall's name, so she nudged Reid in the side with her elbow as she'd done to Ianthe countless times. It was a strong hint he should stop or change the subject, and thankfully he caught on.

"So what about your family? Callie's told me some, and I'm sorry to hear about your mom. Do you remember much about her?" Reid asked.

The question threw her and she glanced at Callie, noting the slight furrow in her brows. She cleared her throat and took a sip of water. "I was pretty young when she passed away, so I have a few memories, but most of what I know came from my dad and my great-aunt." *That explanation shouldn't give much away.*

"That's too bad. I'm sure you miss her like crazy." He offered a look that showed he understood the pain of losing a loved one too well, and it confirmed her suspicion that he'd spoken the truth about his brother's death earlier. His amber eyes brightened to gold and sparked with anger as he spoke, betraying the emotions he was holding back and making her wonder how his brother had died.

Callie stood. "Okay, enough sad talk. I'm going to go to the bathroom and then unfortunately, we need to go study or we'll have to cancel our date Friday night because I'll be grounded for my grades." Ianthe could tell Callie was giving her the opportunity to threaten bodily harm to Reid or scrutinize him further. She also knew Callie would grill her about what she thought about Reid the moment they got in the car. She wasn't sure how Callie would react to Reid not receiving the BFF seal of approval.

The minute Callie walked away, Reid's entire demeanor changed. "I wonder what makes you so special," he hissed under his breath. She wasn't sure if he meant for her to hear or if he was mumbling to himself.

"I'm sorry?" She tried to act confused, and it didn't take much because she was rather taken aback.

Reid cleared his throat. "I said I can see why Callie thinks you're so special," he corrected.

"Oh, well…" She wasn't sure how to respond. She shifted gears, hoping to throw him off balance. "Listen, before she gets back, I need you to understand something." He gazed at her, curious as to what she would say next. She dropped her voice into a low growl. "Callie means the world to me. If you hurt her in any way, I *will* come after you. You *will* suffer. Do you understand me?" She was tempted to raise her sunglasses so he could see the threat in her eyes, but she didn't want to expose herself on the off chance he didn't already know who she truly was.

The surprise on his face was priceless. Thankfully Callie chose that moment to make her reappearance.

"All right, let's roll," Callie said, face beaming.

"It was nice to meet you, Reid." Ianthe turned her pageant smile on full blast before giving him a wave and leaving Callie a few minutes to say goodbye in private. She sat in her car while Callie walked around the corner of the shop with Reid.

A few minutes later, Callie returned with swollen lips and slightly mussed hair. Ianthe quirked her eyebrow at her appearance. "Not a word." Callie giggled, smacking her friend's arm before pressing the fingers of her right hand to her lips as if to savor the feeling. Ianthe remembered doing the same thing after kissing Conall. *Man, I miss him.* She threw the car in reverse and drove toward home.

It didn't take long for Callie to bring up Reid. "Sooooo…what did you think?" she asked excitedly, leaning over the center console. Ianthe pursed her lips, still unsure of what to say. Callie didn't take her silence well. "What? What is it? Did he do something while I was in the bathroom? Did he say something?"

"Look, Callie…" She sighed. "I love you. I'm just trying to look out for you, okay?"

Callie fidgeted in her seat anxiously. "Seriously, Thee, you're freaking me out. Did he do or say something to you?"

"No, not exactly. I just…I don't trust him. He kind of gives me the creeps, like a bad vibe. I don't think he's good for you." It was the best excuse she could come up with and the closest to the truth.

"A bad vibe? Seriously? What are you talking about? He's great. He's hot, he's a good kisser, and he treats me like a princess. What do you mean he's not good for me?" Callie's voice rose, obviously getting pissed with Ianthe, just as she had feared.

"I don't know how to explain it, Cal. I just don't trust he's who he says he is. He seems dangerous. You should stay away from him."

"Dangerous?!" Callie scoffed. "Do you even hear yourself? Are you jealous? That's it—you're just jealous because I'm starting to spend time with him and not spending every freaking minute with you."

*Well, that escalated quickly.* She took a deep breath and tried to ignore the bite from Callie's words. "That's not it at all. I don't want to see you get hurt," she tried to reason.

"Oh, like you did? Look, not all guys leave girls brokenhearted. They're not all Conall."

Ianthe drew in a sharp breath, Callie's words cutting deeper than she'd thought possible. "I'm going to forget you said that. Look, just trust me on this one, please," she begged.

"Stop the car," Callie demanded.

"What?"

"I said STOP THE DAMN CAR!" Callie screeched.

She pulled over to the side of the road, and Callie threw the door open. "Callie, wait—don't do this."

"Look, I know you've had a hard time with guys, but that doesn't mean I should be miserable and alone too. You can't hang on to a ghost for forever, and ruining my relationship isn't going to bring him back." *And the punches keep coming.* "I don't understand you sometimes. You need to take a serious look at yourself before you lose the only friend you have." With that, Callie slammed the door shut and started walking back toward the yogurt shop.

"Callie!" Ianthe rolled down the window and yelled, but Callie just kept walking. *Shit.* She had totally not expected that. Instead of driving Callie away from Reid, she'd pushed her right into his arms—into the arms of a Fae.

# CHAPTER 13

*Ianthe*

**E**VERY TEXT SHE sent Callie that night went unanswered, and she practically chewed her nails down to the nub thinking up all the possible scenarios where a Fae was involved. For all she knew, Reid could be just like Casimir—or worse. She was too upset to call Aunt Grace and didn't want her to worry before she found out exactly who Reid was and what his intentions were. As she lay down in bed, she focused her mind completely on Conall, hoping with every inhalation and every heartbeat to finally reach him, but she was left disappointed with empty dreams.

Before school the next morning she decided to grab an *"I'm sorry"* latte and scone for Callie. She waited at Callie's locker, breakfast in hand, but she never showed. Ianthe checked her phone and sent off a rapid text, asking Callie to at least tell her she was okay, her anxiety rising when she didn't receive a response. By the time fourth period came around, her anxiety had risen to a panic as Callie was still nowhere to be seen. *What the hell?*

She asked to use the restroom and called Callie's house from the hallway.

No answer.

There was no way this was a coincidence. She felt the truth tugging at her gut so hard she couldn't ignore it any longer. Ensuring that Callie was safe was more important to her than class or the Spanish test. She rushed back into the room, gathered her things, and walked out the door, claiming a family emergency.

In record time, she pulled up to Callie's grandmother's house and jumped out of the car. She rang the doorbell.

No answer.

She knocked on the door.

No answer.

*Shit, shit, shit.* She pounded on the door and yelled, "Callie! Open up! Callie!"

No answer.

Her hands were shaking. *Where is she?* With no other option or lead to follow, Ianthe slumped down onto the porch and waited. An hour or so later, Callie's grandmother pulled up to the house.

"Oh, hello, Ianthe. How are you, dear?" she called out, stepping out of the car.

"Um, I'm okay. Do you know where Callie is?"

Callie's grandmother frowned. "I thought she surely would have told you."

"We...um...kind of...had a fight yesterday," Ianthe stammered, hanging her head in shame.

"Ah, that explains it. Well dear, it seems you're not the only one she fought with yesterday. She got into it with her mom last night as well. I'm not sure exactly what the argument was over, but she packed a suitcase and snuck out in the middle of the night, leaving only a note that said she was going to stay with her dad. I'm sure we'll hear from her soon. Maybe she just needed some time to cool off."

Ianthe knew there was no way in hell Callie would have run off to her dad. For one, Callie wouldn't have left her brother Sean for anything in the world; she adored him and made it her mission to keep him happy. Two, Callie was still heartbroken that her dad had decided to leave their family for a younger woman. Ianthe didn't care how pissed Callie was at her and her mom; she wouldn't have left.

"Okay thanks," she mumbled before leaving the porch. "When she gets home, can you tell her I'm sorry and ask her to call me, please?"

"Of course, dear," her grandma replied as Ianthe walked away.

Sitting in her car, she took some deep breaths, trying to control her rising panic. For the first time since Conall broke her of the habit, she felt the need to snap an elastic against her wrist. Instead she pinched the skin tightly next to her leather bracelet and released a scream of frustration. She slammed her hands on the steering wheel a couple of times. *Where is Callie? How can I find her now?*

Ianthe drove home knowing there was no way she could go back to school and sit in class while Callie was most likely out there with Reid. Then it came to her. She knew what she had to do, and she could only hope they hadn't gotten too far.

She hadn't tried using her Mara abilities on a human other than her Aunt Grace, and she always did it at times when the woman was already asleep. She could only hope she was strong enough to pull Callie under if needed. She knew a full-blooded Mara could lull a human to sleep with very little effort. She just didn't know if she had enough juice as a half Fae to pull it off, but she was sure as hell going to try.

She went inside the house and threw herself onto her bed. She focused on Callie and took deep breaths, trying to get herself to relax, which was hard with the amount of adrenaline pumping through her veins. She rubbed Conall's strap against her wrist and tried again.

Deep breath in—she pictured Callie.

Deep breath out—she imagined Callie's voice in her head.

Deep breath in—Callie's fiery red hair and crazy style.

Deep breath out—Callie's laugh and smile.

Deep breath in—

*Success! Well, partially. Ianthe felt herself relax enough to enter the dream realm. She was at Yogurt Land sitting at an empty table, and the place was completely deserted. She repeated Callie's name over and over in her head like a siren's call, to no avail. She had almost given up when the chimes above the door dinged and Callie stepped inside. Ianthe jumped from her table and rushed toward her, throwing her arms around her and holding her tight. "You're here! Are you okay?" She breathed into Callie's hair before shoving her back so she could look her up and down to make sure she was unharmed.*

*"Ianthe?" Callie asked. Her voice sounded so small,*

*like that of a scared child.*

*"I'm here, I'm here," Ianthe repeated, hugging her again as Callie started to cry.*

*"Tell me what happened, please. I'm so sorry, Cal. So sorry."*

*Callie sniffed. "I'm the one who should be apologizing." She cast her eyes toward the floors and her cheeks flushed with embarrassment. "You were right about Reid."*

*"What did he do?" Ianthe growled, pulling Callie to sit down at the nearest table because she looked so weary. Ianthe's anger stirred her Fae side more than she wanted to admit, something that had recently been causing her teeth to sharpen slightly. It was a reaction she was learning to cope with. She hadn't noticed it when she was in the Fae realm, nor had it been pointed out to her (probably because sharp teeth and glowing eyes were a natural appearance there), but she could feel them prick against the inside of her lips. She tried to calm herself so she wouldn't frighten Callie even more. At least there in the dream realm, she already had quite a bit of practice controlling her appearance.*

*"Well, after I left you, I called Reid. We met up and I told him about our fight. He kept asking about you and some guy, like wondering why this guy was so interested in you. It confused the hell out of me, and frankly I started to get pissed. No offense to you, but he shouldn't be worried about you when he's dating me, right? Anyway, he convinced me to go to his place until I calmed down so we could talk more. We were walking together and then all of a sudden I felt dizzy and we were there. It was like I blinked and suddenly we were standing in front of a log cabin in the middle of nowhere. It was the weirdest thing.*

*"I still felt a little lightheaded when we went inside*

*so he got me something to drink and sat me down on his couch. He brought me a cup of liquid. I'm not sure what it was—I had never tasted anything like it. It was like juice, so sweet, but not like any fruit I've tasted before."*

That prick gave her Fae nectar. Ianthe knew how buzzed it had made her, and she'd only had a little. She'd seen the effects on humans at her bacchanalia (Fae version of a wild frat party and debutante ball all in one), so she could only imagine what it might have done to Callie. She tried not to release the growl building in her throat so she wouldn't interrupt Callie's story.

Callie continued, *"The next thing I know I'm passed out and dreaming of you. Am I really dreaming? This feels so real."* She grabbed Ianthe's hands across the table. *"You feel incredibly real."*

*"This is all my fault. I'm so sorry, Cal. You don't even know. I should have done something to protect you."* Her eyes filled with tears as the guilt weighed her down.

*"Your fault? Seriously, Thee?! You're the one who tried to warn me about him, but did I listen to you? Of course not! I was blinded by his extreme hotness. Now, how the hell do I get myself out of this mess?"*

That right there was one of the many reasons Ianthe loved Callie like her own flesh and blood. That girl was not a quitter, and from the looks of it, she was gearing up to kick some ass.

*"Listen, Cal, I don't know how much time we have, but there are some things I should have told you a while ago,"* Ianthe started. Callie had to know. There was no way around it. If she had any chance of getting out of this mess unharmed, she had to know what she was up against and that she wasn't alone. *"This might sound crazy,"* Ianthe continued, *"which is why I haven't told you any of it be-*

70

*fore, but I'm not exactly human."*

Callie threw her head back and roared in laughter. Once she could stop laughing long enough to speak, she said, "Look at you, trying to cheer me up in my dream. My subconscious rocks."

Ianthe's lips were drawn into a tight line; she'd known Callie wouldn't believe her.

Callie took one more look at her friend's face, studying her eyes closely, and whispered, "Oh, shit."

Ianthe took that as her cue to go on. "I know what you're thinking, but you have to believe me. You've never had a reason to doubt me before so please don't start now. I have to get this all out quickly in case someone wakes either one of us up, so just listen, okay?" Callie nodded her head in agreement. "I found out this summer I'm part Fae." Callie's puzzled expression lead her to believe Callie either wasn't processing what Ianthe was saying or was in denial, so she tried to clarify. "I'm part fairy. I know how it sounds, believe me, but it's true. My dad is not really my biological father. I'm not sure if he knows that for a fact, but I'm pretty sure he's had his doubts about my paternity. My real father is Fae, but not just any Fae. He's like the king of Fae, and not the good kind either, no matter how much I wish he were. Nope—he's the kind that likes to torture humans for fun."

Callie's eyes grew wider with each piece of new information, but to her credit she didn't interrupt, even though Ianthe could see a million questions brimming in her eyes.

Ianthe pressed on. "I think Reid came after you as a way to get to me. I'm not sure exactly why he's doing this because some serious shit went down this summer and I'm not exactly welcome back in Fae. In fact, if I return and am caught, I will be sentenced to death, but that's another story for another time."

"Oh, I can't wait to hear that story later," Callie murmured. Ianthe rolled her eyes and Callie motioned zipping her lips so she could finish.

"Reid is Fae—I knew it the moment I saw him. That's why I acted so weird at the froyo shop and why I tried to warn you about him." Callie looked like a kicked puppy at the reminder of their fight. "You need to know he's not human. I'm not sure what he's capable of because I don't know what kind of Fae he is, but it's probably safe to say he's extremely dangerous. Please don't do anything that will get you harmed. I don't know what I'd do if you were hurt because of me." She grabbed Callie's hands in her own. "I promise you I will figure this out. I will find you and get you back."

"Okay." Callie exhaled jaggedly. "But you know me—I can't just sit here like a damsel in distress and do whatever he wants. It's not who I am. I have to fight for myself."

Thankfully, the beginning of a plan had begun forming in Ianthe's mind while she was recounting her story. "I get it. Actually, I've been there. If you want to help get yourself out of this, I need you to do some serious recon. Listen and observe everything around you. I will visit you in your dreams as often as I can and you can feed me whatever information you have. That way we both know what we're up against. Perhaps once we know what his plans are, we can formulate a plan of attack that doesn't get either of us hurt. Do you think you can do that for me?"

"I don't know, Thee." Callie looked down at the table.

She gripped her friend's hands harder. "Listen, I don't want you to stay with him either. When you wake up, if you know where you are and you get the chance, run, but if your surroundings look weird—if the sky seems too blue or the flowers too vibrant—stay put. He hasn't hurt you *yet, and if he takes you to the Fae realm, there are worse Fae out there—much worse."* Ianthe shuddered, imagining Callie in Casimir's hands. *"It's just not safe to run off. As hard as it is to believe, you might be safer with Reid."*

*Callie's face paled with that bit of information and she sighed.*

*"I will find you and bring you home, I promise. Okay?"* Ianthe said softly, attempting to reassure her.

*"Okay,"* Callie squeezed her hands in return.

A loud knock at the front door pulled Ianthe from her dream. *Damn*, she wished she had been able to give Callie more information or even more reassurance before either of them had woken. She glanced at the clock: 5:00 pm. She didn't think her dad was home yet, so she stumbled downstairs to see who it was. She glanced in the peephole and was met with the face of a familiar Greek Adonis.

*Well fudge sticks.* She didn't want to see Kyle at all, let alone right at that moment. She stood perfectly still, hoping he wouldn't be able to see her. Thankfully the blinds were closed on the window by the door. He knocked once again—forcefully this time, startling her—but she stayed silent as a ghost. She stared through the peephole. He was shirtless (again) and slightly sweaty, which lead her to believe he had been running by her house and decided to stop, but why? He ran his fingers through his hair roughly and gave a frustrating huff before turning and stomping down the driveway. *What the hell was that about?*

She walked into the kitchen to get a glass of water. How was she going to get Callie back? She needed to call Aunt Grace; perhaps she would know what to do.

# CHAPTER 14

*Ianthe*

**S**HE PICKED UP her cell and called her great-aunt. The phone rang, but Grace didn't answer. *Where is she?* Her voicemail picked up, so Ianthe left a message.

"Hi, Aunt Grace." She took a deep breath. "I really need you to call me as soon as you can. A Fae has kidnapped my friend Callie. I'm not sure exactly why, but I know it has something to do with me. I need your help. Call me, please. I love you, bye." She sighed. She was hoping Aunt Grace would answer and they could figure out what to do together, but it looked like she might be on her own. She sat on her bed and started to work through the situation.

Ianthe didn't think Casimir had anything to do with Callie's disappearance; he would revel too much in letting her know if he did, never one to shy away from his deeds, always wanting credit where credit was due. So then why had Reid taken her? How could she find out? She had no way of reaching Alfie or Conall without crossing back into Fae, and the only entrance she was aware of was in the woods by Grace's house several states away. She thought there might be a closer portal, but she had no clue how to locate it. She could contact Casimir in her dreams again, but she doubted he would help her. *He would probably laugh in my face and celebrate my misery.* She was pretty sure Callie was still in the human realm since her powers had worked on her, so maybe she could contact Reid. She didn't want him to know she was Fae, but it seemed from his questions he already knew more about her than she realized. She bounced her knee, trying to come up with a safe solution, and then the thought struck her. *That's it!* She'd call Reid into her dream, but she'd disguise herself as Callie.

Before she could put her plan into action she needed to get herself something to eat because she couldn't remember the last time she had eaten that day. She sprinted to the kitchen and popped a frozen pizza into the oven. She was fairly certain a missing best friend was a great reason to stuff oneself full of comfort food. After devouring four slices, she wrapped the leftovers in aluminum foil and set it in the fridge. She scribbled a note to her dad then ran back upstairs to get ready for bed.

Face scrubbed, teeth brushed, and pajamas on, she was ready to attempt to reach Reid. She tried to calm her nerves and center herself as she lay down to sleep. She closed her eyes; this visit would take a little more prep than her earlier dream with Callie. At least when Ianthe had pretended to be her mom, she was able to practice her appearance with Conall ahead of time. Now, she had no such option, so she kept Callie's image fresh in her mind, and focused on calling Reid into her dream.

*Ianthe blinked her eyes open, imagining herself in her room. She studied her reflection in her mirror, visualizing herself with Callie's face and eyes. It took an immense amount of concentration, but after about half an hour, she finally had it down. "All right, think like Callie. You can do this," she whispered. Crap, my voice is too high. She focused harder and kept talking until she had it just right. The only thing left was to act the part. Instead of calling Reid into her dream, she decided to try to visit his dream like she had done that summer when she visited Conall at his home. She closed her eyes and concentrated all of her energy on Reid, hoping and praying he was still with Callie.*

*Ianthe opened her eyes to find herself standing in the living room of a log cabin. There was a fire lit, radiating warmth throughout the cozy interior. She didn't see Reid right away, so she explored her surroundings. There was an oversized sage green couch that tempted her to sit and rest, but that wouldn't help her find Reid. She opened a door to discover a bathroom. Glancing in the mirror once more to make sure she still looked like Callie, she saw a fiery redhead staring back at her. It was pleasing and eerie at the same time. She quietly closed the door behind her as she left the bathroom.*

*Soundlessly she crept down a hallway and found another door at the end. She opened the door as silently as she could. There was Reid sitting on the bed with his head in his hands. He looked so broken and lost that sympathy momentarily overshadowed her need to hurt him for taking Callie. Why does he look so heartbroken? She stepped forward and the floorboard creaked under her feet. His head shot up, capturing her with his intense amber eyes.*

*"Callie?" he whispered, as if she was a mirage.*

*"Hello, Reid." Ianthe smiled coyly, slipping into Callie's character easily. He stood quickly and strode toward her, threading his fingers through her hair to cup the back of her head and pull her into his arms. He held her tightly against his chest, the fingers of his right hand running down her neck to her back. His cheek pressed against hers.*

*"Oh, Callie. I'm so sorry," he whispered into her hair. What is he sorry about? She was so beyond confused by this whole situation.*

*"What's wrong Reid?" she said breathlessly against his neck.*

*"Everything." He squeezed her tighter and his shoulders started to shake. She realized then he was crying. No, not crying—sobbing—huge, grief-racked sobs. Well, this is not at all what I was expecting. She had to keep reminding herself this was the guy who had kidnapped her best friend, because all her other instincts demanded she comfort him. She was human after all—well, at least half human. As it was, she found her body betraying her mind, her right hand rubbing his back soothingly. Screw it, if I'm going to play the part of his girlfriend, I might as well go all in.*

*"Shhh, it's okay," she soothed.*

*"No, it's not." He pushed away from her grasp so he could look into her eyes. She hoped they were still Callie's eyes he was seeing. His own amber gaze glimmered gold with tears. "I don't know who I am anymore. I never should have taken you. Reid would kill me if he were still alive."*

*Wait....what? She froze, unsure of how to respond. Af-*

ter a few moments, she shook her head slightly to clear her thoughts. *"Wh-What do you mean Reid would kill you?"* she asked.

*"Oh my Callie, my sweet Callie, how did I let things go this far?"* He searched Ianthe's eyes pleadingly, but she knew his question was a rhetorical one.

He gently grabbed her shoulders and guided her toward the bed, pushing down slightly so she would sit. Reid—or whoever he was—released her and sat down to her left. He reached over and picked up her hand, holding it in his own firm grip, stroking his thumb across the back in a tender caress. She stared at his hand. She was bewildered by his actions and emotions. Everything she had assumed she knew about Reid and his possible motivation for taking Callie was proving to be false. He was so remorseful, not even a hint of malice. There was no way he could be an Unseelie.

*"Reid..."* Ianthe started, hoping to coax an explanation from him.

*"Evin,"* he corrected, speaking as if he were lifting a huge weight off of his chest. She glanced up toward his face, but his head was down. *"My name is Evin."*

*"Evin?"* she asked, and he nodded in replied.

*"My brother's name is—was Reid."* He raised his chin and met her gaze with an apologetic look in his eyes. *"I'm sorry I've lied to you, Callie. I didn't know any other way."*

*"Any other way for what?"* she inquired, attempting to put the right amount of ire in her voice, as Callie would have.

*"Let me start from the beginning,"* he stated as she glared at him in a very Callie-like fashion. He continued to run his thumb across her hand in slow affectionate circles.

"I never meant to hurt you, I swear." He looked into her eyes, pleading for forgiveness, and she nodded so he would continue. "Reid was my older brother and best friend. I worshiped him, and he died because of me." Pain etched every one of his features. His voice grew thick with emotion, and he swallowed thickly, trying to hold his tears at bay. "One night we were drinking at a tavern. I'm not exactly sure how it started, but I ended up having a fight with this other guy. Reid jumped in to defend me, and the other guy, Casimir, killed him." She sucked in a sharp breath at Casimir's name. Thankfully, Evin took her gasp as sympathy for his pain. "It should have been me. Casimir's sword was aimed at me, but Reid moved so quickly. He was in front of me before I could react." His thumb had stilled and he stared at the wall of the cabin lost in his memory. "I tried to save him, to get him help, but it was too late. He was gone." He swallowed hard and closed his eyes. This time it was Ianthe's thumb that caressed his hand. She knew what it was like to feel as if Casimir had taken your world away; she knew it all too well. However, unlike Reid, she had been able to save Conall in time.

"I'm so sorry, Evin," she whispered, and she truly was.

He took a few minutes to compose himself before continuing his tale. "I vowed to hurt Casimir the way he hurt me by taking Reid's life. Unfortunately, where I come from, Casimir is well protected. The only way I could think of to hurt him was to take something from him that he cherished. So, I tracked him to your town." Her eyes widened with the knowledge that Casimir was so close. She was sure Evin could read the fear in her eyes. "He seems to have a thing for your friend Ianthe. I'm not sure why, but I thought if I could get her, I could hurt Casimir." And now it's all beginning to make sense.

"But, you didn't take Ianthe," she replied, quirking her

*eyebrow in a silent question.*

*"No." He frowned at her. "She is too guarded."* Guarded? What's he talking about? How am I guarded?

*"So you took me instead?" she asked, although she already knew the answer.*

*"I did. I'm hoping she will come after you herself. I'm sorry, Callie. I really do care about you. I just...I just need to do this—for myself, and for Reid." To his credit, he looked genuinely torn between his feelings for Callie and his need for revenge.*

*"And what will you do if Ianthe comes for me?" She shook her hand loose from his. She was not going to comfort a man who wanted to kill her.*

*"I—I don't know yet. I'm hoping Casimir will come for her and I can take his life to pay for Reid's. I don't want to hurt an innocent." His eyes brimmed with guilt, and she swallowed against the underlying threat in his words. Even if Evin didn't want to, he might hurt Callie or Ianthe if he needed to, if it brought him closer to exacting his revenge on Casimir.*

*"I see..." She wasn't quite sure how to respond. This situation was far more difficult than she had imagined. How am I going to get Callie out of this mess?*

*"I know what you must think of me now, but truly I don't want anything to happen to you. I just didn't know what else to do."*

*She refused to meet his eyes as she racked her brain for where to go from there. "Where are we, Reid—I mean Evin? Where did you take me?" She looked up at him like a little lost puppy, hoping to gain information through feigned innocence.*

*"Um, well..." Evin actually blushed and looked slight-*

*ly nervous. "You're at my place. My king, King Lachlan, gave this place to my father many years ago for his years of service. My father in turn gave it to Reid and me when we came of age. We use it to spend time in the human realm from time to time as a vacation home of sorts. Mostly we check in every so often to make sure the place looks inhabited. The gateway to Seelie land is close by and the king wants humans to believe they are on someone's property so they don't stumble into our realm by mistake."*

*She gasped. A gateway nearby—is that how Casimir ended up here? "I don't—I don't understand—" Well, she did, but she couldn't let him know that. Callie would be confused by this information. Thankfully he took her cue and attempted to explain that he was not human, that a race of people still capable of using magic remained in this world—the Fae. It was a rather good explanation, one that would have saved Ianthe a lot of confusion in the beginning had she heard things explained that way. She was grateful that he was being so kind and patient with Callie for now, but that didn't mean things couldn't change.*

*"How long do you plan on keeping me here?" she asked, pleading with her eyes.*

*Evin dropped her gaze. "Um, I'm not sure...maybe just a day or two to try to work something out." Crap. That doesn't leave me with a lot of time. "If I bring you to my world, I can't let anyone find out about you. They...won't understand." Well that's the understatement of the century, Ianthe scoffed internally. How can I get to Callie before he crosses over to Fae with her? She knew if she crossed into Fae, she risked everything, including her own life, but she would do it for Callie. She was about to question him further when she heard an alarm beeping in the distance. Damn.*

# CHAPTER 15

*Conall*

CONALL WAS GROWING increasingly more antsy and anxious. Sometimes Fae were known for being rash and rushing into things, and other times they seemed to take forever to reach a decision. This was one of the latter times, and it was driving him crazy. Every day King Corydon spent in meetings with his advisors was a day Conall wasn't with Ianthe. Of course, he was required to attend the meetings, but he wasn't allowed to speak unless spoken to directly by Corydon, so mostly he stood in the background and observed while biting his tongue or trying not to die from boredom. This time it was a difficult task to not say exactly what he thought about Casimir and how he should be dealt with any time one of the advisors brought up concerns about what the prince would do next and where he was at the moment.

King Corydon had always let the boy have a lot of freedom, since Corydon's younger brother—Casimir's father,

Rodric—had gone missing a couple years after Ayanna left. Conall had often wondered what had happened to Rodric. Many surmised that he went to search for Ayanna after seeing his brother so devastated by her departure. It was an odd occurrence for a Fae to disappear the way Rodric had. Conall's thoughts were interrupted by King Corydon asking, "What do you think, Conall?"

Conall realized all eyes were on him, and he wasn't sure how long they had been focused on him. "I wouldn't want to see our peace treaty with the Seelie ruined by Casimir's carelessness. Perhaps we should send a tracker to find him and bring him back. Maybe he didn't realize the severe consequences his actions had." King Corydon looked impressed with Conall's objectivity. Of course, Conall secretly hoped he was the one sent to track Casimir, but that was unlikely, given their history. However, he did know enough about Casimir to realize he probably had no clue as to the identity of the Seelie he had killed and the effects it could have. He probably just assumed he was fighting a peasant or a lower class Fae. He might be a lot of things, but Casimir was surprisingly sharp about politics, and in that aspect he could have made a decent Unseelie leader, if it weren't for his many other flaws.

Several of the advisors murmured their agreement with Conall's suggestion, including Drummond. No one wanted to go to war with the Seelie. Finally, King Corydon arrived at a decision. "Very well, let's send"—Conall held his breath, his hope hanging by a thread—"Jaeger to track Casimir down." Just like that, his hopes were dashed. He wondered where this left him. "However," Corydon continued, "if a Seelie so much as sets a toe across the line, upsetting this delicate balance, I will not hesitate to be merciless. We are known for our ruthlessness, and I'd hate to disappoint anybody." A cruel smile tilted King Corydon's lips up, and his violet eyes sparked with bloodlust, craving the violence that would come with war.

The advisors quickly left as the meeting ended. Drummond went in search of Jaeger and the others had business to take care of around the palace for Corydon. Conall, too, rose to leave the meeting. He was eager to find Alfie and hopefully learn something about Ianthe, but the king's voice halted his steps. "Conall."

He turned to face Corydon, who looked a little worse for wear. Perhaps these recent events were taking a toll on him. He bowed in acknowledgment, waiting for the king's command.

"If Jaeger is unable to locate Casimir or convince him to come home, I will need to send you to help. I know the two of you have history, but he is heir to my throne and should be treated with as much respect as you treat me."

"Of course, sire," Conall replied, still bowing.

"I will call for you if we do not hear from Jaeger in two days' time," Corydon added before waving his hand to dismiss Conall. Everyone knew Jaeger was an excellent tracker. He could find anyone or anything. Everyone who lost something went to him to find it. He usually led the royal hunts as his abilities also aided in tracking game. Hopefully, Casimir would be located quickly and Conall could sneak away to find his love.

He exited the war room and turned toward the stairs. He eagerly climbed them, ascending steps two at a time, and rushed into the library. "Alfie," he called.

"Back here, Sir Conall," Alfie replied. Conall followed the voice to find him searching the shelves for a book. "Glad to see you made it back okay, lad." Alfie smiled.

"Glad to see you're still around, old man," he teased

before pressing on to the matter weighing heavy on his heart. "Have you any word of Ianthe?"

Alfie's smile slipped and Conall knew his answer before he spoke it. "No, I'm afraid not. I have been able to gather she went back to her father's house. I believe she should have started school again, but I do have some news that might be of interest to you."

Conall raised his eyebrows, intrigued. "Do tell."

"It appears your lady love has been asking about you."

Conall didn't realize how much he had doubted her feelings for him would remain until that single sentence made his heart soar. *If she is asking about me, she obviously still cares.*

"Enora paid me a visit while you were gone," Alfie began.

"The healer?"

"Yes. It appears she has contact with Grace, Ianthe's great-aunt."

*This is excellent news.* If he couldn't sneak away, perhaps he could pass a message to Ianthe through Enora and Grace. "I, of course, told her you made a full recovery and to please let Grace know how much we both miss Ianthe, and that the minute you can get away, your first stop will be to find her."

Conall sighed and smiled, feeling lighter. "Thank you, Alfie. You have no idea how much that means to me."

Alfie grinned. "Oh, I think I do. Just remember, I care about our princess as well. I'll do anything in my power to help the both of you." Conall couldn't help himself—he quickly grabbed Alfie into a brief hug. When he stepped back, Alfie blushed, slightly embarrassed by the affection, but his grin had widened and his eyes shone with warm affection. "I will let you know if I hear anything else."

"Thank you. I'll check back in with you once I know what King Corydon has in mind for me next," Conall replied, and Alfie's eyes softened with sympathy. Alfie could sense how restless Conall was becoming from being unable to pursue Ianthe. He hoped Conall would be able to keep himself in check or his need to be with Ianthe might be his downfall, especially if Corydon were to discover the depths of Conall's feelings toward her. Even though Corydon had exiled her, Alfie doubted he had cut all ties. In fact, he was almost certain there was a small guard placed on her right then, tracking her and reporting back to Corydon. While many saw King Corydon as a ruthless and coldhearted Fae king, Alfie knew better.

He knew that once upon a time, Corydon had truly loved Ayanna, and that as much as Corydon tried to fight it, part of him loved Ianthe too. Of course, she would never make a good Unseelie ruler, as she was too much like her mother. It wouldn't surprise Alfie if part of the reason why Corydon exiled her was to make her happy or to keep intact her innocent ways that reminded him so much of Ayanna.

# CHAPTER 16

*Ianthe*

**T**HE BEEPING CONTINUED, pulling her from her encounter with Evin. It was her alarm, of course. She supposed she had forgotten to turn it off the night before. She knew on her limited time frame, there was no way she was going to school that day, but how would she find the cabin in the woods? The task seemed daunting, almost impossible. The first thing to do would be to try to get ahold of Aunt Grace. Someone should know what she intended to do, and perhaps Grace might have an idea of how to deal with the Seelie.

Ianthe jumped out of bed. She rushed through her shower and put on jeans and a well-worn Harry Potter t-shirt, throwing her hair up into a messy bun. The morning sun cut through the slats of the blinds, casting a striped pattern across her room. She grabbed her cell phone and scrolled through her contacts until she landed on Grace's name. The phone rang in her ear, once…twice.

"Hello?"

She hadn't realized she was holding her breath until it rushed from her lungs at the sound of her great-aunt's voice. "Aunt Grace?"

"Ianthe, dear. Good morning. How are you, sweetheart?"

She was slightly taken aback by Grace's casual conversation. "Did you get my voicemail last night?"

"Voicemail? Oh, no. I didn't realize I had one."

*Well, that explains it.* She spent the next 10 minutes telling Grace everything she had learned about Callie's kidnapping and Reid's true identity as a Seelie Fae named Evin. She didn't find herself any closer to forming a plan of rescue, but just being able to share the burden with someone else was quite a relief.

"What do you think Evin meant when he said I was too guarded, Aunt Grace?" she finally asked, voicing one of her main concerns.

"Well, to be honest, it doesn't really surprise me, sweetheart. I didn't think Corydon would leave you completely alone." She could almost hear the small sympathetic smile Grace's expression most likely held. "I suppose he has a few of his men keeping an eye on you, although you wouldn't have noticed them. I'm positive that after protecting your life, their second goal is to never be noticed by you. It makes sense when you think about it."

She was still a little floored. *Why would Corydon have his men guard me? Does that mean—does he actually care about me? No, surely not. He let me go after all. In fact, he exiled me on threat of death if I ever return to the Fae realm.* Therein lay her major dilemma with Callie's capture. "Aunt Grace, what am I going to do about Callie? I have to find her before Evin has a chance to take her into Fae. Do you have any clue where the Seelie gateway might be?"

"I'm afraid I don't, love," Grace said with a sigh.

A sudden idea sparked in Ianthe's mind. "Do you think Corydon's guards may know where it is?"

"I'm sure they do, but I don't know how you will find them. After all, they're probably under orders not be noticed by you. I definitely don't think you should go after Callie. Maybe you can send word to Conall and he can take care of it," Grace suggested.

"I have to do something. She's my friend—my best friend—and I'm the reason he took her. I have to get her back."

"I know, sweetheart, and I can't imagine what you're feeling right now, but I don't want you to get yourself killed, and if you follow them into Fae, that's exactly what will happen." She could hear Grace worrying her lip. She knew her aunt was only looking out for her, but that was not what she wanted to hear. She needed someone's help and support right now. *What would Conall say? Would he tell me to stay out of it and keep myself safe? He probably would, and meanwhile he'd be the one risking his life to get Callie back and make me happy.* The thought made her smile, but it quickly faded. *I'll be damned if I let someone else risk themselves for my sake.* She knew what she had to do.

"I understand, Aunt Grace, but I have to try. I love you. If anything happens"—she swallowed against the sudden lump in her throat—"know that I love you, and please tell Dad I love him too, and I know he loved me the only way he knew how. Also, if you could get word to Conall…" She paused to regain her composure. She did not want to cry, but the thought of saying goodbye to Grace and everyone else was breaking her heart.

"Ianthe, this is not the end. You are not going on a suicide mission. Think this through, please. You don't even know what you're up against. Do you know this Seelie's powers? His father must be well off if the king gave him the land with the gateway."

"Aunt Grace, I will be careful, but I have to go. I know she would do the same for me."

Grace sighed in resignation, knowing there was no way to keep Ianthe out of it. "Okay. Keep in contact as much as you can. Try to hide who you are if you must return to Fae. You already changed your hair, but you'll definitely need to do something about your eye color. If no one recognizes you, you won't be executed for breaking your exile."

Ianthe flinched at the idea of being recognized. Sure, the Seelie may have no idea of her existence, but her eyes would quickly clue them in. Even Conall had admitted that her eyes had given her identity away when he first met her. She wondered if any other Fae besides her father had violet eyes. If there weren't any others like her, her eyes would be a dead giveaway. So many things could go wrong with her plan, but she owed it to Callie to try.

"I love you, Aunt Grace."

"I love you too, Ianthe. Be safe." Ianthe hit end on the conversation before she or Grace could change their mind. She knew she was disappointing her aunt, but really what choice did she have? She grabbed an old blue backpack from her closet and threw in some extra clothes and necessities then went into the garage to retrieve a flashlight and pocketknife. She raced back upstairs for her phone charger and made sure Conall's leather strap was tied securely against her wrist. She was as ready as she was going to be.

She ran back down to the kitchen and grabbed some bottled water, protein bars, and a few apples. At the last minute, she decided she should probably leave a note for her dad. She didn't want him to think she had run away or slipped back into old habits, even if there was a chance that he might not notice her missing at all until she returned. She decided it would be best to let him know, especially if something happened while she was gone. She grabbed a pad of paper and a pen from his office.

Dear Dad,

I know there are things about me you don't know. I wish I could change that, but now is not the time. Sometimes I wish I could be the daughter you want me to be, but that's not who I am. You may not understand why I left, but please know I didn't have much of a choice. Callie got into some trouble because of me, so it's my job to get her out of it. I'm not sure how long I'll be gone. Please don't call the police. They won't be able to find me where I have to go. Don't worry, I haven't fallen back into any bad habits that might disappoint you.

I think part of you may have always known this was coming. I think you've always had an idea about just how different I am, how unique Mom was. I know we don't talk about her anymore, but I know her secrets now. I learned all about them during my summer away. I hope one day we can sit down and have an honest conversation. I think we've both been ignoring the elephant in the room for way too long. I will come home as soon as I can. I love you

Love,

Lola

P.S. There's leftover chili in the freezer for you.

She decided to sign with the name her father had given her, knowing that was the version of her he loved the most. She folded the letter and set it on the kitchen island where she knew he would find it. She fished her wallet and lip balm from her purse, slipping them into the front pocket of her backpack, and then she grabbed her keys and took one last look around her comfortable home. It almost felt like a goodbye. She kissed her fingers and touched them to the letter for her dad before she left. "I'll be back," she whispered to the empty foyer before pulling the front door closed behind her. She locked the door and paused for a moment, struck with the finality of her decision.

She sighed, still unsure of where to begin her search or how to convince her Fae guards to reveal themselves. As she walked to her car with single-minded determination, she heard her name called. She glanced up to see a shirtless Kyle headed her way. *Great, just great.* She didn't want to play nice right then; she just wanted to find Callie. She sighed as he jogged her way, and she knew she couldn't just get into the car and ignore him.

"Hey Kyle. I'm kind of in a hurry this morning," she explained as she opened the car door, placing her backpack on the passenger seat. He stopped right in front of her, blocking her path to the driver's side of her car.

"Running late for school?" he asked with a teasing smile as he quirked an eyebrow.

"Something like that," she mumbled.

"Is everything okay?" Kyle asked. She looked up and pasted on a pageant smile.

"Sure, just have to get to school, you know."

"Hey, listen, why don't you skip today and come hang out with me?" Kyle offered. She smiled, knowing exactly how Callie would have responded to this invitation. She realized too late that Kyle mistook her smile as acceptance of his offer. His blue-green eyes brightened with mischief and lust, and he licked his lips in an oddly familiar gesture. Ice ran through her veins and warning bells rang through her head. She backed herself into the car door and tried to edge around Kyle. Her eyes widened as he stepped closer, pressing his body against hers and pinning her to the side of the car. He plucked a strand of her hair and brought it to his nose, his eyes closing as he inhaled her scent. *Now I am officially weirded out. I don't care how gorgeous he is—this is just creepy.*

"Um, Kyle…" She tried not to let her panic show. If she'd learned anything from her time with the Unseelie, it was not to show a predator any sign of weakness. "I really can't today. I have a chemistry test that counts for twenty percent of our grade." The lie slipped easily past her lips.

Kyle seemed to come back to his senses. He dropped the lock of her hair he had been smelling and stepped back. "Of course. Do you think I can take you to dinner tonight instead?"

"Yeah, that would be great." She smiled before making a quick retreat to the other side of the car. Obviously there would be no dinner date because she wouldn't be here.

Kyle beamed. "Great. I'll pick you up at seven."

"I can't wait." She climbed into the car and waved to

Kyle before pulling out of the driveway. *What was that? Why does the thought of a date with Kyle send me into a panic and what is with that look he gave me?* It tugged at her subconscious as if she should recognize it from somewhere, but where? She hadn't seen that look from Kyle before. She shook her head. She shouldn't be worried about him; she should be focusing on rescuing Callie. *All right, focus Thee. Where would the Seelie gateway be?* She stewed over possibilities, taking the quickest route out of town. As she drove, she knew her task would be impossible. Her only hope would be of the Fae variety.

# CHAPTER 17

## Conall

ONALL AWOKE TO someone pounding on his door. His night had been a quiet one, and he was still trying to shake the disappointment of not being able to contact Ianthe when he opened the door. In front of him stood a tall, elegant Fae with long, moss green hair and silver eyes. She was wearing a brown lacey sundress, her cheeks were flushed, and there was a light sheen of sweat glimmering on her skin, as if she had been running.

"Sir Conall?" she managed between heavy breaths.

"Yes," Conall replied hesitantly.

"I am Enora," the Fae woman replied, as if that would explain everything, and in a way, it did—she was the healer who was in contact with Ianthe's aunt.

Movement beyond her caught his attention as a family passed by in a wagon. He smiled widely and spoke loudly for the benefit of anyone who may overhear. "Enora! I'm glad you stopped by. I was hoping you could…" He opened the door, allowing her to pass so they could carry on their conversation in private.

"Conall," she whispered, placing a hand on his arm. "Grace sent me."

The words froze him mid-step. He could hear an edge of panic and desperation to her tone. *Something happened—something bad.*

"What's going on?"

"I—perhaps we should take this inside," Enora said, glancing around as if worried they may be watched.

"Yes, yes, of course."

She hastily entered his home and he closed the door behind her.

"Please tell me she is okay." He couldn't handle it if something terrible had happened to his Ianthe, his violet flower, while he wasn't there to protect her.

Enora didn't realize how much her words had sent poor Conall into a panic until his hands grabbed her biceps, desperately seeking reassurance that Ianthe was okay. "She's okay for now, Conall," she reassured him.

"Okay for now? What's that supposed to mean?"

She gently removed his hands from her arms. "It means she's fine for the present. What happens next is completely up to her."

"Why did Grace send you?"

Enora remembered how upset Grace had been when she last saw her. She had been running low on several herbs and decided to pay Grace a visit early that morning. What a surprise it was when she arrived to find a distraught

Grace raving about her suicidal great niece who had taken it upon herself to rescue a human from a Seelie Fae. Enora knew this would not end well, and guessing by Grace's reaction, Grace also knew where the situation was headed. Grace pleaded with Enora to get Conall. She insisted that he was the only one who would be able to help, so Enora set off right away to find him, practically sprinting most of the way there. Based on how on edge he already was, she knew she had to explain the situation carefully or he might do something rash and endanger them all.

"Please, have a seat, Sir Conall." She gestured for him to join her in the living room and they both took a seat, although his posture was stiff and he sat on the edge of his chair, as if to spring into action at any moment. "When I went to see Grace this morning, she was rather upset. It seems Ianthe has chosen to do something rather dangerous."

Conall sprung from his seat. "Where is she?" he demanded.

Enora sighed. This was going to be harder than she thought. "Conall, sit," she ordered in her sternest voice. "You cannot just jump into action. You must hear me out all the way through. You'll do her no good unless we figure out a plan of action first. Moreover, last I heard, you were still needed at the castle. Are you really going to defy the king?"

Conall leaned toward her, his emerald eyes darkened, and he lowered his voice to almost a growl. "You have no idea what I would do for her, Enora. Do not ask me questions you are afraid to have answered."

Enora was slightly taken aback. What he'd just admitted could be considered treason if she were to report him to the king. Of course, she wouldn't do such a thing. While she was Unseelie, she wasn't one to meddle in politics and preferred to remain an unknown subject to the king. She would have to speak to Grace about this. She knew Grace had underestimated Ianthe and Conall's relationship. If Corydon were to catch wind of it, she was not sure what the repercussions would be, but they wouldn't be good, that was for sure. "All right, Conall, your point has been made and noted. Sit, please."

He grudgingly took his seat again, mumbling curses under his breath.

"Grace is concerned about Ianthe's safety." Conall looked as if he were going to leap into action again, so Enora reacted the only way she knew how: by humming a soothing tune under her breath until she saw him visibly relax.

"Do not think you can hold me here as long as you like, siren," Conall spat. He wasn't anything like Enora had thought he would be. The stories she'd heard from Alfie, though, were beginning to make a little sense. This sounded more like the young boy Alfie had spoken of so long ago, not the man he had become.

"I do not wish to hold you here, but you must keep your anger in check, and if I have to use my powers on you to help the situation, I will." She smoothed her hands across her lap before looking back at him. She hated to use her powers against him. She wasn't cut like most Unseelie and while her beautiful voice could bring men to do terrible things under her control, she didn't like to use it. She liked to be known as a healer instead.

Conall's cheeks flushed slightly, ashamed at his own outburst. "My apologies, Enora."

"Now, shall I continue?" She looked at him, and he nodded. "It appears a Seelie Fae has kidnapped Ianthe's best friend, a human girl by the name of Callie. Grace mentioned something about it having to do with Casimir."

Conall snorted. "Of course it does."

"Yes, well, apparently Ianthe has taken it upon herself to rescue her friend from the Seelie." Enora put her hand up, sensing his impending outburst, and hummed under her breath slightly. His clenched fists relaxed as he sagged back into his seat. "So far, we know the girl has yet to enter Fae. Ianthe was hoping to reach her friend before he could take her across through a Seelie portal."

"That's it? That's all we know?"

She swallowed hard and nodded. She'd known the lack of information would upset him, but not as much as knowing his love had planned to break her own exile. She waited for the moment when the realization hit him.

His face dropped. "Ianthe plans to follow her into Fae, doesn't she?" His voice was barely above a whisper as if he was afraid he already knew the answer to the question.

"She does, or at least Grace believes she does."

*Enora confirmed his worst fear—if Ianthe set foot back in the Fae realm, she would be facing her own execution. Conall felt like someone had plunged a knife into his chest. How could she do this to me? Doesn't she know I won't survive her death? He took a moment to wallow in pity before shaking some sense into himself. Of course she will go after her friend—would I expect anything less from her? Her strength, compassion, and determination were part of why I fell in love with her to begin with, not to mention she is protective and fearless when it comes to saving those she cares about. Hasn't she shown me that through her own actions the night I was nearly killed? Guilt seeped into him.*

Enora's voice cut through his thoughts. He had almost forgotten she was there. "So, Conall, what do you plan to do with this information?"

"Do we know who took her friend? The Fae's name?"

"Ah, yes—that would be some fellow by the name of Evin."

His eyes widened in surprise. He had been expecting to hear Casimir's name, not the name of the young Seelie he had met recently. *Of course, the connection to Casimir now makes sense, but what led him to Ianthe? Does he know who she truly is—that she is the Unseelie princess?* Conall didn't think so—Evin wasn't suicidal enough to anger Corydon through his daughter.

Enora studied his expression carefully. "I take it you know this Evin."

"I do," he replied. "Casimir murdered his brother not too long ago."

"Ah, it always comes back to Casimir, doesn't it? I never liked that little twerp." Her comment caught him off guard, and he released a bark of laughter despite the grave situation they now faced. He wasn't sure how to find Evin, but he did know who would—Torin.

# CHAPTER 18

## Ianthe

**IANTHE HAD HOPED** her scheme would lure her guard out of hiding. When she made it, her plan had seemed brilliant, but now she was doubting her sanity. She had found a young guy at the gas station willing to make some quick cash by pretending to attack her. Her first clue it wasn't the smartest idea should have been how easily the guy agreed. He took her cash with a smile on his face and arranged a meeting time a few streets over, in an alley behind a bar the guy knew. He didn't ask any questions about why she had hired him to do it. In fact, he didn't ask any questions at all, and that was perhaps the most frightening realization as she stood in the alley behind the bar an hour later.

She was checking the time on her phone when a hand clamped down over her mouth and yanked her back against a large body. A startled scream tried to work its way out of her throat when she felt a cold blade pressed against her skin.

"Don't make a sound," a man's voice hissed in her ear. He smelled of greasy food, stale cigarettes, and body odor. His voice was gruff and raspy, as if he smoked a pack or two a day, nothing like the young man's musical tenor. She tried to discreetly move her fingers toward her pocket where she had shoved her own knife before leaving her backpack in the car. Her plan may have been foolish, but she was not a complete idiot.

"Now, don't try anything stupid, princess," the voice warned. She hoped and prayed Evin was right and she did have an Unseelie guard following her. She didn't know how else she was going to get out of this. A dark figure rounded the corner into the alley and she held her breath.

"Are you okay, miss?" a man called out as he strode toward them. She swallowed and felt the blade of the knife prick her skin. A small droplet of blood rolled down her neck, and she involuntarily whimpered.

"Don't step any closer or I'll slit her throat," her attacker warned.

The man kept approaching. "I wouldn't do that if I were you." His face came into view and she could see his glowing silver eyes. He smiled, revealing a set of sharp teeth, and then he whistled. Quick as a flash, another man appeared at her right, holding a crossbow aimed at her attacker. His eyes were a brilliant, shimmering gold.

Her attacker dropped his knife and backed up, shoving her forward. He hastily made his way to the back door of the bar, threw it open, and rushed inside. Ianthe released the breath she was holding and swayed on her feet. The Fae to her right grabbed her arm to steady her.

"Are you okay, Lady Ianthe?"

"Yes, I just need a moment," she said, leaning against the nearest brick wall.

"Why did you let him get away? I could have had some fun with that one," the silver-eyed Fae complained to his companion.

"Don't worry, I got his scent. We can hunt him down later."

Well, even though it wasn't her original plan and she'd narrowly escaped being attacked, she had succeeded in making contact with her Fae guard. She didn't know the Fae by name but she did recall seeing the golden-eyed one around the castle once or twice during her stay the previous summer. With a second glance at them, she revised her observations to include the silver-eyed Fae. She definitely remembered him from her trip to the Unseelie dungeon. He was tall and rather lanky where his companion was shorter and muscular. They made quite the pair of opposites. The silver-eyed Fae had dark skin that made his metallic eyes look completely otherworldly. His black hair was pulled back in a mass of dreadlocks while his companion had alabaster skin and a short mop of unruly curly red hair.

The redhead placed his hands on Ianthe's face and gently tilted her head to the side so he could rub something against her neck where the knife and pricked her skin. "There. All better, milady," he replied.

"Thank you..." She paused, hoping he would supply his name.

"Quinn." He smiled, flashing his sharp teeth.

"Thank you, Quinn," she repeated. Her head was spinning from the attack, but she needed to get her thoughts together. She had to figure out how to get the information she wanted without letting them know her intentions. She was quite positive if they were sent to guard her, they wouldn't let her waltz back into Fae to face her execution. She decided to try to play it cool. "I take it my father sent you." Quinn smirked as if to humor her while the other Fae looked bored by their conversation. She didn't wait for a reply before continuing, "Of course he did. I wouldn't expect anything less from King Corydon. Can you tell me anything about why he sent you? Are you only here to protect me from harm?"

"I'm sorry, Lady Ianthe, but we're not allowed to reveal our orders to you," Quinn replied.

The silver-eyed Fae rolled his eyes in annoyance. "She's fine. We should go back to our posts, Quinn."

"Wait," she stalled. "How can I thank you properly? Can I tell my father to reward you perhaps?" The silver-eyed Fae grimaced. *Bingo.* She batted her eyelashes innocently.

"Ah, no, that's not necessary, m-milady," Quinn stammered. Ianthe tilted her head aiming for a perplexed expression. "You see, it wouldn't look good if he were to hear how close we let the attacker get to you."

"You mean, how close *you* let her attacker get," the other Fae interjected.

"Well, if you hadn't distracted me…"

She let the two of them squabble for a moment because the conversation was currently playing to her advantage. "All right, Quinn, I won't say anything," she finally conceded. The men faced her and smirked in relief. "If"—the darker one's eyes narrowed suspiciously—"you can answer a few questions for me."

Quinn swallowed and paled slightly. "I'm not sure we can, milady." She frowned. "Well, you can ask them and we'll see if we can answer them," Quinn suggested as a sort of compromise.

"Very well, I know you can't tell me about your orders, but do you know if there is a gateway nearby?" Quinn's lips tightened into a thin line as his companion's expression grew dark.

"Why do you want to know?" the silver-eyed Fae asked.

"Well, I was thinking the other day about how silly it would be for me not to know. I mean, what if I stumbled into one by mistake?" Ianthe could see how unlikely this might sound. Her mind whirled for a reason why this would be plausible when the idea clicked. "I heard some kids at my school talking about bonfires and parties in the woods. I'd hate to go to one of the parties, have too much to drink, and not realize I had stumbled into the Fae realm until it was too late." That sounded like a reasonable excuse—at least it did to her.

Silver eyes narrowed even further. He wasn't buying it, but Quinn, on the other hand, seemed to be relieved. "Well, milady—"

"Quinn," he growled.

"No, no, it's a good reason. She probably should know. It's not like she's stupid enough to go back voluntarily. She knows she'll be captured and executed if she sets foot in Fae. Besides, it's not like she'd be able to get through. We'd keep her from going in," Quinn reasoned to his companion.

"Which is exactly why we *don't* need to tell her."

"Ahem," Ianthe interrupted with what she hoped was a doe-eyed look of innocence.

Thankfully, Quinn ignored his companion's advice. "Well, there is one not too far out of town off of Windsor

Road. So, if you're going to party, just try not to go out in that direction." Silver Eyes shook his head in disapproval, but Quinn merely shrugged as if his vague directions wouldn't deliver her right to the gate.

Inside, she smirked in triumph, but she didn't let it show. Instead she smiled appreciatively and said, "Okay, thank you."

*"Is that it?" Silver Eyes asked. Oh right, I should probably have more than one question, otherwise it will look too suspicious.*

"Are you the only two who watch me?"

"Currently, but you never know with His Majesty."

*She nodded her head. While this has been informative, how can I get rid of them in order to find Callie?* "What will happen to the man who attacked me?"

Silver Eyes' smile widened predatorily. "Nothing you need to worry your pretty little head about. Just stay out of trouble tonight so we can take care of him. Think you can handle that, princess?"

"Of course. I was only planning to go to the library to work on a school project. I'll probably be there late and then go straight home. I really shouldn't put off these huge projects until the last minute," she lied. "Okay, well I should get going. Thanks for the rescue, guys. It was nice to meet you, Quinn." She hastily made her retreat to her car. *Hmmm...they will be occupied tonight—sounds like the perfect time to go after Callie.*

She got into her car and decided to go the library until then. There was no way she could go home and risk running into her father or Kyle. She would just find a place to hunker down at the library, hopefully get in a short Mara visit to Callie to fill her in on the plan. She decided that was exactly what she needed to do. She needed to get ahold of Callie so she could stall Evin from taking her into Fae until tomorrow, unless she was too late. No, she wouldn't think that way. She had to stay positive. She would do everything in her power to reach Callie before Evin could take her into Fae.

Later that evening, Ianthe sat in a cushy, green, paisley chair in a secluded corner of the library, wondering how she could check that her guards had left her to go after her attacker. She knew they would wait until dark, so she was hoping eight o'clock would be late enough. She would have to leave the library by then anyway. She sighed deeply. There were so many risks involved with her plan, but she knew she had to do something. She couldn't just sit there and let a Fae take Callie from her. Callie had nothing to do with this. She snarled in frustration. It was her fault, after all. If Callie hadn't been hanging out with her, Evin would have had no reason to take her. She gripped the arms of her chair, trying to calm herself down. *Come on, Ianthe, you can do this. You can get her back. You just have to think.*

She needed to get in touch with Callie again. It had been too long and too many things could have happened to her. Pulling herself together, she settled in to meditate, calling on her Mara ability and focusing on Callie's beautiful face and spunky personality.

*She blinked her eyes open. She was in the yogurt shop again—the perfect place to put Callie at ease. She sat at the table and willed Callie to walk through that door. Every second that passed with no sign of her best friend*

*increased the panic growing inside. Her heart started racing. What if I'm too late? She took a few deep breaths. Maybe Callie wasn't asleep. As soon as she tried to reason with herself, the words she didn't want to utter crept into her mind. What if he's already taken Callie through to Fae? She gripped the table tightly.*

*"Shit. Shit! SHIT!" she yelled, the volume of her voice increasing with each word. This was not how she had pictured the day going at all. Every bone in her body screamed for Callie to show up, for them to be able to figure something out. She knew all too well the risks of going back into the Fae realm. If she were discovered and sent back to the Unseelie, she would be executed. She couldn't let that happen. Some part of her felt that her father would either cause an upheaval with the Unseelie by not being able to follow through, or he would have her executed and it would drive him further into his own darkness. She knew even though he hid it, part of King Corydon cared for her more than he would ever admit. If only there was a way to get ahold of Conall; he would know what to do.*

*She took a deep breath and refocused her energy. Her heart sank knowing Callie was a no-show, but maybe she could reach Conall. She closed her eyes and pictured the clearing surrounding Aunt Grace's house. She opened her eyes to find herself sitting on Grace's porch. She stood, gripping the railing of the steps, and flung herself into the clearing, racing toward the tree where they had first met. "Conall?" she called to the night air, but the only thing she heard in reply were crickets chirping. "Dammit! Where are you?" Her steps faltered, and she threw her head back to yell toward the sky. "Where are you, Conall?" Her voice cracked on his name. "I need you!" When they left her lips, her final words were just above a whisper. She collapsed into the grass and released the sobs that were building up in her chest. She was alone...completely alone.*

*She wasn't sure how long she had been kneeling in the grass and sobbing into her hands. She felt spent after shedding so many tears, but at the same time, she felt a little bit lighter. Now that she'd had a good cry, she could think a little more clearly without the desperation and panic setting in. She searched her memory for anyone who might be able to help her get to Callie. She knew she wouldn't be able to reach Alfie, as he never really left the palace, let alone the Fae realm. She already knew her guards would refuse to do anything that might put her at risk and couldn't have cared less about a human life. Casimir's name unexpectedly flashed through her mind. She flinched with the knowledge that her thoughts led to him. He shouldn't have been a welcomed thought on any occasion, and she wasn't nearly that desperate yet. She knew he wouldn't help her without a price—one she was certain she wouldn't be willing to pay. She shuddered as the possibilities of what he would request raced through her head.*

*She gave herself a short pep talk before standing up. "All right, Ianthe, you can do this. You can save her. You've got no one else, and neither does she. You're all she has, and she's your best friend. Pull yourself together and let's get this show on the road." She brushed her hands clean on her jeans, and with a hardened resolve, began to wake herself up. It was time to go save Callie.*

# CHAPTER 19

*Ianthe*

S HE BLINKED HER eyes. She was once again seated in the paisley green armchair in the library. She plucked her phone from her purse and checked the time: 7:50 p.m. She knew the library would be closing soon, so she gathered her things and headed toward her car. She sat in the driver's seat, contemplating if it was clear for her to leave. She decided the smart thing to do would be to at least let one person know where she was headed. She didn't want to talk to Aunt Grace, because she knew how upset she'd be and knew she'd try to talk her out of going after Callie. She decided to settle on an email. She typed up a quick note saying she was going after Callie and not to worry. She would be extra vigilant and not let anything happen to herself or her friend. After she hit send, she felt her stomach drop, knowing the message would disappoint her great-aunt. She hated to disappoint the one person who had shown the most faith in her, but she had made up her mind.

She turned the engine on and put the car into drive. Pulling out of the library, she headed East on the two-lane road toward the edge of town. Curious if Quinn and his partner were following her or out "hunting", she swerved into the opposite traffic lane. She quickly swerved back and didn't notice any change—no glowing eyes in sight. She tried once more, this time when a car was heading down the opposite lane, playing a risky game of chicken. The other driver laid on the horn as she jerked the car back into her own lane just in time to avoid the oncoming traffic. Surely her guards would have shown up by now if they were watching her. Her heart pounded in her chest and the adrenaline surged through her veins after the near collision. She smirked, pleased that they were not being vigilant, and took a left onto Windsor Road. She craned her head into the darkness, searching for what could be the log cabin from her dream visit with Evin. She saw a dirt driveway off to the right and turned down it, hoping to hit the jackpot.

Several failed attempts later, she turned back onto Windsor, feeling more and more discouraged with every wrong house. She drove for another ten minutes, getting farther away from town and deeper into the woods. Finally, she saw another driveway coming up on her left. She took a deep breath, crossed her fingers, and turned. She bounced along the dirt road until a porch light came to view. The breath rushed from her lungs and she hit the brakes, staring at the moderate log cabin in front of her. *This is it.* She quietly climbed out of the car, retrieved her backpack from the back seat, and made sure to grab her knife, sliding it into her pocket.

Silently, she crept up to the front door of the cabin. Every step seemed to snap twigs or disturb rocks loudly, giving her location away to anyone or anything within ear-shot. Even though the porch light was on, she noticed all the interior lights were off. It was too early for everyone to be asleep (if this was indeed Evin's place), and dread settled into her gut like a ball of lead. She tried to peek into the windows, but couldn't see much as the curtains were mostly closed. She tried the front door handle and—surprisingly—it turned, opening with a loud creak. She cringed and held her breath, straining to hear any sign of life. After she was certain no one was coming to investigate, she tiptoed inside and silently crept through the house, not encountering a single person or Fae. Her breath caught as she stepped into one of the bathrooms. In the corner of the mirror was a lipstick print—a bold red lipstick print to be exact—in the exact shade Callie wore. She placed her hand over her heart. It ached with the knowledge that Callie had been there and wasn't any longer. There was only one place they would have gone, and the thought turned her stomach sour. If they weren't there at the cabin, they were most likely on their way to or already in Fae. She raced back through the house. As her feet hit the dirt path, she yelled her friend's name as loudly as she could, hoping beyond measure Callie might still be around, hoping she would hear her and be able to break free of Evin.

Silence resonated around her. *Damn. I need to find the gateway and fast.* She could practically feel Callie slipping away with each second she hesitated. She grabbed her flashlight from the backpack, illuminating the ground around the house as she prayed Callie might have left some clue for her to follow. Her eyes widened and she couldn't help but grin when she realized that Callie had done even better. It appeared she put up quite a struggle as Evin forced her to leave. There was a scuffle of footprints and a path through the dead leaves that seemed as if someone had been dragging their feet the entire time they walked. Ianthe could almost imagine Callie doing exactly that with an exaggerated pout on her face, and a giggle bubbled out of her mouth before she could stop it. *Man, do I love that girl.*

She followed the tracks into the woods. Now that she knew the direction of the gate, she thought it shouldn't be too hard to find it. She had probably been walking for a good 30 minutes, following a sporadic path of disturbed dirt and foliage when she noticed a familiar archway of intertwined trees, this time birch. It was somewhat surprising that this one was so similar to the one outside her Aunt Grace's house. She had thought it might be harder to spot or might use trees that were more native to the area, and it made her wonder if the gateways were glamoured in a way that humans couldn't see them, but she could. She sighed, realizing that since Callie and Evin's path ended here, he had already taken Callie to the Fae realm. *Well, this blows.* The realization of just how bad things were struck her, and she staggered against a large maple tree. *There's no way to reach Callie now unless I cross over. However, if I cross over and am discovered, I'm totally screwed.* She knew she could be executed if she were caught, but there was no way she would leave Callie in the hands of the Fae. This was literally a matter of life or death, for the both of them.

She knew she had to act fast, before the guards returned. "I'm sorry, Dad. I'm sorry, Aunt Grace. I'm sorry, Conall. I love you all. I know you may not agree with what I have to do, but I have to do it," she whispered into the breeze, hoping her words might somehow be received. She reached for her knife, reassuring herself that she was armed, slid her flashlight back into her bag, and tightened the straps of her backpack so it wouldn't bang against her while she ran. Lastly, she took a deep breath and stepped forward into the gateway. "Hold on, Callie. I'm coming for you."

# CHAPTER 20

## Conall

**NORA LEFT CONALL'S** house after she felt her message had been properly delivered, and she would return to Grace's home to inform her of what he intended to do. Conall wasn't sure how he'd be able to get ahold of Torin. He considered informing King Corydon about Ianthe's predicament, but he worried the king would either not care at all, forbid him from going to her aid, or start a war with the Seelie over it. None of those options sat well with him. Of course, there was always the off chance that King Corydon just might let him go to her side and rescue her human friend, but the odds were too slim to risk it, especially since Conall suspected King Corydon was intentionally keeping him close by so he couldn't pursue Ianthe.

He was in quite a predicament. He knew defying the king's orders would make him a traitor, but he also knew when it came to Ianthe, there wasn't anything he wouldn't do for her. He sighed and ran a hand through his hair roughly. He felt as though he could rip it all out. The whole situation was so frustrating. Finally, he decided to pay the king a visit. Perhaps, on his way to the palace, he could come up with a reasonable excuse for taking leave and traveling to Seelie territory.

He stepped into the throne room where King Corydon sat, looking as bored as ever. He waited to the side until his presence was acknowledged. The king's gaze finally seemed to settle on him as he slightly raised an eyebrow. "Ah, greetings, Conall. What news do you have for me today?"

"No news, Your Majesty," Conall replied, rising from his bow. He cleared his throat before continuing, "I was merely wondering if you've heard from Jaeger yet regarding Casimir's whereabouts."

The king's expression turned dark and stormy, his lips flattening and tugging downward. "I have not. His last communication stated that he was crossing into Seelie territory, and I fear Casimir's blood debt may have more severe effects than we had anticipated."

Conall nodded his head slowly. The situation had presented itself with a unique opportunity. "I would be happy to go after Jaeger and Casimir. I do not fear the Seelie since they know me well from all our negotiations. I think if they are going to cooperate in any way with an Unseelie, it will probably be with me."

Corydon rubbed his lower chin like an evil supervillain. Conall tried to make it look as if he considered the task stupid and beneath him, and not exactly what he was hoping for.

After several long minutes, King Corydon released a sigh, and the calculating chill left his violet eyes. "I suppose that would be for the best. You will follow Jaeger's trail to Seelie land. If for some reason you need to cross into the human realm"—Corydon's eyes narrowed suspiciously—"you will send word and wait for further orders before crossing. Is that understood, Conall?"

He bowed his head. "As you wish, sire. Will anyone be accompanying me on my journey?"

"With peace hanging so precariously in the balance, I cannot afford to allow any more soldiers leave." The king studied his second's body language closely. "I know Casimir may be resistant to returning with you—for understandable reasons. It's no secret he despises you, especially after your most recent disagreement. In fact, it wouldn't surprise me if that were the reason he left in the first place. However, I'm most certain if you tell him I order him home, he will return of his own free will. I'm trusting you with his safety, Conall. Do I need to remind you what will happen if you fail to return with him?" Corydon's long silver hair glimmered in the trickling sunlight. His face became a cold mask of indifference, and Conall knew without a doubt that Corydon's words were not a warning, but a threat. The thought that the man he had been loyal to for so long would so quickly dispose of him sent a chill down his spine.

"I understand." Conall met the king's eyes to show he acknowledged the veiled threat underneath his words.

"Then you may go. Leave at once." Corydon waved his hand dismissively, and Conall turned to leave, taking several strides away from the throne before Corydon's voice halted his steps. "Oh, and Conall…" He turned around to see the king's eyes narrowed upon him. "It would be best for everyone if you did not have any contact with my daughter. She's no longer part of our world, and I would like to keep it that way." For the first time, Conall saw

Corydon's usually cold eyes flicker with something else. He couldn't put his finger on it exactly, but it seemed like a mixture of sadness, regret, and resolution.

"Of course, Your Majesty." He forced the lie past his lips, and it was easier than he had anticipated. There had been a time before Ianthe when he would never have thought about lying to the Unseelie king, but now he knew where his true loyalties lie. He only hoped King Corydon didn't notice the shift.

He left the palace to gather supplies from his home and in town for his journey then retrieved Rain from the palace stables and saddled him. Finally, he mounted his steed and set out. He wasn't sure how long it would take to find Casimir, and even if he did follow through with finding him, all that mattered was that he was heading toward Seelie land, the same place Ianthe was heading toward. He hoped he would arrive early enough to prevent her from doing something foolish like crossing over to Fae. Only when she was safe would he decide what to do about everything else.

# CHAPTER 21

*Ianthe*

IANTHE STUMBLED AND fell to her knees. She felt the world spinning around her as if she was riding a tilt-a-whirl at the fair. She closed her eyes and dug her fingers into the soft earth. It was cool beneath her fingertips and the blades of grass were a soft blanket covered with dew. Slowly, she regained her bearings and blinked her eyes open then tugged her backpack off. Her stomach rolled, and she closed her eyes again quickly, turning over onto her back. Once she was positive she wasn't going to puke her guts out, she opened her eyes slowly and stared at the night sky above her. She could tell at once she was in Fae by the way the stars glimmered brighter, sparkling like diamonds against the night sky. The moonlight lit up the forest around her, and even in the dark she could see the silhouettes of brightly colored flowers. After a few minutes, her eyes adjusted to the dark, and her nausea dissipated. She pulled herself up to a standing position, peered around, and found herself in the middle of a wood similar to the one she had left behind in the human realm.

*What am I going to do? How will I ever find Callie now?* She hadn't really stopped to consider the consequences of her actions, but at that moment they slammed into her like a speeding train and she staggered back against a tree. If anyone were to discover her and who she was, she would be killed. While the Seelie were not known to harm humans intentionally, there were always exceptions to the rule, so even if they didn't know who she was and found her, she still could find herself in extreme danger. *Think of Callie— what chance does she stand against them? She needs you. You're here for her.* The reminder of why she had crossed into the realm in the first place was as effective as dumping a bucket of ice water on her fears. She instantly squared her shoulders, ready to face whatever may come.

She plucked her backpack from the ground and slid her cell phone out of her pocket, powering it off. *Not like I'm going to get a signal in Fae anyway.* She chuckled as she safely stowed her phone in the front pouch of her backpack. She took inventory of her supplies and even though she was beginning to get thirsty, she convinced herself to wait and ration her water wisely. She had no idea where to go from there because she didn't have any clue where Callie was. She could just start walking, or she could take some time to try to reach her friend. She figured running off without a real plan probably wouldn't be the smartest idea, so she lay back down on the soft grass. She stopped to listen for creatures, both animal and Fae, but when she was only met with the sounds of insects, she relaxed and placed her backpack on top of her chest as a sort of shield before closing her eyes and focusing her mind on Callie.

*This time instead of the yogurt shop, Ianthe found herself at Callie's house—on her front porch, to be exact. She smiled, knowing if she was there it was because Callie was dreaming and she had entered Callie's dream instead of pulling Callie into her own. Her powers were still alien to her, and they came with a huge learning curve. She never quite knew what to expect or how to control where she first started from.*

*She stepped toward the door and knocked, waiting for a response. When there was no answer, she grabbed the door handle and turned it. Releasing a sigh of relief, she stepped inside. "Callie, are you here? Hello...Cal?" she called out as she walked through the living room. She had just turned toward the hallway that led to Callie's room when a flash of red hair tackled her in a strong hug.*

*"Ianthe! Oh my god! Is it really you? Are you really here?" Callie practically yelled in her ear while holding her in a death grip.*

*"Yes, Cal. It's me. Can you let go a bit? I can't breathe," she wheezed.*

*Callie's grip instantly loosened and she stepped back from Ianthe. "Oh, Thee, I was so scared. I thought I'd never see you again once we left that cabin. Did you find my clues?" A sly smile tilted her lips up.*

*Ianthe smiled in return. "Yes, you were amazing. That lipstick print, the drag marks—it all helped me. I know he took you into Fae, and that's where I am now too. Can you tell me what happened after you guys left the cabin? I'm trying to track you, but I'm not sure where to go from where I am."*

*Callie took a deep breath and nodded her head. She tugged Ianthe's hand, pulling her toward the couch in the living room, and they both sat down. "Okay, so Reid—I* mean Evin—well, he pulled me through the woods, which I guess you know since you followed us—"

"Wait, he told you his real name?"

"Oh, yeah. It was the strangest thing." Callie smirked at her. "So, the morning after you visited me in my dreams he tells me he had a dream about me. You wouldn't know anything about that, would you?" She teasingly elbowed Ianthe in the side, while Ianthe blushed and nodded. "I thought so. Anyway, he decided he should come clean with me. He told me his real name was Evin and he was sorry he had lied to me" Her voice cracked slightly, letting Ianthe know Reid's betrayal hurt more than she let on. "He told me what happened to his brother and that some guy named Casimir is like obsessed with you, so Evin was using me to get to you." She swallowed, her voice growing thick with emotion. "It sucks, ya know? Knowing this amazing guy I was falling for was just dating me to get to my bestie."

Ianthe reached over and grabbed Callie's hand, holding it to offer comfort and show her support. A few tears managed to escape Callie's eyes before she pulled herself back together. "Of course, he also told me what a huge mistake it was. He said he really does care about me, but honestly, how am I supposed to believe that now? He kept apologizing, but he still won't let me go, said he doesn't have any other choice, and he already made decisions that'll have consequences, so there's no going back now. I still don't get it. How could he do this?" Callie started crying again. It was obvious she hadn't dealt with what she had experienced and learned yet. Ianthe dropped her hand and folded Callie into her arms, allowing her to sob freely and take comfort in the embrace. She stroked Callie's hair as her Aunt Grace had done for over the summer whenever she awoke sobbing and calling out Conall's name.

Conall! That's right, now that I'm in Fae, I should be

able to use my Mara powers to communicate with him. That thought brought her more comfort in that moment than she could have imagined. Callie sniffed and pulled free of her embrace.

"Thanks. I guess I kind of needed that. I hope you don't think any less of me. I'm not quite the badass I pretend to be sometimes," she apologized.

Ianthe shoved her shoulder playfully. "Whatever. I always knew you were a big softie under that hard exterior. Besides, no one can master resting bitch face the way you do without having some deeply buried emotions." She winked, and Callie glared at her.

"Hardy har har. You're so hilarious, Lola," Callie teased right back, placing emphasis on her friend's less preferred name.

"All right, now that we've gotten the lying bastard part out of the way, do you remember what happened after you were dragged through the woods?"

"Well, we got to this strange set of white trees that formed a kind of arch..." Ianthe nodded her head to show she understood what Callie was saying. "Then he tells me it might be better if I were asleep, and I was like hell no! I wasn't going to let him knock me out and do whatever he wanted with me, and I told him that."

A small giggle escaped Ianthe's lips. Picturing Callie telling Evin off was definitely something she wished she could have seen in person. "Man, I love you, Cal." She smiled. "So what happened next?"

"Well, believe it or not, he was actually really kind about the whole thing. He kept apologizing. He said he only thought it would help if I were unconscious, but he wouldn't force me. He looked really pitiful, honestly. I don't know what to think about him. It was like he didn't

want to hurt me, but then why take me in the first place?"
Callie wondered aloud.

Ianthe stared at her hands, guilt seeping through her
pores. She couldn't even look her in the eye, knowing all
of this was her fault. "It's because of me," she whispered,
and Callie sucked in a quick breath. "I'm so sorry, Cal.
You don't even know how sorry I am."

Callie grabbed one of Ianthe's hands in her own. "It's
okay. I don't blame you. You're not the one who took me.
There's nothing to apologize for. Now, why don't you start
at the beginning and tell me what the hell is going on?"

Ianthe smiled weakly and complied. Callie already
knew bits and pieces about her summer with Aunt Grace,
so she filled in all the holes. When she finished, Callie was
sitting there with her mouth hanging open.

"So, let me get this straight—my best friend is a princess?! An actual freaking princess?!" Of course that would
be the part of the story she focuses on. Ianthe nodded and
Callie squealed. "This is so damn cool! I can't believe it.
You're half fairy—that's so freaking wicked. So, what do
we do now?"

"Well, that's where I need you to tell me everything you
can remember from the time you went through the gate."
Callie scrunched her eyebrows in confusion, so Ianthe explained, "You know, the white tree arch thingy."

"Oh yeah, so Evin pulled me through, and I swear I
tried to fight and get away like you told me to, but he is
freakishly strong. Anyway, that gate thingy—yeah, that
sucked major ass. I felt like that one time I drank way
too much at Danny's party and ended up puking all over
his shoes—not my finest moment, but you get the point."
Ianthe snickered, and Callie continued. "So, Evin was all
like, 'I told you it would have been better if you were un-

*conscious.' And I was like, 'Not helping, douche.' So then he picked me up and carried me." Callie's eyes widened, "Oh! I know what his power is!"*

*"Really? What?"*

*"He can travel freakishly fast—like, one second we were standing by the arch and the next we were by a stream. It was like he teleported—like, 'Beam me up, Scotty.'"*

*The Star Trek reference made Ianthe's heart ache for Conall and remember how she called him Spock on account of his pointed ears.*

*"So we stopped at a stream and he helped me drink some water to help settle my stomach, and then he picked me back up and BAM! I blinked and suddenly we were standing on a dirt road. I could see a town in the distance. He kept me close and wouldn't put me down. He seemed to be scanning the area to make sure we weren't seen. Then he teleported us in front of a cottage near the edge of the town."*

*"Do you remember any details that may be able to help me find it?"*

*Callie thought for a few moments. "Oh! There was a large cherry tree full of pink blossoms across the road. I remember thinking how beautiful it was. The cottage is two stories with dirt brown walls and a moss-covered roof. Is that right?" Callie's eyebrows scrunched again in concentration.*

*Ianthe thought of Conall's cottage, "Yep. That sounds about right for Fae. Most of their roofs are some sort moss or thatch, at least the ones I've seen. Do you remember anything else that might help?"*

*"Oh, it had a blue door, like a sky blue color."*

*"So, cherry blossom tree and sky blue door? Got it.*

*How are you doing otherwise? Are you okay?"*

*"Yeah...I think I was exhausted because after we got into the cottage, he showed me to a room and I collapsed on the bed, and now I'm talking to you."*

*"But are you okay?"*

*"Not exactly, but I will be. Even though he is a lying bastard, I really don't think Evin will hurt me. If anything, he's been extremely attentive and almost doting. Just try to hurry so we can get the hell out of here. I don't want you to get caught. Promise me you'll not put yourself at risk for me, Thee."*

*"You know I won't promise that. I will do everything in my power to get you back home safe and sound."* Callie looked disappointed by Ianthe's response. *"But I'll also do my best not to be seen or caught. Besides, I have a little trick up my sleeve that might help me out."*

*"You do?"*

*"Yep, I picked up a pair of colored contacts, and hopefully the blue will help disguise the violet enough that no one will know who I am."*

*"I sure hope so."* Callie sighed.

*Ianthe reached over and squeezed her tightly. "Don't worry, I'll be there before you know it, and I'll keep in contact with you as much as I can until then, 'kay?"*

*Callie nodded. "Love you."*

*"Love you more."*

Ianthe blinked her eyes open. The grass was slightly damp beneath her and her arms were still clutched around her backpack, which was draped across her chest. She stood up. It would be hard to find the exact direction they'd gone in since there were no tracks to follow and very few markers due to the Evin's unique ability. Ianthe thought briefly about trying to contact Conall, but then she realized how bright it had gotten. She wasn't sure how late in the morning it now was. That was the thing about her Mara ability—time in the dream realm was unpredictable. What felt like five minutes there sometimes turned out to be five hours in real life, and other times it was the exact opposite. She could never tell for sure. She was torn, but Callie took precedence over contacting Conall. She couldn't afford to waste any more time. She slung her backpack over her shoulder and started hiking in the direction away from the gate, looking for any sign of a stream.

She moved cautiously, darting behind trees and listening for sounds of water or anyone approaching. After an hour or so, she noticed a particularly thick copse of trees, which made her think she might be nearing a water source. Sure enough, she could hear a gentle trickling. She rushed toward the trees and found a rather large stream snaking through the forest. She sighed as she bent her head toward it and sipped some of the cool refreshing water. She took a water bottle from her backpack and refilled it to the top, unsure when she might be able to get water again. Carefully she plucked the colored contacts from her bag and gently slipped them in her eyes, using her reflection in the water to guide her. Once they were in, she blinked several times, waiting for them to settle in the right place. This time when she glanced at the water, she was no longer struck by her violet eyes, instead seeing a deep blue. The violet bled into the colored contacts so perfectly she hoped they might be enough to deter anyone from realizing who she was at first glance, and perhaps even upon closer inspection. She took a moment to rest and devoured an apple from her backpack, tossing the core to the forest floor when she was finished. She gathered her belongings and took one more sip from the stream before continuing on her way. She figured since most towns were built near a water source, her best bet was to keep following the stream until she encountered signs of the town Callie had mentioned.

Luckily, it seemed the weather in Fae was always the perfect temperature so she didn't start to sweat during her hike, instead enjoying every cool breeze that caressed her skin. There was part of her that felt more alive now that she was in Fae. Perhaps she hadn't noticed what she was missing when she was there the first time, but after being away, she felt renewed, almost like the land called to her. She yearned to stop, to soak up the beauty, to smell every fragrant flower, but Callie and her mission were foremost in her mind.

She also felt her powers surging within her, almost as if she had energy crackling just below her skin, waiting to be released. She hadn't realized how they had dulled in the human realm, but the feeling was definitely noticeable now. She itched to use them, the feeling so reminiscent of when she would crave a high from drugs that she automatically reached down to snap a rubber band against her wrist, encountering Conall's leather bracelet instead. She dug her nails into her skin a little more forcefully than normal, leaving pink crescent marks behind, but the effect was the same. The pain centered her attention and drove the addiction away. She heaved a sigh. She never would have thought about her power becoming something addictive as well. This was an unexpected side effect she'd need to monitor as she learned to use and control her ability.

She was so lost in her own thoughts she stumbled over a tree root and went sprawling onto her stomach. It was then she heard them—the low tones of two men talking.

She held her breath, hoping they hadn't heard her, as she dragged herself up and crawled toward the tree in front of her. Farther ahead, down the next slope, were two Fae soldiers watering their horses by the stream. She assumed they must have been Seelie because they didn't quite look like the soldiers she had seen around the Unseelie palace. Their uniforms were more earth-toned, warm and bright, where the Unseelie wore shades of blue, grey, and black.

She slowly released the breath she had been holding. They didn't seem to have heard her, thank goodness. She crouched behind the tree with her heart in her throat. If it were just one soldier, she could have tried to steal a horse, but there was no way she would win a fight against two of them. It wasn't like they were human, so she couldn't lull them to sleep using her powers. She'd found with Fae she could pull them into her dreams or invade theirs only if they were already asleep or unconscious, as had been the case with Casimir the previous summer. Maybe they wouldn't notice her, but what if they did? What would she do?

Her mind spun, searching for ideas. She hoped she had disguised her violet eyes well enough they wouldn't immediately give her away as Unseelie royalty. She could claim to be human, but then she shuddered remembering how the Unseelie had treated the humans at her bacchanalia. *No, that won't do.* A whinny broke through her thoughts, and she peeked around the tree once again.

The Seelie soldiers were mounting up. This was it; they would leave or they would discover her. The horses trotted toward her instead of away. *Crap. I'm a sitting duck.* She held her breath as they approached and tried to squeeze around the side of the large tree trunk, keeping herself out of view. It would have all worked out had she also paid attention to where she was stepping. She stepped on a large stick, causing it to snap with a cracking sound that echoed through the quiet wood. The soldiers halted immediately and swung their heads in her direction. She lined herself up with the tree, back pressed flat against the trunk, praying they couldn't see her and would move on.

"Halt! Show yourself!" one of the soldiers called. She held deathly still, her heart pounding against her chest. She didn't even dare breathe. "We know you're there."

"If you don't come out, we will be forced to take action," the other soldier warned.

*Crapola.* She took a deep breath. *Well, I guess it's time for plan "just go with it".* She pasted on her best doe-eyed damsel-in-distress look and stepped cautiously from around the tree. "Um, hi, I don't mean to be a bother, but do you guys think you could point me in the direction of the nearest town?" She hoped her words or language wouldn't give her away. *Do they even call it a town?* She cautiously approached the soldiers. One had golden hair that was longer on top and so short on the sides it almost seemed shaved. It was swept back as if styled that way by a hairdresser, not blown back by the breeze. It was an unusual style for a Fae, but with his five o'clock shadow and tanned skin, he was a striking example of male beauty. It was his eyes that really caught her attention, a shade of burnt orange she hadn't seen before.

The other Fae had fair skin with what looked like a tuft of red hair on top of his head and blood-red eyes. The combination was even more startling than the other soldier's beauty. You would think she had gotten used to what Fae looked like, but these Fae…there was something hypnotizing about them. While different in color, their skin seemed to shimmer like when she applied her sparkly body spray. Their horses were rather large and imposing, the kind she remembered seeing on the Budweiser commercials. *What are they called? Oh, right—Clydesdales.* They were magnificent creatures but rather intimidating when paired with the soldiers on their backs, one of which had his sword drawn. Once he got a closer glance at her, he decided she wasn't a threat and slid the sword back into its scabbard.

"What can we do for you on this fine day? I haven't seen you around here before," the redhead stated, still moving closer on his horse.

Ianthe's brain scrambled for a plan of action. She tried to hide the panic by coyly acting as if she were embarrassed to be stranded in the woods. "It seems I may have gotten turned around. I'm...um...I'm looking for..."

"I've got what you're looking for right here," the blond guy interrupted suggestively, pulling up next to his friend as he motioned to his own body and grinned widely, showing off the sharp teeth she was growing accustomed to seeing.

She rolled her eyes as the redhead elbowed the presumptuous boy in the ribs then she smiled sweetly. "While I'm sure what you have is a fantastic offer, I think my *boyfriend* would disagree," she deflected, hoping that would help him lose interest.

"Boyfriend, eh?" The flirt shook his head. "Why is it that all the pretty ones are taken?" He hopped off his horse and handed the reins to his friend. He strode toward her but stopped a little short in front of her and narrowed his eyes slightly. "You're not from around here, are you?" She noticed the flicker of interest and the predatory way he was staring her down. She quickly tamped down her fear, remembering what Conall had told her when they first entered the Unseelie town—that her fear would only draw them in. She wasn't totally sure what the differences would be between the two factions of Fae, but it would be best to err on the side of caution.

"I'm pretty sure I'm a long way from home. See, my boyfriend brought me here last night to his place…and I, um…" She swallowed and licked her lips before continuing, stalling for time as her brain spit out lies. "I know he told me not to leave his place, but it was such a pretty day, and I wanted to walk around and pick some flowers to take home with me."

The soldier's gazes were scrutinizing her every action. "I don't see any flowers," the redhead observed, dismounting his steed.

*Crap sticks.* She glanced down to her own empty hands and noticed some scrapes across her palms from her earlier fall. "Oh, yes—well, see, I'm a little bit of a klutz. I tripped and dropped them." She blushed, as if embarrassed, and held her hands up in front of her for proof.

"Why do you need a pack to pick flowers?" His eyes narrowed in on her backpack. *Damn.* She'd almost forgotten about that. The red-haired boy approached quickly and clutched her wrist, studying her palm. He stepped in closer and inhaled deeply. "You smell different—sweet," he commented.

"Um, thank you?" She wasn't sure if that was a good or a bad thing. He looked directly into her eyes, studying her gaze for several minutes. The red of his irises swirled as he inhaled once more.

"She's not one of us," he called over his shoulder to his companion. "Are you human?" He might have whispered it, but he was so close now, she could feel the exhalation of his question. He inhaled her scent again and licked his lips. Her heart raced as his eyes flashed a brighter red.

She pretended to look confused. "Um, of course—what else would I be?" She released a nervous little giggle, adding to her girlish innocence act. The Fae's eyes narrowed once again. She took a small step back but maintained eye contact so he wouldn't mistake her retreat as a sign of fear, more of an act of regaining her personal space.

The tan Fae jumped off of his horse. "So, who's your boyfriend?" he asked.

"I'm sorry?" As soon as the words left her lips, she wanted to smack herself on her forehead.

"Your boyfriend? You said you were at your boyfriend's place." He quirked an eyebrow, studying her expression.

"Oh, yes…sorry. It's just…has anyone ever told you that you could be a model?" *Holy hell where did that come from?!* She hadn't meant to say that. *I mean, sure, the guy is attractive—I have yet to meet an unattractive Fae—but seriously?* She wanted to kick herself for blurting out something so stupid until she saw his face. He looked shocked for a minute, but then a wolfish grin overtook his expression.

He elbowed the red-eyed Fae and waggled his eyebrows. "Did you hear that? She thinks I could be a model." He straightened his posture and it reminded of her of the boys at school when they would get a boost of self-confidence and it seemed to overinflate their egos. The other Fae snorted in reply. He looked less amused and not as easily distracted.

"So, your boyfriend?" She stood mutely, trying to think of what to say. The soldier must have taken her silence as confusion about the question being asked because he clarified, "What's his name?"

She smiled shyly. "Oh, his name is Evin." There, that might get them to lead her in the right direction. The redhead's eyes widened, and they both took a step back.

"Evin, you say? Are you sure?" one of them sputtered.

"I'm quite sure. Why? Is there something wrong with Evin being my boyfriend?"

They exchanged a knowing glance, and the blond shrugged. "Sure would explain why he's been disappearing so much. I thought he was just having trouble dealing with...things, but this is much better, don't you think?" The redhead merely studied her instead of giving his friend a reply.

"So, if you know Evin, do you think you could give me directions back to his place?" She pulled one arm behind her back and crossed her fingers, hoping this stupidly reckless plan of hers just might work.

"Oh, we can do better than that," the redhead sneered, but he quickly schooled his features into an overly polite smile. "We can take you there."

"Oh, no. That's unnecessary, really. I'd hate for you to go out of your way to get me back there. It was my stupidity that got me lost in the first place."

"Which is exactly why you should let us take you—to make sure you don't lose your way again." The redhead motioned for her to head toward his horse. The last thing she wanted to do was get within touching distance of him. She suspected his red eyes meant he was Lampir, a Fae who acted much like a vampire, feeding on human blood or energy. She had only met one other Lampir during her stay at the Unseelie palace, Killian, and while his eyes were more pink than red, the mannerisms were very much the same. She shuddered, remembering her close encounter with Killian and how she had almost become his food. She tried not to show her panic. Being human, they would expect her not to know what they were.

The burnt orange-eyed Fae approached her, perhaps

sensing her hesitation or the hungry gaze of his companion. "She'll ride with me." He spoke the words as if there were no room for argument, and really, there wasn't. She opened her mouth to insist she didn't need their help, but he swiftly picked her up and set her on the back of his chestnut Clydesdale. She resigned herself to the ride, hoping they would indeed take her to Evin, but even if they did—what then? *How will I rescue Callie without getting myself killed in the process?*

# CHAPTER 22

*Conall*

CONALL AND RAIN raced across the Seelie border. He had been tracking Casimir, and his direction did not bode well—he was approaching one of the Seelie gates to the human realm. He stopped for a short moment by a stream to let Rain drink. Something in the air felt off. He wasn't sure what it was, but it tugged at his gut. It was as if he could feel Ianthe there with him in the woods. He was just about to mount Rain again when something caught the animal's attention. The horse was pulling fiercely toward an object on the forest floor. He walked closer to it and plucked it from the ground: an apple core. He glanced around, noticing the lack of apple trees in the area. What he found most interesting was the color. It seemed dull in comparison to the vibrant apples found in Fae.

As he glanced around for more clues, he noticed footprints by the bank of the stream. He sprinted toward them, already knowing exactly who they belonged to. No Fae would be caught dead wearing human tennis shoes, and the slender width indicated they'd been made by a female. His heart sank. *I'd bet my life they belong to Ianthe. That's why I can feel her—she's been through here.* He whipped his head to and fro, searching for evidence of where she might have gone from there. *This is not good. If she was here, her life is in danger. Screw Casimir, and screw the king's orders.* Conall knew without a doubt he now had a new person to track. He needed to find Ianthe.

# CHAPTER 23

*Ianthe*

IANTHE TRIED NOT to hold on too tightly to the Fae in front of her, but she really had no choice. If she didn't hold on, she would fall off, especially at the speed they were moving. She wondered why they were so eager to take her to Evin's place. The nervous butterflies fluttering in her stomach quickly turned into a colony of bats. *What if my plan backfires? If they want to go inside Evin's house, they could discover Evin and Callie.* She had to find a way to make this work. She had to reach Callie and get her out of there alive.

She could see houses in the distance. "So tell me, how did you manage to wander so far from Evin's house?" her traveling companion asked, glancing back and studying her reaction.

"I guess I didn't realize how far I had walked. It was all so beautiful. I just wanted to keep exploring." She tried to maintain her *silly me* expression. The horses slowed as they reached the edge of the town. Ianthe searched for a cherry blossom tree and sighed in relief when she found it. "There's his place. I remember that tree," she said, pointing toward it and the cottage that stood just beyond.

She expected the Fae to head over in the direction she was pointing, but instead they kept going straight on a dirt road toward the center of the town. She held on to her hope they would turn until she caught sight of the sky blue door just as they were passing by. "Wait!" she yelled. "You passed it. It's back there with the blue door!" The Fae in front of her grabbed her wrists in his hand where they were wrapped around his torso. She struggled to break free. "What are you doing? That was his house!"

"Ah, my dear, I don't know how much Evin has told you. He's not permitted to tell you much unless there's someone who can erase those little memories." He tightened his grip painfully. "So, before we can let you go back to him, I'm sure the king would like to ask you a few questions."

*Oh, shit. This is way worse than I thought. There's no way I'll survive an encounter with the Seelie king.* She tried to calm the rising panic and stopped struggling, continuing with her clueless girl ruse. "King? What do you mean king? We don't have kings anymore."

He shook his head like he pitied the poor idiot behind him. "I hate to be the one to break this to you, sweetheart, but we're not anywhere you've been before. This land has a whole new set of rules—rules your *boyfriend* should have considered more seriously before bringing you here. You see, little *human* girls don't belong in our world."

"I don't know what you're talking about. Can you please let me go? You're hurting me." She tried to add a little whine to her voice, but it stirred no sympathy in the soldier in front of her. "Evin will be mad when he finds out about this."

The Fae chuckled. "Oh, I'm sure he will, but he'll only be mad at himself. He knew the rules of the game when he started playing."

"Please, let me go. I won't tell anyone, I swear." She imagined what any girl would say to try to get herself out of this situation.

"I'm afraid that's no longer up to me, sweetheart. Just be a good little girl, answer a few questions, and we'll make sure you get home, okay?" This time when he looked back at her, his gaze softened as if he really did want her to do as he asked, as if he really would return her home—most likely with a few gaps in her memory.

She sagged against the Fae in resignation. The only thing she could think of doing was crying as any human might do in a scary situation. She thought about Conall and Callie, about what might happen to them if she were discovered and executed, about both of her fathers (Unseelie and human), and her great-aunt. She wasn't sure when it happened, but her acting morphed into real tears. "P-Promise?" she stuttered.

He sighed wearily and his voice was gentle, reassuring. "Yes, sweetheart, I promise I will do my best to make sure you get home." *Well, that's a refreshing change from how an Unseelie would handle a human.* His hands clasped hers a little less tightly, firm enough she wouldn't get away, but not the death grip he had before. Still, this was quickly turning into a worst-case scenario kind of situation. Perhaps she could fool the king into buying her innocent human act, although she was certain that if they attempted to erase her memories, it would be game over.

"Wh-What's your name?" she asked through her sniffles.

"Maddock."

"Can I ask you a question?"

"Seems like you already have." He chuckled.

"Oh, yes, well…what will happen to me at the palace?"

Maddock's demeanor instantly changed. He stiffened, tightening his grip on her wrists once more. He pulled his horse up short and turned around, holding her arms up high. His orange eyes narrowed suspiciously. "No one said anything about going to a palace." His redheaded companion seemed to have noticed their abrupt halt and stopped a few yards ahead, debating whether Maddock needed assistance.

Ianthe's eyes widened as she realized her mistake. "I—um—I assumed if we were going to see your king then… well, usually kings live in palaces, do they not? I mean, I wouldn't personally know as we don't have any where I'm from, but from what I've read—" She realized she was nervously rambling and closed her mouth, hoping he might buy her excuse. He scoffed and she wasn't sure how to read it. *Was it an "I don't buy the bullshit you're selling" scoff or an "Oh my god, could this human girl be any stupider" scoff?* She held her breath and counted her heartbeats until he made up his mind.

He slightly narrowed his eyes once again, realizing there was probably more to this girl than met the eye, but he lowered her arms. After two more beats and without a word, he turned back around and nudged the horse to continue.

It wasn't long before they slowed down as they neared a more populated part of town. Most of the Fae wandering around ignored her, but a few short sent curious glances at the strange girl. It was a completely different feel from when she had first entered a Fae town. She remembered how terrified she had been when she went to the Unseelie castle, how the Fae had looked at her with hunger and malice. She was still a little scared, knowing what was at stake, but she didn't get the same uneasiness from the Seelie. There was no hunger in their gazes—well, except for the red-eyed soldier. He definitely stared at her as if he wanted to take a bite. The Seelie townspeople were merely curious, and they seemed happy with that same shimmery glow as her traveling companions. She held her head high and took in everything she could that might help her formulate an escape plan. She was not going to be a passive prisoner—oh no. Every moment she would be working toward finding Callie and getting them the hell out of there.

She was so caught up in studying her surroundings she almost missed the castle ahead, although to call it a castle did not seem to do it justice. No, this was more of a palace, not a grey medieval structure like where her father, the Unseelie king, lived, but more like something out of a Jane Austen novel. In fact, it looked a lot like a cross between the Biltmore Estate in North Carolina and the estate in *Downton Abbey*, which Aunt Grace watched religiously. She smiled, remembering many nights she had spent snuggled against her aunt on the couch, watching the drama unfold around the Crawley family. It seemed like ages ago, though really it had only been a few months.

Maddock pulled his horse to a stop as the redheaded Fae dismounted ahead of them. "You will not try to run," he commanded, "because my friend there loves a good chase before dinner." He nodded his head toward the red-eyed Fae, and a shiver ran down her spine. She had no desire to be anyone's prey, so she reluctantly nodded her acquiescence. He released his grip on her wrists and dismounted the horse before reaching back up to grab her. He lifted her gently off of the horse as if she weighed nothing and set her on the ground before steering her toward the entrance. The redhead took his place in front of her while Maddock followed closely behind.

Her mind raced. She didn't think she could keep up her charade for much longer. *What will they do with me once they find out? Will they give me back to my father, use me as a pawn in their game, or execute me themselves?* While she knew the Seelie were known to be kinder to humans, she also had to remember that they were still Fae—deadly beings who were known to make humans dance until they dropped dead from exhaustion with a smile upon their lips.

The soldiers marched her through the many rooms and hallways of the palace, up and down stairs, until she was completely turned around. She tried to pay attention, but the rooms and hallways all looked so similar. Perhaps this was their intention—to get her so confused that if she did try to escape, she would get hopelessly lost. Finally, they led her to a small, plain room. It had a single bed, a wooden desk, a small table, and a chair—not what one would expect from such a fancy exterior.

Maddock plucked her backpack off of her so quickly and effortlessly she swore he could have been the world's best pickpocket. He then patted her down, frowning as he discovered the knife she had hidden in her pocket.

"That was to—um—cut the flowers I was picking." She wished she didn't sound so doubtful of her own explanation. His expression remained unfazed.

"You will wait here until the king can see you," Maddock explained before closing the door. She heard the small click of him locking her inside the room. Of course, this was her holding cell. *Well, it could be worse,* she thought, remembering the Unseelie dungeon and her time spent on the hard rock floor with a pile of straw and a blanket as her only comfort. Powerless to do anything else, she lay down on the bed, stared at the ceiling, and then closed her eyes, focusing on the one thing she always did before she let herself drift into her dreams, the one person she hoped would do anything to save her, the one she missed with every fiber of her being—Conall.

*She blinked her eyes open. She was by the tree where they'd first met. She glanced over her shoulder to see her great-aunt's house in the distance, offering her comfort. She traced the bark of the tree with her hand, feeling its roughness. "Oh Conall, where are you? What am I supposed to do?" she whispered aloud. Her eyes fell to the forest floor, and that was when she spotted it. There on the grass by the trunk of the tree was a violet flower. Its vibrant color, cut stem, and amazing scent were identical to the flower Conall had left for her by the exact tree after she first started dreaming about him. She took it as a sign he had been thinking about her as well, but then again it could have just been wishful thinking on her part, a sign her imagination created because she so desperately yearned to hear from him. She waited around, still hoping he might show up. She wasn't sure what time it was, but she knew there was a slim chance he would actually be asleep.*

*She remembered the last time she had seen him in the woods after his fight with Casimir, how broken he had looked. At the time, she hadn't thought he was going to make it, but Alfie had managed to save him. Alfie! That's it! Conall may not have been asleep, but Alfie was notorious for falling asleep in the library while reading. She closed her eyes and concentrated all her thoughts on him—his wrinkled affectionate smile, the way he looked at her like a loving grandfather, his shoulder-length white hair and Dumbledore-ish beard. When she opened her eyes, she was in the library at the Unseelie palace. "Alfie?" she called.*

*His worn face appeared around a shelf of books. "Lady Ianthe! Is it really you?" He strode toward her more quickly than one would imagine a man of his age could move and grasped her into a firm bear hug. "Oh my dear, it is so good to see you." He sighed in contentment as he released her. Suddenly his expression clouded over and turned disapproving. "Wait a minute, if you can visit me, that means..." He trailed off as he put the pieces together. "Please tell me I am wrong. Tell me you aren't here."*

*"Well, I'm not where you are exactly," she replied, trying to smooth over the truth.*

*"But you're in Fae." It was more of a statement than a question.*

*She took a deep breath. "Yes."*

*"You knew what would happen if you returned. Why would you ever come back? It isn't safe."*

*"I know, Alfie, I know. Believe me, if I had any other choice, I'd have taken it, but the situation is desperate."*

*"Conall's fine, I told you. Wait—does he know you're here?" Alfie responded.*

*"I know, I trust you, and no, he doesn't know. I haven't had any contact with him since I left him with you." She sighed. "It's a long story."*

*"Well, lucky for you, I have plenty of time," Alfie replied, motioning for them to sit at the long wooden table instead of standing. She told him everything that had hap-*

*pened, how Casimir was following her, Evin pretending to be Reid and kidnapping Callie, meeting her guards and using them to find the location of the portal, and finally crossing over and being caught by Seelie soldiers.*

*"Who brought you to the palace?" Alfie asked.*

*"He said his name was Maddock. I didn't get the name of the other one, but I did figure out he's a Lampir."*

*"Well, it has been a very long time since I was at the Seelie palace, but I do remember those two. Stay away from the Lampir—even as a child, he could easily pass for an Unseelie, and he will not hesitate to carry out your execution order for the king." Alfie's eyes were serious. "As for Maddock, when he was younger, he was always a very pleasant, caring boy, but that was a while ago, and people change, so be wary. The best course of action would be to try to talk to the head of the guard, Torin. He's basically the equivalent of Conall for the Seelie, although quite a bit older and more experienced. He's Evin's father and will be very interested in correcting any wrongs on his son's behalf. He'll help you reach Callie and get home."*

*"Find Torin, got it."*

*He grasped her hand affectionately across the table. "You must be safe, my dear. Let no one know who you are, other than Torin. Try to contact him as soon as you can, and I'll do my best to reach Conall and send him to you."*

*"Reach Conall—what do you mean? Isn't here there at the castle or at his house?"*

*"No, I'm afraid not." Alfie sighed. "He was sent to track Casimir, although I suspect he was only using it as an excuse to find his way to you. He seemed like a man on a mission before he left."*

*"Oh, I see. So he could be in the human realm right*

*now?"*

*He nodded and squeezed her hand reassuringly. "He could be, but I'm sure the minute he finds out where you are, he will be there. I'll send a discreet messenger to find him. I'll also let your aunt know what's happening." She opened her mouth to disagree, but he cut her off. "She will fret more if I don't." He raised his eyebrows as if challenging her to contradict him.*

*"Okay, but please tell her not to worry. I will make it home safe." She heard a distant knocking. "Crap, I'm out of time. Take care of yourself, Alfie, and I promise to do whatever I can to keep myself safe." She could no longer feel his hand on hers as the dream faded.*

She blinked her eyes as the door was opening. Maddock stood in the doorway. "The king will see you now." She rose and took a breath to steady her nerves. Following him out of the room, she steeled herself for whatever the Seelie king had in store.

# CHAPTER 24

*Ianthe*

"**YOU SHOULD NOT** speak unless directly spoken to, understand?" Maddock asked her as they approached the giant double doors. She nodded. "It would be in your best interest not to lie, either. King Lachlan does not take kindly to liars. The fastest way for us to get you home is for you to answer all of his questions as honestly as you can." He gave her shoulder a slight, almost painful, squeeze before shoving her forward through the open doors. She wasn't sure if the gesture was meant to be a reassuring or a threatening.

She entered a throne room similar to the one at the Unseelie palace. It was a grand hall with an ornate golden throne on top of a dais. However, where everything in the Unseelie palace had seemed dark, gothic, and heavy, the opposite was true here. The throne room was lit with a natural light flowing from countless large skylights, which created a warm, bright, and airy feeling within the space.

The walls were a rich brown accented with tapestries and curtains in vibrant golds, greens, and sky blues. Seated upon the golden throne was who she could only assume to be the Seelie king. She took a minute to study him. His black hair was short, almost buzzed in a militaristic cut. It was an unusual style for a Fae, but it seemed to suit him. The shortness of his hair made his strong facial features even sharper. He sat straight forward with his tanned elbows resting on his thighs, his fingers laced together underneath his chin, his bright lavender eyes studying her intently. They were a shade or two lighter than hers and her father's, but still, the undeniable shade of violet was there. She remembered Conall telling her he had never seen her eye color outside the royal family, but she hadn't considered that it also applied to Seelie royals. Now more than ever, it was imperative that no one see the true color of her eyes.

The king surveyed her with an intense expression, like she was a jigsaw puzzle he was trying to assemble.

"King Lachlan, here is the girl we found stumbling around in the forest. She said her boyfriend brought her here and she was just taking a walk." Maddock almost snorted, indicating he didn't believe her story one bit. *Damn*, she had hoped he would be her supporter.

A man to the left of the king spoke. "Did she say his name?" He was stocky and muscular, as she would expect one of the king's guards to appear, and his black hair was greying along his temples. It was straight and long but gathered back in a ponytail, and his amber eyes gave her a hint as to who he might be.

Maddock glanced down at his feet sheepishly. "She did, sir."

"And?" the man prompted.

"She said it was Evin, sir," Maddock admitted reluctantly. He had no desire to be in a 'don't shoot the messenger' kind of situation.

The older guard stepped forward as if to defend his son, confirming his identity. "That can't be."

"Do you know anything about this, Torin?" King Lachlan asked his first in command.

"Of course not, Your Majesty. Evin would never do such a thing," Torin countered.

"Torin, even you must admit that Evin hasn't been making the best of decisions lately. First, fighting with Casimir, and now…" He gestured toward Ianthe, who was standing there as innocently as she could.

Torin heaved a heavy sigh. His lips drew into a tight line and his brow furrowed. "Who are you?" he asked, directing his attention to her.

Maddock gave her a nudge, indicating that she should answer the question, but she didn't know what to say. She couldn't give them her real name in case word got out that she was there. She wondered if she should make up a name and pray Evin thought it really was Callie, or if she should give Callie's name to convince him that Callie had been caught. She sighed; she didn't know if what she was doing would doom them both or be what saved them. "Callie," she replied. She tried to keep a tight rein on her facial features lest she give away the fact that she was lying. She really didn't want to find out what a Fae king would do to someone who lied to him.

"Callie, would you step forward, please." The king motioned for her to come closer. She gulped as Maddock practically shoved her. "Now, tell us how you came to this fine place."

*Time to turn on the naïve human act.* "Well, um, you see, my boyfriend Evin brought me here."

"Yes, we already established that." She could practically feel the king rolling his eyes. "Please, tell us how you met *Evin*." He said the name as if he could see right through her lies.

She searched her memory for how Callie had described their meeting. "We, um, met outside this coffee shop, Roots, by my house. I was sitting out there one day and he came over to talk to me." She didn't want to say the part about singing and playing a guitar because she was terrified they might want her to demonstrate her abilities, and tone deaf was probably a generous description of her musical talent. "He was super sweet and we seemed to hit it off, so I gave him my number." She tried to leave things vague so she wouldn't be caught in an outright lie. "After that we would talk or meet up, ya know, and then the other night he asked me if I wanted to go back to his place." She gulped nervously. "I...um...I said yes." Her eyes widened slightly, realizing how that must have sounded, and she tried to recover. "I mean, I don't, like, just go home with guys all the time, but we had been dating for a while, and so I, um...I thought it would be fine." *Jesus, the whole Seelie court probably thinks I'm a slut now.*

King Lachlan held up a hand to stop her nervous rambling, his eyes raking over her with an intensity that made her want to break out in a sweat. She worked hard to contain her nervous tremors and any other indicator that might reveal her hand. It could have been only moments, but it felt like he held her gaze for hours, looking for anything that might reveal the truth. She thought the king really should have considered a career as a professional poker player because she couldn't read a damn thing off of him.

Finally, he spoke. "Maddock, return the lady to her

room please. I would like to speak to Evin before we decide what to do with her. I'm not entirely sure she is telling us truth."

*Well, damn, guess I won't be winning an Academy Award after all.* Maddock gripped her shoulders and pulled her back toward him.

"Torin, I suggest you find your son, and do so quickly. I would like this matter resolved before dinner," the king commanded with a flick of his hand, dismissing them all.

Maddock pulled her from the room, shoving her roughly in front of him. He manhandled her back to her quarters and stopped in front of her door, where he heaved a sigh of frustration. "What did I tell you? Yet you still thought it would be smart to lie. Why would you do that?" He spun her around so she faced him. "If you had told the whole truth, he would've let you go. You would be on your way home right now."

"With a few gaps in my memory, right?" She arched her left eyebrow. "Well, who's to say you would've taken the right memories?"

"I would have—" Maddock growled before catching himself.

Ianthe's eyebrows shot to her hairline. *That's an interesting revelation.* She hadn't meant him personally, but it was good to know Maddock was a Skepseis. She swallowed. "Well, nice to know it wouldn't have been your redheaded friend," she tried to joke.

"You're a stupid, *stupid* girl. Do you have any idea what you've done?" His fingers tightened, digging painfully into her shoulders.

She smiled sadly. "Actually, I do." She met his gaze head on. "Some memories are worth fighting for." Of course, he had no way of knowing what she was talking about, but she knew there was no way she could let anyone go poking around her memories. The moment she did, she would be dead, either by the hands of the Seelie or her father.

"You think he's worth it, but he'll turn you over in a second if it means saving his own hide. You think you're the only one—you think you're special." Maddock shook his head and laughed. "Sweetheart, you are nothing to him, and you're an idiot if you think he'll save you."

She knew Maddock was referring to Evin, but she couldn't help but think about Conall. She grinned up at her captor, knowing he was wrong.

She was special, and Conall would save her.

# CHAPTER 25

*Conall*

CONALL GALLOPED TOWARD the Seelie palace. He had tracked Ianthe's trail to where she must have encountered two Fae on horseback. He didn't know what to think then. Part of him hoped they were honorable Seelie soldiers who would take her directly to King Lachlan, and the other part hoped they were just Seelie villagers who might take her for their own reasons, giving her a greater chance of escape. He knew if she made it to the palace, she would be safe until the king decided what to do with her, but there wasn't really much hope for escaping on her own.

He approached the town cautiously, thinking he really should stop and come up with a plan. It wasn't like he could storm the castle. One false move on his part could lead to war between the Seelie and Unseelie. He stopped at the edge of the village and saw a familiar figure approaching in the distance. He watched as Torin raced toward a house near a cherry tree, dismounted his steed, and approached the blue door.

Torin knocked forcefully for several minutes before yelling, "Goddammit, Evin! I know you're in there! Open the damn door!" He huffed in frustration before kicking the door, which startled Conall, who had never seen Torin so upset. He decided it might work in his favor and approached cautiously.

"Oy, Torin!" he called out, waving as he brought Rain to a halt next to Torin's mount. "What seems to be the problem?"

"Oh, Conall, you haven't by chance seen my ungrateful, idiotic son anywhere, have you?"

"Can't say I have. Is there anything I can help you with?"

"Not unless you can produce him out of thin air. I swear I have no clue where that boy's head is at, but he will be the death of me. How could he be so foolish?" Torin banged on the door again.

"What has he done?"

Torin faced the door again. "Evin, I swear if you are in there, I'm coming in to get you out myself!" he yelled before entering the house. Unlike humans, most Fae didn't see the need for locks on doors. Torin stepped through before addressing Conall over his shoulder, saying, "You're welcome to help me look for him. Actually, I'd appreciate the assistance as I may throttle him when I find him."

Conall followed him into Evin's home. Torin stormed through the living room while Conall was drawn to the kitchen table.

"Torin, you may want to see this." He had noticed two glasses sitting on the kitchen table, which would have been fine and completely explainable, except one of the glasses had bright red lip prints on it. He carefully picked the cup up and held it closer to study it. He ran his finger on the lip print, noticing that the red smeared across the glass and onto his finger. Fae women used magic and stains, so their lip color never came off on what they drank, which meant this had to have come from a human. For a brief moment, he considered if it was Ianthe's lips on the glass, but in all his time observing her, she had only worn lip balm, and nothing in a color so bold. It must have been from her friend who had been kidnapped, which confirmed that Evin was the one who'd taken her. Conall drew in a sharp breath as Torin peered at the glass over his shoulder.

"Stupid, foolish boy," he muttered. "What am I going to do? He brought a human girl over without permission. She's in the king's custody now. I had hoped she was lying, but..." Torin exhaled sharply, shaking his head in disbelief. He appeared as if the weight of the world were on his shoulders as he sat at the table and placed his head in his hands.

Conall briefly rested a hand on his shoulder. "I'm going to check out the rest of the house." He didn't feel Ianthe anywhere near, but there was something off in the house he couldn't quite explain. Well, at least if Evin was involved, Torin was likely to help him rescue Ianthe and her friend without bringing anyone else into it, but if her friend was already in the hands of the king, things had just gotten a whole lot more difficult. He approached the wooden staircase, admiring its craftsmanship for a moment before climbing up. He poked his head into each of the rooms, searching for any sign of Evin or the human girl. Finally, he reached a closed door that was locked from the outside. *Interesting.* Luckily, it didn't require a key; he simply had to turn the lock.

He opened the door and drew in a sharp breath. There on the bed was a sleeping girl. She appeared to be around Ianthe's age, with her copper red hair spread around her like a halo. Her lips still held traces of the bright red lipstick. *If the girl is here, who the hell is at the palace?* Knowledge slammed into Conall like a horse galloping toward him at full speed, knocking the breath out of him. If she was here, that meant Ianthe was the one at the palace. He dragged his hand across his face. Things were so much worse than he'd thought. *What am I going to do?* He quietly crept out of the room, locking it behind him as he stumbled down the stairs.

"Torin? What did the girl look like—the one at the palace?" He hoped Torin didn't hear the tremor in his voice.

Torin raised his head from where he still sat at the kitchen table, looking momentarily confused.

"The human girl?" Conall prompted.

"Oh, she had long, almost white blonde hair with stripes of purple throughout."

"What about her eyes?" Conall asked. He knew they were her tell, that they would figure out exactly who she was by those alone.

"What does it matter?" Torin asked, rubbing his temples as if he were trying to soothe away a headache. He glanced at Conall and noticed he was still awaiting an answer. "Blue. They were dark blue like sapphires, but with a hint of…"

"A hint of what?" Conall felt as if his heart was waiting on Torin's answer to start beating again.

"A hint of violet, but that couldn't be right, could it?" Torin shook his head. "No, they were probably just a dark blue."

Conall released the breath he hadn't realized he was holding and his heart started beating again. No one knew who she was yet, but this could go all kinds of wrong in an instant. *Can I trust Torin? And why did Evin kidnap Ianthe's friend?* Conall tried to think back to what Enora had told him, something to do with Casimir. In that instant, it all seemed to click into place. *If Evin kidnapped Ianthe's friend, he was or is after Ianthe herself. Casimir must still be following Ianthe, and he led Evin right to her.* Conall growled.

"What is it, Conall?" Torin asked, looking puzzled as to why Conall would be standing there brooding and growling when it was Torin's son who was in trouble.

Conall didn't know how much he could trust Torin, but he really wasn't left with much choice. "Do you remember Alfie?"

"Of course I remember him," Torin stated, as if offended that one could ever imagine forgetting a person such as Alfie.

"Then I beg you to think of him now. He is my closest friend at the Unseelie palace, and someone he cares for greatly is in grave danger."

Torin swallowed. "Who?"

"I cannot tell you who just yet, but Evin is mixed up in this as well."

Torin nodded, fully aware that his son had gotten himself involved in something. "I've gathered as much, but what does it have to do with Alfie?"

Conall wasn't sure how much he should reveal, but he didn't see any other option. He was either condemning her or saving her, and he wouldn't know until it was all done. "I believe the girl you have at the palace is not, in fact, the one Evin took."

"And what makes you think that?"

Conall chuckled. "Probably the human girl sleeping upstairs." Torin's eyes widened as he jumped up from the table. Conall knew Torin would have to see her with his own eyes so he waited for him to return. He got a glass of water and sat down at the kitchen table.

Torin came down the stairs with his lips set in a grim line. "I'm listening."

Conall took a deep breath and explained what he had surmised from the situation. Evin had been following Casimir to get revenge for Reid's death when he stumbled across Ianthe. The mention of Ianthe caused Torin's eyes to widen and he inhaled sharply, opening his mouth to say something, but instead he thought the better of it and motioned for Conall to continue. Conall told him how Evin had kidnapped Ianthe's friend to get to her, probably not realizing who she was, for if he had, he never would have attempted something so idiotic. If he had kidnapped the Unseelie princess intentionally, it would have been a death sentence for him and for his father, along with the start of war between the two courts.

"So, you see, if either king were to discover who she truly is, it could mean the end for us all," Conall finished, looking into his ally's eyes pleadingly.

Torin seemed to mull things over for a few minutes before reaching a decision. "All right then, what do you suggest we do to get everyone out of this mess?"

Conall sighed in relief, knowing from Torin's use of "we" that he wasn't alone—they were in this together. They sat down and came up with some sort of a plan. Torin would work to free Ianthe from the Seelie palace while Conall waited for Evin to appear, though it took every ounce of his willpower not to storm the palace and demand his beloved be released. His arms ached to hold her and his heart longed to see her again, but he knew his presence there would only make things worse. For the time being, his best option was to trust Torin would uphold his end of their mission.

He was too antsy to sit still, and his stomach rumbled. While Torin remained at the table lost in thought, Conall searched the kitchen for something to eat. After looking at the contents of Evin's pantry, he decided to make a vegetable omelet. As he was cooking, he heard the girl stirring upstairs and thought he should probably take her something to eat. *Who knows the last time she was fed?* He finished the omelet, split it in half, and plated the halves on a tray, which he carried upstairs and set down before knocking on the girl's door. After he unlocked it, he poked his head inside but didn't immediately see her—the bed was empty. He crept farther into the room and caught a flash of movement to his left. He spun quickly and instantly clasped his hands around a vase that had been inches from striking him on the head. Her hands were clutching its sides as she swung, but now she froze.

"Oh, shit." She dropped her hands immediately and scrambled backward. Conall was impressed; the girl was a fighter. *Of course Ianthe's friend would be as fierce as she is.*

He smiled at her like she was a skittish animal he was trying to soothe. "It's okay, I'm not here to harm you."

"Wh-Where's Evin?" she asked.

"That's a great question, to which I would love to know the answer. I was hoping you would know." He paused and took her silence combined with the previous question as an indication that she had no clue where Evin had gone.

"Are you hungry?" He turned back toward the hallway and grabbed the tray.

"Um…" The girl appeared torn. Her stomach rumbled loudly, but she eyed the food as if it were a coiled snake waiting to strike.

"I've been told I make a decent omelet." He took a bite to show her there was nothing wrong with it. She still stared at him suspiciously but took the plate when he offered it and sat on the bed. "I'm here to help get you home. I'm a friend of Ianthe's," he explained.

"You know Thee?" the girl asked, her eyes wide with disbelief. She set the plate on the bed beside her as he smiled at her nickname for Ianthe. Then her doe eyes widened even further. "Wait, wait! What's your name?"

"Conall," he replied.

The girl released a high-pitched squeal before jumping up and down. "Oh my god! Oh my god! You're Conall?! *The* Conall?!"

He nodded and chuckled. His heart warmed knowing her reaction meant Ianthe had mentioned him. "Please, eat before your meal gets cold."

The girl excitedly sat back down. She wasted no time, shoveling the food into her mouth now that she knew who he was. "I can't believe I'm meeting you in person," she said around bites and chews. "You're gorgeous. I can definitely see why Thee is so taken with you. For a while there I wasn't sure you even existed. I mean, she hasn't heard from you in months." Conall swallowed hard and the color leeched from his face at the stark reminder of how much more quickly time passed in the human realm.

"Yes, well, her father has made it fairly impossible for me to get away, and I can't really contact her from the Fae realm." His brow furrowed in frustration. It wasn't like he was intentionally staying away. He thought about her every moment of every day.

"Her father? Mr. Grayson?" the girl repeated incredulously. "How has he kept you away?"

"Not her human father, her biological father, King Corydon," he clarified.

"Holy crap, so she was telling the truth! I mean, I didn't want to doubt her, but it was a lot to process all at once, finding out your BFF is not only part fairy, but also considered royalty. So she really is a princess?" The girl didn't even pause to let him answer, and he was amazed she could manage to eat and talk so much between bites. "Holy smokes, this is so awesome! I can't believe I'm finally meeting you. Wait, how did you know I was here? Where's Ianthe?" Her excited expression instantly shifted to concern. She placed her fork on her now empty plate and peered up at him expectantly.

He had to hold in his laughter. This girl was something else, and he could see why she meant so much to Ianthe. "Before I begin, I would love to know your name."

"She didn't tell you?" Her brows drew together, concern weighing on her features.

"I haven't spoken to Ianthe since we parted ways in the summer. She doesn't know I'm here," he replied.

The girl's jaw dropped. "She doesn't know you're here?! But—but she—she said she was coming to get me. That's why I thought she sent you to help. Holy crap! She's going to flip when she finds out you're here. She misses you like crazy."

Conall smiled. "I will explain, I promise, but first I would love to know who you are."

"Oh my gosh, of course! I'm Callie. Thee and I met on the first day of school and have been inseparable ever since."

"Well, it's an honor to meet you, Callie." He extended his hand to her. "It brings me great joy to know Ianthe has someone like you as a friend." She blushed and shook his hand, and he couldn't resist sending her some calming, positive vibes as he grasped her hand before releasing it. He knew she would need it for the next part of the conversation.

"When was the last time you spoke with Ianthe?" he asked her.

"Um, just this morning, actually. She wanted to know where I was and what I had seen to help her track me, so she came to me in my dreams. Did you know she could do that? Wait, of course you knew she could do that. Can you do that too?"

"Yes, I know she's capable of manipulating dreams, and no, I cannot. My powers are a little different." She opened her mouth to speak, but he beat her to the punch. "I can alter emotions, make you feel whatever I want through just my touch." He pressed on, hoping to avoid any more interruptions because time was of the essence, and Torin was waiting downstairs. "Do you have any clue where Evin is or when he might be back? Did he say anything to you before he left?"

She shook her head. "No, he didn't tell me. I haven't seen him since he made me drink that really yummy fruity stuff you guys have." Conall's eyes widened. Evin had given her ambrosia, a strong Fae wine, to knock her out.

"You really shouldn't drink that stuff if it's ever offered to you again. It's a Fae wine, and it affects humans differently than Fae, as I'm sure you've figured out. Do you know why Evin brought you here?"

"Oh, um…" She paused to think, and then her eyebrows rose. "Wait, I do! He told me. See, Evin pretended to be his brother Reid when we first met, but after Ianthe pretended to be me in one of his dreams, he decided to come clean with me. He told me he was trying to get Ianthe, because this dude named Casimir is obsessed with her, so he kidnapped me to lure her here because he couldn't just take her. She's like guarded or something, whatever that means. Oh wait, I bet she is guarded because she's a freaking princess. Am I right?"

"Yes, she usually has Fae guards protecting her, but she doesn't know about them. I wonder how they allowed her to cross realms," Conall pondered aloud. He didn't like where this was headed. He had already surmised that this was some plot to get revenge on Casimir and the knowledge that Casimir was so fixated on Ianthe was definitely unsettling, but he didn't want to show Callie how deep his worry ran.

"Well, the good news is we're going to get you out of here. Unfortunately, that means I also have some bad news. Evin's father is downstairs, and it appears while Ianthe was coming to rescue you, she was captured. She lied to the guards about who she is and why she's here. She's pretending to be you, so it's even more important we get you out quickly. We can't let anyone know her true identity. You can't tell anyone, do you understand? Her very life depends upon it."

She nodded her head solemnly. "I promise. I'd never do anything to hurt Thee. She means the world to me."

"Good. Now, let's go downstairs and figure out what's to be done next." Conall held the door open and motioned for Callie to go first. She did, most likely happy to be out

163

of that room and curious to see the rest of the house. Based on the lock on her door, he didn't think Evin had given his captive the freedom to roam when he was there.

She came to an abrupt halt at the bottom of the stairs when she caught sight of Torin. He was sitting exactly as Conall had left him, at the table with his head in his hands. Conall stopped behind her and placed his hands on her shoulders, sending her calm, protected feelings. He watched as the tension left her body and her shoulders sagged slightly forward. "It's okay. That's Torin. He's Evin's father, and he's here to help. Don't worry," he assured her. "Torin, this is Callie," Conall said as they both approached the table.

Torin stood and bowed his head toward her. "I apologize for any trouble my foolish son has caused you, my dear. We'll get you out of this mess, I promise. No harm will come to you as long as I have a say in the matter."

Callie smiled politely. "Thank you, sir."

"Conall, there is one thing I'm curious about," Torin stated, as if he had been pondering this very point. "If the girl at the palace is exactly who you say she is, why does she look and feel so human?"

"Well, she only recently passed her 17th birthday, and as a half Fae she hasn't fully developed into her powers. I've discussed this with Alfie before and we believe her physical Fae features aren't well developed because of how little time she has spent in Fae. When she was here the last time, we did notice a slight change by the end of her trip. Her ears and teeth were starting to sharpen. We're not quite sure if she will develop more with time, but I know the magic in the land will also pull those features out of her the longer she stays, which is why it's imperative we get her out of the Seelie palace and out of Fae as soon as possible." Conall glanced at Callie to see how she was taking this information. Thankfully, she looked curious instead of frightened.

"Okay, that makes sense. However..." Torin paused. "If she's truly King Corydon's child, as you say, why doesn't she have his eyes?"

Now Conall was the one who was confused. "What do you mean? She does have his eyes. They're the royal shade of purple."

"Then perhaps it's another girl at the palace, because this girl's eyes were blue," Torin replied.

"Did she have pale blonde hair with purple streaks?" Callie interrupted.

"Yes."

"Then it's Ianthe. She's probably just wearing colored contacts. She told me she used to do that a lot to hide her unique eye color," she explained. Conall was intrigued. The last time he had seen Ianthe, her hair was a dark brown with blue streaks. He imagined she looked even more like Ayanna with blonde hair. He smiled at her cleverness and foresight to protect her identity with colored contacts. They had probably already saved her life.

"I see," Torin acknowledged. "I forget how easily humans can disguise themselves these days."

They all took a seat at the table and started figuring out what should be done. Torin wanted Conall to take Callie home, but Conall refused to leave Seelie territory without Ianthe by his side, and no one could guarantee her release from the palace. Torin's absence would be noted if he were to take Callie, so the only solution they could think of was to convince Evin to escort Callie home. If no one could find Evin to question him, this would give them time to find a solution to Ianthe's imprisonment. Now, having figured out a plan, the only thing left to do was wait and hope Evin was discreet enough that no one else caught him before he made it home.

# CHAPTER 26

## Ianthe

IANTHE PACED HER room anxiously. *What the hell am I supposed to do now?* She had already checked every possible point for an escape. There was a window, but it wouldn't open, and she wasn't sure it would do her much good even if it would as she was on an upper floor of the palace. She could tell it was getting late in the day, and she didn't think she wanted to find out what the Fae forest was like at night. There was no evidence that there was a lock on the door or she would have tried to pick it, but she was positive there was at least one guard posted in her hall, if not right outside her room. How was she going to get herself out of this mess? She couldn't just sit around and wait to be rescued, especially if no one knew she was there. She had to find a way to speak to Torin alone.

She wasn't sure how long she had been locked inside when there was a knock at the door. She had been facing the window and spun around to see who it was. Maddock entered, carrying a tray with food and drink. "I thought you might be hungry."

"Really, you're serving the prisoner now?" Ianthe snapped at him. "I thought you guys forgot that the little human needs to eat." Her voice dripped with sarcasm.

"Well, I suppose if you're not hungry, I can just enjoy it myself." He set the tray down on the table and sat in the chair. It looked like steak, mashed potatoes, and some sort of green vegetable she was unfamiliar with. He picked up the silverware, cut off a small piece of the steak, and took a bite.

"Hey!" She rushed over and grabbed the fork as it was reaching his mouth for a second bite. She swiftly put the fork into her own mouth, savoring the explosion of flavors on her tongue. She may have even moaned, but she wasn't going to admit it. *Damn, this is so much better than the protein bars I had stuffed into my bag.*

She plucked the plate off of the table and sat down on the bed, balancing it on her lap while she shoveled another mouthful of food into her mouth. "When...an I...et my... uff ba...?" she asked.

Maddock smirked, trying to hide his amusement at the baffling human in front of him. "I'm sorry. Can you repeat that when your mouth is not full of food?"

She swallowed and took a breath. "When can I get my stuff back?"

"Your stuff?"

"Yeah, my backpack."

"Oh, that. Well, that's rather interesting. See, I could understand how you would take water and food with you while you were picking flowers. However, the clothes, flashlight, and knife..." He paused, retrieving the pocketknife from his pocket. "Those are a little harder to explain."

She swallowed the food in her mouth. "You went through my bag?"

"Of course. Did you really expect me not to?"

"No, I suppose not." She shrugged casually while her mind raced. How could she explain her supplies? She didn't trust him enough to come completely clean, but she had to give him something. "Okay, okay, you caught me. I wasn't out picking flowers."

"Really?" Maddock scoffed. "I would have never guessed." *Seems I'm not the only one with a sarcastic streak.*

"You see, I met Evin in the woods by a cabin before he brought me over here, so I needed the flashlight to find my way, because it was night and all, and the knife, well, my father taught me to always have a way to protect myself from boys who get a little too handsy." She tried to keep the doe-eyed, innocent expression on her face instead of the smirk she felt on the inside because she was pleased with her own quick thinking.

Maddock didn't look like he bought her story, but he didn't press her for more. She had offered him a reasonable explanation.

"So when can I get my bag back?" she asked, hoping to shift the focus of the conversation.

"When I'm escorting you back to your home."

Her face fell. "Can I at least get my clothes? Surely there's no harm in that."

"That seems like a reasonable request, however, I must check with the king before I can give you an answer. Depending on how quickly we locate Evin, you may be home before nightfall, or you may be here for some time."

"What do you mean how quickly you can locate him? Isn't he at the house where I left him?" She was dying to know where Evin was. If he were brought to the palace, he would immediately know she wasn't Callie, and she wasn't sure what he would do with that information. *Would he try to get me released? Or convince the Seelie king I'm the quickest route to Casimir?*

"His father went to check, but since he has yet to return, I have a feeling Evin isn't there. Perhaps your *boyfriend* is out looking for you." Maddock quirked an eyebrow, as if challenging her to contradict him.

"Perhaps, or he found out what happened and decided to leave me here to fend for myself and avoid any punishment for any rules he may have broken," she countered indifferently as she continued to eat the delicious meal before her.

"That is definitely a possibility."

"So, I'm supposed to just wait around, locked in a room until he shows up or you guys decide what to do with me?"

"Pretty much. You don't seem heartbroken that he isn't banging down the palace doors to rescue you," Maddock observed, his eyes narrowing in suspicion.

"No, I suppose not. I mean, he's gorgeous and a great boyfriend and all, but I'm kind of used to guys letting me down." She smiled sadly. She hadn't realized how much truth bled into that statement until she said it out loud. She stared down at her plate and took another bite of food, swallowing hard. It was true. She was used to men letting her down—first her father back home, then her biological father. She didn't want to admit it, but she was a little disappointed Conall had yet to come after her, and her heart ached at the reminder. *Has he forgotten about me?*

She released a sigh. She shouldn't be there pining over Conall when there was so much to figure out. She couldn't depend on a white knight to come to her rescue. Nope, she would have to be the white knight in this scenario and rescue Callie on her own. She also knew the more time she spent in Fae, the harder it would be to hide her identity. Any little slipup could lead to her death. She needed time to figure out a plan of action to get herself and Callie out of this mess. She was a ball of contradictions, feeling both hope and dread at the thought of remaining in the Seelie palace. She reminded herself yet again that the comfort of the room was a hundred times better than the Unseelie dungeon. She shuddered at the sharp memory of the hard floor and leering guards after she'd denounced her claim to the Unseelie throne.

She had paused with a forkful of mashed potatoes mid-air, lost in thought. Maddock must have mistaken her shudder as related to her current situation and not memories of the past. He rose from the chair and cautiously approached her. He sat down beside her on the bed and took the fork out of her hand, placing it gently on her plate.

"It's okay, Callie. We will figure this out, and you'll return home," he soothed. He was such a contradiction—cold and indifferent one minute, flirty and tender the next. She didn't know what to make of him. She definitely couldn't trust him—he was too unpredictable—but it was still nice to be comforted when she was out of her element.

"I'm all right, just tired and a little homesick. Thank you for the meal," she replied, hoping he would catch the hint and leave her room. Maddock apparently had other plans as he scooted himself back on the bed, leaning against the headboard. He raised his arms so his hands locked behind his head and crossed his feet at the ankles, looking relaxed and comfortable.

She rose and placed the now empty plate on the table. Keeping her back toward him, she picked up the glass of orange liquid and sniffed cautiously. It smelled of honeysuckle and tangerine. Deciding it was not ambrosia, so she lifted the juice to her lips and drank. It tasted just like it smelled—fruity and sweet. She finished off the entire glass and placed it on the tray along with the plate. She spun back around toward Maddock and unconsciously licked her lips to remove any residual traces of the sticky juice. His gaze narrowed in on her mouth and sparked with interest.

She cleared her throat as he continued to stare at her lips. "Are you going to stay in here all day? Don't you have better things to do?"

"Would you prefer to spend your time alone?" he countered.

She shrugged. "It depends on which version of you I'm going to get."

His lips tugged downward into a slight frown. "What? Am I not entertaining enough for you? You humans are so strange."

"Strange? Really? *We're* the ones who are strange?" she asked incredulously.

"Yes. I mean, just look at you. What are you wearing? There are much more comfortable clothes to travel in, clothes that are more flattering for a woman. You look like a man in that outfit." He motioned toward her t-shirt, jeans, and Converse. "And your hair—why would you want to alter that beautiful color? Who puts purple in their hair when you have such a lovely shade of blonde? It's the perfect combination of sunshine and snow."

She couldn't help the blush that spread on her cheeks. She had never heard her pale blonde hair described that way. After the initial fluster from his compliment, anger began to simmer under her skin. *How dare he insult my choices and my outfit? He has no right.* "Whatever. *My* outfit is completely normal where I come from. I can't help it that *you're* so weird." Maddock raised his eyebrows at her accusation. "I mean, look at you with your bizarre orange eyes. Who has orange eyes?"

He snorted softly. "I'll have you know the ladies love my shade of orange. Many have compared it to a warm sunset." He raised his chin arrogantly and batted his eyelashes at her as if to accentuate his point.

She rolled her eyes at his cockiness. "I'm surprised you're still able to sit down with all that hot air inside your head."

He tossed his head back and laughed—a rich, warm sound. "Oh, you are a treat, sweetheart. I can definitely see why Evin's interested in you." *What is that supposed to mean?*

She crossed her arms in front of her and glared at him. "I'm not sure I like your assessment of me," she retorted.

"Oh, you do—trust me." He swung himself off of the bed swiftly and effortlessly, stalking toward her. "Well, while this has been entertaining, I have some work to get done." He tugged gently on a lock of her purple-streaked hair. When she opened her mouth to tell him off, he winked at her and picked up the tray of dirty dishes. "I'll check on you in the morning. I'm sure even *little humans* need breakfast." His raised the pitch of his voice to mock her tone and closed the door behind him before she could reply.

She huffed out a sharp breath of air. He was so frustrating and confusing. She flung herself back on the bed. *Now is not the time to worry about some Fae boy. Now is time to plan how the heck I'm going to get out of this mess.* She thought through all her options. Until she could get a one-on-one with Torin and convince him to help her, her first priority needed to be trying to contact Callie or Conall. She had a strong feeling Evin wouldn't hurt a hair on Callie's head, but that didn't mean they hadn't run into trouble elsewhere. Callie could've tried to escape already and been found by another Fae or some strange creature. If she could get ahold of Callie, she could explain this mess. Maybe together they could get Evin to take Callie home, especially since now Ianthe was right in Evin's reach. She would turn herself over to him in a heartbeat if that guaranteed Callie's safety and return.

If she couldn't get reach Callie, she needed to let Conall know about her predicament in case he hadn't received Alfie's message yet. She wanted to keep believing what she had with Conall was real, but she couldn't stop doubt from creeping into her head. It had been months since she'd talked to him, let alone seen him. There was that, and the fact that it seemed like their relationship had developed so quickly. *Is it possible to love someone so quickly?* She knew he had tried to say the words the last time she had seen him, but she had stopped him instead, making him promise to save them for a time when they weren't saying goodbye. It was all so confusing, and of course her own insecurities were fueling her doubts. *It would be so much easier if Conall had made contact with me. Shoot, Casimir has broken who knows how many rules to track me, but Conall can't manage it? Maybe I don't mean as much to him as I thought.* She slapped her hand down on the bed in frustration. She wanted to scream out loud but was afraid the redheaded Lampir might be the one who came to investigate. She huffed loudly and threw herself back on the bed. With a loud sigh, she closed her eyes and concentrated on using her Mara abilities to contact Callie.

# CHAPTER 27

*Conall*

ORIN LEFT TO report back to King Lachlan shortly after they devised a general plan to get Callie and Ianthe home safely without anyone discovering Ianthe's true identity. Now, Conall was left sitting at the table with Callie. She was an interesting creature, full of life and ferocity. He could already see she loved Ianthe fiercely and would do anything for her, which pleased him to no end. Ianthe deserved someone who would fight for her. He remembered how lonely she'd seemed when he'd first started observing her at her great-aunt's house. Come to think of it, he couldn't recall her ever mentioning friends back home other than to tell him how they had all turned their back on her.

A thought suddenly occurred to him and he interrupted Callie's story about the night she and Ianthe toilet-papered some boy's house from school. "Callie, did Evin ever meet Ianthe in person?"

"What? Oh, um, yeah, we got frozen yogurt together so she could meet him, why?" Callie's features clouded with concern as she noted the sharp intake of breath from Conall and the color leaching from his skin.

"This is really important. I need you to think back and remember as clearly as you can for me—did he ever look her in the eyes? Does he know hers are violet?"

Callie chewed on her lower lip as she thought. "I don't think I ever mentioned it. I mean, I guess I'm so used to her eyes I hadn't even thought about how unique they are in quite some time."

"What about when she met him in person?"

Callie's brow furrowed in concentration for a moment before smoothing into relief. "No! I remember now—she wore her sunglasses the whole time. She does that sometimes if she doesn't want people to stare at her. She didn't take them off once while we were there."

Conall heaved a sigh of relief. *So Evin really doesn't know who Ianthe truly is.* There was hope that he could be reasoned with and may even help salvage the debacle he had created.

Callie's voice interrupted Conall's thoughts. "I take it that's a good thing."

"Yes. Her unique eye color is indicative of her royal Fae blood. Had Evin truly seen her for who she was, I'm not sure what kind of a situation we would be in right now. I don't think he would have made the same decisions, but I could be wrong. Any Seelie Fae could see Ianthe as an opportunity to strike against the Unseelie king."

"Seelie? Unseelie? What does that even mean?" Callie asked curiously.

Conall tended to forget how little humans knew when

it came to Fae. He shouldn't have assumed she would understand. "There are two main courts in Fae: the Seelie and the Unseelie. Ianthe and I both belong to the Unseelie court. These are Fae you would not want to cross paths with. Most of our kind see humans as a meal or a plaything. They have no respect for human life and usually take great pleasure in causing pain or chaos. On the other hand, the Seelie court—where we are now—still use humans, but in less harmful, more positive ways. Where an Unseelie Mara usually creates nightmares in her victims' dreams and feeds off of their fear, a Seelie Mara is more like a muse and uses dreams to inspire or induce positive emotions and feeds off of the human's joy."

She seemed to be absorbing everything he said. He barely heard her when she hesitantly whispered, "So Ianthe causes nightmares and feeds off of fear?" It was the first time he had seen her appear worried or afraid, despite the situation.

"No. Most Unseelie Maras do, but Ianthe and I are different. We're both only half Fae, so our human emotions and perspective influence how we use our powers. Just like humans, Fae always have the choice whether to act in a negative or positive manner. Most prefer what they are born into, but there are some who are exceptions to the rule. For instance, not all Seelie are good, just as not all Unseelie are evil. Does that make sense?"

She nodded her head and sighed. "I get it now. So even though both of you might have been born with these tendencies, you choose not to use them, like when Dean has the mark of Cain and he fights against his desire to kill."

"I have no idea who Dean is, but it sounds like you got the gist of it."

"How could you not know Dean? Dean Winchester?

Oh my gosh! Surely Thee has talked *Supernatural* to you."
His face remained blank, and her jaw dropped in disbelief.
"It's only like the greatest TV show ever!"

"Ah, that makes sense now. I'm not familiar with your
TV shows—we don't use your kind of electricity here."
He smiled, remembering the times Ianthe had called him
Spock, referencing some TV show where the character had
pointy ears.

"Aw, I feel a little sad for you. You're missing out, bud-
dy." She was about to say something else when the front
door opened. He stood from the table before she could
even blink and pulled her up from her chair, thrusting
her behind him, effectively shielding her from whoever
stepped inside.

"What the hell are you doing here?" Evin sneered as
his hand went immediately toward his sword.

"It seems you've made quite a mess of things, Evin.
I'm just here to help clean up," Conall stated, resting his
own hand on the hilt of his sword, ready to answer Evin's
challenge.

"What are you talki…" Evin's voice trailed off as he
noticed Callie peeking around Conall's shoulder. Evin's
features contorted into anger and he growled, drawing his
sword and holding it in front of him, ready to lunge. "Step
away from her this instant."

*Well, this is interesting.* Conall quickly removed his
hand from his sword and held both of them palms up.
"Callie, can you please reassure Evin that I mean you no
harm?"

Evin roared, "Do not speak to her!"

Quickly sensing that things were about to get ugly,
Callie stepped around Conall. "Evin, Conall's here to help.

It's fine. He would never hurt me, I swear."

"How would you know?" Evin snarled, stepping forward.

"Evin! You're scaring me. Stop it right now! You boys can have your pissing contest later. We have more important things to deal with at the moment," she yelled.

Evin, appearing stricken when she mentioned him scaring her, quickly sheathed his sword. "I'm sorry, Callie. I didn't mean to scare you. I'm only trying to protect you. *He* shouldn't be here." He shoved an accusatory finger toward Conall, as if he were the one to blame for this whole mess.

"Yeah, well, he is. In fact, he was here when I woke up this afternoon, unlike you. If you're so concerned about me, why weren't you here?"

Evin didn't really have an answer to that, or if he did, he didn't want to share.

"May I speak?" Conall asked, hesitant to break up what appeared to be a lovers' quarrel.

"Of course," Callie replied as Evin nodded.

"I don't know how much time we have before someone shows up to escort you to King Lachlan. Did anyone see you come home?" Conall inquired.

"No. No one saw me, but why is that any of your concern? Why would someone be here to escort me to the king?"

"Well, it seems they found a human girl wandering around the woods outside of town. When they questioned her, she told them her name was Callie and said you had brought her here." Evin's confusion showed clearly on his face. "Of course, she's not actually Callie, but her friend, Ianthe," Conall continued. He wasn't sure if he should reveal Ianthe's true identity to Evin, but he was also fairly certain had Evin known who she really was, he would have found another way to Casimir from the start.

"Oh," Evin replied.

"Yeah, *oh*. We have to do something," Callie jumped in. "We can't just leave her there. You had to figure something like this might happen when you went about this stupid kidnapping." Evin had enough good sense to appear embarrassed after Callie's scolding, but she wasn't finished. "This has gone on long enough, Evin. It's time to take me home. Obviously, this is not the way to get to Casimir. You'll have to figure out something else—although from what I've heard about that guy, perhaps you should just give up on this foolishness right now."

"It's not foolish," Evin countered, shifting quickly from ashamed to furious and anguished. "Casimir *murdered* my brother. He deserves to pay! He should feel the same loss he inflicted upon me. I shouldn't be the only one suffering here. He needs to feel pain, needs to know what it's like to lose someone he loves."

"But he doesn't love Ianthe," Conall interrupted, hoping to clear things up. Evin narrowed his gaze at Conall, showing he didn't believe him for one second. "Sure, Casimir is obsessed with Ianthe, but he doesn't *love* her. He would probably pout because you took away his favorite toy and may even be angry about it, but he wouldn't feel her loss—not the way you want him to."

"How do you know?" Evin sneered.

"Because…" He knew the only way to get through to Evin would be to tell him the truth. He hoped it was the right thing to do and wouldn't backfire on him. "Because I love her. If anything happened to her, I would be the one devastated by her loss, not Casimir."

Evin's features softened. "How do you know her?"

"I met her last summer at her great-aunt's house a few miles outside the Unseelie portal. She is...she's—"

"Oh for crying out loud. Ianthe is the Unseelie princess, you doofus. That's why this Casimir dude wants her so bad," Callie interjected, clearly frustrated that the boys were taking so long to get to the point.

"Unseelie princess? But...but Corydon doesn't have a daughter," Evin stuttered.

"Oh, but he does," she replied.

"I don't understand."

"It's like this: sometimes when a man gets horny, he has sex with a woman, and if they don't use any sort of protection, they can create a baby," Callie explained, speaking as if she were explaining it to a child, complete with some rather interesting hand motions Conall hadn't seen before.

"I understand how babies are made, Callie," Evin retorted, rolling his eyes.

"Ayanna was her mother," Conall explained. "None of us knew Ayanna was pregnant when she left Fae. In fact, no one knew about Ianthe's existence until this summer when I discovered her at Ayanna's aunt's house. Of course, after my initial shock, I surmised she was Corydon's child. She has his eyes."

"Shit," Evin cursed under his breath. Conall was relieved to see how seriously Evin took this information. Evin's face paled and filled with panic. "Conall, I swear I didn't know. I didn't know who she was. If I had I wouldn't have—"

Conall placed a hand on Evin's shoulder. "It's okay. I figured as much, but now you see why it's imperative we figure out a way to clean up this mess immediately." Evin nodded in response, looking nervous but nowhere nearly as panicked as before. "I think the best thing in this situation is for you to take Callie home. If you are seen and taken to the palace, I don't think that would help our situation at all. The best thing for Ianthe is if you aren't found so the court cannot confirm who she is and hopefully won't suspect her of being more than human." Evin nodded in agreement while Callie scowled.

"You're crazy if you think I'm just going to leave her here. She risked her life to rescue me," she interjected.

"Exactly, Callie. She is risking her life for you, so she wouldn't want you to waste this opportunity. What's most important to her is that you are returned safely. That's what I'm trying to do. I know you want to help, but trust me, I will not let anything happen to her. I'd give my life to save her," Conall replied, soothing her fears. He loved how fiercely she wanted to protect Ianthe, but the best thing would be to remove her from the equation. If the Seelie discovered Callie or Evin, Ianthe's cover would be completely blown, and her cover was the only thing saving her.

"Fine, but that doesn't mean I have to like it," she retorted.

"Understood," he acknowledged before turning his attention back to Evin. "Your father is already aware of what's going on. He's going to help us get out of this mess. I only hope Casimir hasn't discovered what you've done, because if he comes for her, it will only lead to the one thing none of us want—war.

"You should probably take Callie and get going. I'll do my best to get in contact with Ianthe this evening and work out an escape plan for tomorrow," Conall stated, observing that the sun was already setting and there was no way they would be able to get her out that day. There were too many variables and so much that could go wrong. Her guards could have already notified King Corydon of what she had done, or they could currently be making their way through Seelie territory looking for her. Casimir could be on his way to storm the castle and start a full-scale war. King Lachlan could discover who she was and hold her for ransom from King Corydon, or decide to go ahead and carry out her execution order himself. So many possibilities, and most of them not good, but he had to hold out hope. He knew how clever his girl could be and that she would do everything in her own power to make sure she wasn't discovered. He fought his instincts to storm the castle himself and demand her release, knowing that wouldn't be the right route to take.

Callie interrupted his thoughts with a poke to his chest. "The only reason I'm leaving, mister, is because I know you will get my girl out of this mess." She accentuated her point with several sharp pokes. "And so help me God, if you don't, I'll find you and I'll castrate you with an extremely dull knife—very slowly."

Conall did his best not to laugh at her threat, as if she could really hurt him. Fortunately, he admired her tenacity. "I promise I will bring her home," he said, taking a step back and extending his hand for her to shake.

"You better," she replied, shaking his hand roughly. She popped her lips loudly before turning her attention to Evin. "All right, baby cakes, let's blow this popsicle stand."

Conall couldn't help but let a small chuckle bubble over at Evin's bewildered expression. Callie, on the other hand, had no patience for it, tapping her foot loudly and putting her hands on her hips. "Are we going or what?"

Evin shook his head as if to clear it. "Yes, we should go." He stepped forward and extended his hand toward

Conall. "You're welcome to stay as long as you need and take whatever may help you. I trust you will indeed get Ianthe home safely without discovery. If not, we both—we all—" He swallowed hard. "We could lose everything."

Conall shook his hand. "I'll take care of Ianthe if you promise to let go of this vendetta against Casimir. Nothing good will come of it."

Evin stepped back sharply. "You cannot ask that of me. Reid deserves retribution."

"Then honor his life with your actions. Become the man he was—the man he would want you to be. He'd never want this of you, and you know it. I have known your father and your brother for many years, and you're absolutely right—Reid does deserve retribution, but not in the form of revenge. He'd never want you to harm an innocent girl. In fact, he'd probably be appalled at your form of retribution."

Evin flinched as if he'd been slapped and hung his head in shame. Callie placed a comforting hand upon his shoulder. He turned, pulling her toward him and burying his face in her neck and hair, almost melting into her. She glanced over Evin's shoulder, slightly shocked by his emotional display, before wrapping her arms around him and whispering comforting words against his chest. Evin was a mess. Conall had a feeling he had not yet properly grieved his brother's death and it was finally catching up to him. Grief had a funny way of doing that. It can sneak up on you when you least expect it, and the slightest, silliest thing can bring you to your knees.

Conall left the couple and walked into the kitchen to give them a little privacy. About ten minutes later, Callie stood in the doorway. "We're going now. We'll do our best not to be seen, and you do your best to get my bestie back, 'kay?" She pulled him in a quick hug before leaving him to contemplate all that needed to be done to ensure his and Torin's plan would be successful. The dark was quickly creeping in upon them, so he resigned himself to spending the night where he was. He scrounged up dinner and ate as he pondered everything that could go wrong. He knew the most important thing to do was to try to contact Ianthe, and the best way to do that would be to lie down and hope she was trying to reach him as well. Noting the night sky and the fact that she'd most likely be asleep now as well, he lay down on the couch and closed his eyes, focusing every thought on his love for her and his need to see her again.

# CHAPTER 28

*Ianthe*

*S*EATED ON CALLIE'S *front porch, Ianthe had been waiting for what seemed like an eternity. She hoped her lack of contact meant Callie was awake or Evin had experienced a change of heart and took her back to the human realm. She sighed heavily in frustration. She still had no plan to escape the Seelie palace and could only hope her disguise would hold before someone realized she was more than human.*

*She closed her eyes and imagined Conall's little cottage, hoping he might be there. She blinked her eyes open slowly, scared she would find it empty. Her heart ached at the sight of his home. They had only spent one night there, but everything about it made her think of him. It was cute and comfortable, rustic yet romantic, just like Conall. She smiled as she stepped toward the door. She took a deep breath, holding all the hope she had within her chest, and opened the front door. She felt her lungs deflate and disap-*

pointment occupied the space where her breath had just been as she stepped into the empty room. She hadn't even realized she was smiling until she felt her face drop.

"Of course," she whispered, crossing the living room toward the little kitchenette. Strong hands grabbed both of her shoulders and pulled her back against a large chest. She would have screamed had his comforting touch not instantly relaxed her.

"You're here," he said breathlessly into her hair, and she sighed in response, melting into him. He took advantage of her languid body and spun her around to face him, his hands gently cradling her face. She blinked up into his glowing emerald green eyes. *Man, how I've missed those eyes, his touch, his voice...everything about him.* "Oh my flower, how I have missed you." His eyes seemed to convey the same torture she had experienced at his absence, and she felt some reassurance that their relationship was not one-sided. She opened her mouth to respond when his lips crashed down on hers. Her eyes closed, and he stole her breath. The kiss was passionate and desperate. Like a man dying for a sip of water, he drank her in. It was overwhelming and perfect all at the same time. She lost herself in his kiss, in the caress of his lips and tongue, and didn't really care if she was ever found again.

He pulled away so they could both catch their breath, and she gazed into his pools of green. "Conall," she said on a sigh. He closed his eyes, savoring the sound of her voice. She brought her right hand up to his face, stroking his jaw with the backs of her fingers then flipping her palm over to cradle his face as she met his cheek. He leaned into her touch and stayed like that for a few moments before pressing his lips against her palm. Overwhelmed, a few tears dripped down her cheeks. His fingers cupped her face as his thumbs wiped them away.

"Shhh, my flower. There is no reason to be sad. I'm here now," he soothed.

She tried to chuckle, but it came out as a hiccup. "I know, Spock—they're happy tears."

"I have never been happier to be called Spock than I am right now." His smile lit up his face as he pulled her into another fierce embrace. "I missed you so much." He clung to her as if he feared she would vanish, and the sad fact was that she could. Either of them could wake at any second and their heartfelt reunion could come to an end.

"I know, Conall—me too. I feel the same way." She pulled back to look him in the eyes. "There's something I should tell you…" She started to speak those words she had kept hidden in her heart since they last saw each other, the same words she had not let him speak as a goodbye, but he interrupted her.

"I know, I know. I have been filled in on your adventures through your Aunt Grace and an encounter with Torin." He mistook her words for a confession of her whereabouts and didn't pause to let her correct him. "What matters most is that you are safe now. I've spoken with Torin, and we're working on way to get you out of the Seelie palace. In the meantime, Evin agreed to take Callie back to her home."

"Really? He agreed to take her back home after all of that?"

"I don't think he would have taken her to begin with had he known who you truly were. I'm sorry, my love, but I had to tell them. I trust both Evin and Torin. They dread a war between our people as much as I do, so they will do anything to help us keep your identity a secret."

"So Callie's home now? Is that why I couldn't contact her?"

*He paused, his glance flicking away from her steady gaze. "Not quite. They left only a half hour or so ago. I can see why she is your bestie." He said the last word like an older person trying out slang for the first time, and she giggled.*

*"I take it you got to meet Callie in person?"*

*"Ah, yes. I got a stern talking to and had to promise your safe return under the threat of bodily harm." His eyes flicked back to hers, sparking with amusement.*

*Ianthe chuckled. That certainly sounds like Callie. "Well, I'm glad you two finally got to meet and she could see I wasn't making you up." The whole time they were talking, he still held her gently in his arms, but with the reminder of what she had been through and how she had been doubting his feelings, she began to pull away.*

*His lips tugged down into a frown. "I'm sorry, my flower. I did not mean to stay away for so long, but King Corydon made sure I was kept busy. I think he meant to keep me away from you. However, once I got the chance to pursue Casimir and instead locked onto your trail, there was no stopping me from getting to you." He loosened his grasp on her, allowing her to step farther out of his embrace.*

*She walked toward the sofa and sat down. He followed behind her, pulling over a chair so he was sitting directly across from her, knees touching, and could look her in the eye, but she kept her head down. "I understand. I won't lie and tell you it has been easy. I knew it would be difficult for you to get away, I had just hoped...well, never mind. There's no point in bringing it up now. It's not like it would change anything." She couldn't help the heartache that laced her voice.*

*"Oh, Ianthe." He sighed regretfully. "I did everything*

*I could, I promise you that. I thought about nothing but you every moment since we were separated, but you and I both know I couldn't just leave my duties. I could not put us both at risk that way."*

*"I know, Conall. I know, I just—it just sucks. I mean, this whole situation sucks when you really think about it. It's like we're freaking Romeo and Juliet here. Two star-crossed lovers fated to never to be together..."*

*He placed two fingers against her lips and his other hand gently tilted her chin up so he could stare into her violet eyes. "I know this hasn't been easy, and I'm not saying it's going to get better right away, but we'll figure it out. We will be together. I'll make sure of that, but for now we have much bigger problems to worry about."*

Damn. He's right. Here I am wallowing over our relationship when my life is in danger the longer I remain in Fae. *She sighed. "Of course."*

*His fingers traced lightly down from her lips to her throat and she swallowed hard, battling against the massive butterflies in her stomach, but he didn't stop there. He glided down her collarbone and over to her left shoulder before using his entire hand to graze down her left arm. Her breath quickened and her heartbeat thudded against her ribs like a caged bird trying to escape. Finally, his hand stopped its torturous path and twined his fingers with hers, pressing their palms firmly together. "You are the most important thing to me. My only mission now is to get you home safe. We can worry about everything else after that." He gave her hand a quick reassuring squeeze and her whole body filled with his warmth and comfort. His other hand came up and tugged on a lock of her hair. "This is different."*

*It took her a moment to realize he was referring to her*

*hair color. The last time she had seen him she was a brunette with blue streaks, not a pale blonde with lavender streaks. "Yeah, um, it's my natural color—well, the blonde is. The purple obviously isn't."*

*"I like it. It seems to fit you better—not that I didn't like your other hair color, I just really like this version of you. It looks like your mom's. If you'd had this color the first time we met, I think you would have had a harder time convincing me you were not Ayanna." He chuckled.*

*She blushed, silently relieved that he liked her no matter the color of her hair. Unsure of how to take his strange compliment, she shifted the conversation back on track. "Well, now that that's out of the way, what's the plan?"*

*He let his fingers drop from her hair, a little taken aback by the shift in conversation even though he knew it was important to deal with the matter at hand first. He was hesitant to let go of their closeness. "Who has been guarding you?"*

*"Maddock," she replied, and he tightened his grip on her fingers as his eyes went wide with fear.*

*"Shit," he hissed. Maddock's name was like a bucket of ice on the conversation, instantly turning Conall's usually warm demeanor chilly.*

*"I take it that's not a good thing. I mean, he's been okay to me, not like his friend the Lampir..."*

*Those were obviously not the words to say as he yanked his hand from hers before clenching both of them into tight fists. "Could this possibly get any worse?" he huffed in frustration to no one in particular.*

*"I could think of a way or two," she joked, trying to lighten his ever-darkening mood.*

*"This is not the time to joke. Do you not understand*

how dangerous this situation is?" He practically yelled the question at her.

She scooted back into the sofa, putting distance between them. *What does he think I am, stupid?* "Of course I understand. One Fae could attempt to read my memories at any point, and the other merely has to take a small drink and they'll both know I'm not who I say I am. I know damn well the danger I am in, Conall. I don't need you to remind me." She crossed her arms against her chest firmly.

He sighed, releasing his pent-up frustration. "I know, my love. I'm sorry. I just—it's so hard not being with you right now, so hard to know you're in a dangerous situation and there's not much I can do about it without revealing who you are or starting a full-out war with the Seelie." He sighed again. "If you had just—"

He didn't realize the mistake he'd made until it was too late. She shoved herself off of the sofa, putting a good amount of distance between them. "If I had just what, Conall? Not gone into Fae? Ignored the fact that one of them kidnapped my best friend? Just let her go?" Her voice rose with each rhetorical question she threw at him. "Or should I have just waited for you? Well, guess what! I did wait. I waited until there was no choice but for me to do something about it. I was not about to let anything bad happen to an innocent girl because of me, let alone my best friend, so if you think for one minute I regret any of my decisions that led me to this point, think again. I don't. Given the choice, I would do it again a hundred times over, because I'm tired of being the little girl who needs rescuing. It was time for me to man up and do the rescuing myself." She paced during her tirade, throwing her hands into the air.

As much as he wanted to remain mad at her, in his heart he knew her decision was not foolish, but was every *bit of why he was so madly in love with her. She was the most selfless Fae he had ever met. She was a complete contradiction to everything an Unseelie was supposed to be, and even though he was not going to say it openly because he knew it would just further fuel her anger, she was really cute when she was angry.*

*"You're right. You're absolutely right," he placated her, stepping toward her slowly. "You did the right thing. I would've done the same thing if someone had taken you. Hell, it's taking everything in my power not to storm the Seelie palace right now and whisk you away. I'm not blaming you for being in this situation at all. I'm just frustrated at my own inability to do something about it, and I apologize for taking that out on you."*

*His words helped her anger slowly melt away. "Apology accepted," she mumbled softly. Even though she knew he was genuine with his words, she still worried about how he saw her. Is he starting to see me as a magnet for trouble or as a foolish, young girl? Her insecurities nibbled away at her, making her doubt her own strength and power. What could she do to prove herself as his equal? She felt so clueless about all things Fae, and perhaps that was what was making her come off as a naïve little girl. There was also the age difference of course, but that really shouldn't matter. He loves me, right? His actions certainly show that, but he hasn't said it yet, so maybe... She shook her head to clear her thoughts. Now was not the time for that discussion. They needed to figure out how to get her home, and then they could talk about their feelings.*

*"What do you know about Maddock?" she asked, hoping to refocus their conversation on a plan for escape.*

*"I know he is powerful. I don't personally know him, not like Torin, but I have interacted with him a few times in my dealings at the palace. He seems to be your average,*

*arrogant Fae—a bit stuck on himself, definitely sees himself above half-breeds like myself, as well as humans. I'm sure he would have no love lost if the order were to come down for you to be executed."*

*She gasped softly. She knew Maddock had seemed that way initially, but after spending time with him, she wasn't so sure. "He promised he would return me to my home."*

*Conall's eyebrows rose. "Did he really? Did he say those exact words? Because Fae take their promises very seriously."*

*Fae take their promises seriously—how have I not realized this before? She thought for a few minutes, replaying all their conversations in her head. "He said he promised he would do his best to get me home."*

*"His best will all depend on whatever is within his power. He will do whatever the Seelie king orders him to do, including reading your memories, erasing them, or even disposing of you if need be. He won't defy his king for you."*

*"What if I could get him to promise to do more than just his best, but to actually help me?"*

*Conall snorted a laugh. "Yeah, good luck with that."*

*"You don't think I could?" She quirked an eyebrow, taking his amusement as a challenge.*

*"And how exactly would you do that?"*

*"Oh, I have my ways," she implied suggestively.*

*His features morphed into a fierce expression. "You will not."*

*"And why not?" she asked, placing a hand on her hip and soaking up the jealousy she could so clearly read on his face.*

"*I thought we agreed to not play games with each other,*" *he replied, narrowing his eyes.*

"*I'm not playing games, Conall.*"

"*Oh yes, you are,*" *he argued, tugging her into his arms. "I'm well aware of your charms, my flower, and I do not wish you to use them on anyone but me." He lowered his mouth with each word until his lips were gently grazing hers. She couldn't resist pressing into him. His kiss was slow and gentle, as if he were savoring the very taste of her. She breathed him in and opened her mouth, exploring his as they shared their next breath, both tongues pressing madly against each other in a slow, hypnotic dance.*

*When the kiss ended, she pulled away reluctantly, but not before he pressed several quick kisses against her lips, eyelids, forehead, and finally the tip of her nose. They rested their foreheads against each other, just taking a minute to soak everything in. She smiled at him and said, "Conall, I—"*

*A rough hand was shaking her awake. No! It's too soon! I haven't told him I love him, let alone figured out how the hell I'm going to get out of this mess.*

"Leave me alone," she grumbled, hoping the shaking would cease and she could quickly return to Conall.

"I would gladly leave you alone, *Callie*, but first you have to tell me how you know Conall," the voice grumbled above her. *Shit.* That woke her up. She sat up quickly, eyes wide, taking in the morning light.

"I—I don't know what you're talking about," she stuttered.

"Don't try to lie to me, *sweetheart*." His orange eyes narrowed on her. "I heard his name muttered from your pretty little lips when I came in here to wake you. I think you have some explaining to do, and you better start right now."

She glanced around the room, searching for a weapon or something to change the discussion, and then she saw the tray of food he had set down. Her stomach grumbled.

"Sure, just let me eat something first," she replied, swinging her legs out of the bed.

He blocked her from getting up. "Nope, you can eat after you tell me how the hell you know Conall."

She swallowed, unsure of how to handle the situation. Could she trust Maddock with the truth? Conall certainly didn't feel like they could trust him. *Maddock has no reason to be loyal to me. Will he want to avoid a war with the Unseelie, or is he looking for a reason to start one?* There were so many ways this could go wrong, but she wasn't sure she had any other options.

"Um, I have a cousin named Conall."

"*Eeeeehhhh*," He made a sound like a buzzer going off. "Wrong answer. Try again." His body crowded her space intimidatingly, anger etching his masculine features.

"Do you know my cousin Conall?" She blinked up at him innocently.

He placed his hands on her shoulders, using his weight to keep her seated. "You don't have a cousin named Conall. It's time to tell me the truth. Who. Are. You?"

*Shit, shit, triple shit.* She took one more shot in the dark, hoping it would appease him. "Oh, I must have been dreaming about *Supernatural* again. It's this TV show about these demon hunters, and one of them is named

Conall," she lied, acting with everything she had.

His hands gripped her shoulders painfully. "You do realize I can just take a walk through that pretty little head of yours and find out for myself, right?"

"Then why don't you?" she challenged.

"Because I'd rather have you tell me. But, if you can't be honest with me, I'll take that walk. Although, sometimes my anger makes me a little careless and I erase the memories people seem to hold most dear—nasty little side effect, can't really be helped." He shrugged his shoulders indifferently, closed his eyes, and moved his hands toward her head.

"NO! Wait!"

He squinted his right eye open, fingers poised in her hair, nearing the back of her skull.

She sighed, defeated. "Fine, I'll tell you. Just don't— don't read my memories. It will only make things worse."

"Make things worse? If I think for one instant you're lying to me again, Callie—or whoever you are—I'm going to take that walk, and I won't be careful. Do you understand me?"

She nodded. He released her and stepped away, getting himself a chair to sit directly across from her. Her stomach growled loudly again. "I swear I'm not trying to stall or change the topic or anything, but do you think I could eat while I tell you?" She blinked her eyes at him, hoping to express her hunger and helplessness.

"Fine," he huffed, walking over to grab the tray of food and placing it beside her on the bed before taking his own seat. "There. Now talk."

"Sir, yes sir," she replied, giving him a mock salute before snatching a slice of bread off the plate and tearing into it. While she chewed, she debated how much to tell and contemplated all the risk involved. Her gut said she could trust him, but could she trust her gut? She swallowed, noting that his patience with her was waning. "Okay, so here it goes…"

# CHAPTER 29

*Conall*

**ONALL BREATHED IN** Ianthe's scent, cherishing every minute in her presence. His forehead pressed against hers. When he looked at her, her smile took his breath away, and she said, "Conall, I—" Then she was gone. He sighed heavily. Someone must have woken her; she wouldn't have woken herself up without giving him a proper goodbye, and she had been in the middle of telling him something. What was she going to say? Oh, how he longed to hold her in real life.

She looked different. Her pale blonde hair was a unique blend of the golden yellow of Ayanna's hair and Corydon's milky silver. He could see how striking it was against her porcelain skin and how it made her violet eyes seem even more ethereal, so he could understand how it would cause the humans to stare at her beauty. And the violet streaks— he smiled at his little rebel. He loved that she had fire in her soul and wanted to be different from others, not re-

*ally caring what they thought about her anymore. It spoke to someone's true confidence when they were happy to be themselves and not worry about what others thought about them.*

*He sat back down on the couch in his cottage. It had felt so right to have her there in his home, like finally everything he could possibly need to make himself happy was in one place, but that would never happen. His smile vanished and his heart ached. She was banished from Fae, so if he wanted to be with her, it would have to be in the human realm. He would have to leave behind everything and everyone he had ever known. Was he ready to do that? He shook his head—of course he was. There wasn't much tying him to this realm. He'd never quite felt like he fit in with everyone else since he was only half Fae, and he didn't really have any close friends. There were his men who respected him due to his position of power as first in command, and at one time he had almost thought of Corydon as a friend, but he was never foolish enough to believe the king would ever see him as an equal. The only one he would truly miss would be Alfie, but Alfie would support his decision to leave in a heartbeat, so what was he really waiting for? With his mind made up, he stood and strode toward the kitchen, but then a thought stopped him right in his tracks.*

Will Corydon let me leave?

*He obviously hadn't thought it would be easy, but what if Corydon wouldn't release him from his position? What if it wasn't as easy as deciding to walk away? He huffed out a frustrated breath. There would be plenty of time to figure that out later. What was most important in the moment was that he help Ianthe return to her home in the human realm without detection. After that they could worry about everything else.*

His eyes fluttered open, staring at the ceiling of Evin's cottage in the late morning light. He hoped everything was okay at the Seelie palace. Torin should have already returned to the king and reported that Evin could not be located. He was going to suggest the release of the human, but they both knew there was a good chance King Lachlan would deny him or it would look as if Torin were trying to protect his own son. However, there was a slim chance that the king could be swayed, and if anyone could do it, it was Torin.

Conall debated staying longer in Evin's house. If he were discovered there by someone other than Torin, it would raise suspicion, and he was sure that even though the king trusted Torin above all others, he would still send other guards in pursuit of Evin. Conall could return to his tracking of Casimir, but could he knowingly leave Ianthe in such danger? No, he knew he couldn't. His only other option was to go to the palace, but that was also a risk in itself. He needed a reason to be there. He didn't want to report back to Lachlan what Corydon thought of his revision of the blood oath agreement, and he couldn't risk upsetting the delicate balance between the two courts. Perhaps he could claim he was on leave or had a message to deliver from Alfie. Whatever reason he was going to give, he'd have to figure it out soon. He couldn't stay at Evin's another day. If he knew which home belonged to Torin, he would have gone there. *Wait, that's it.* He could visit the palace under the guise of visiting Torin to pay his respects for his loss. No one could argue with that reason, and it would give him a chance to scope out Ianthe's situation and make contact with Torin to let him know Evin was returning Callie to the human realm.

With his decision made, he gathered his things and tracked back to where he'd left his horse in the forest. He found Rain grazing in a field of flowers and mounted up, quickly trotting toward the Seelie palace.

# CHAPTER 30

*Ianthe*

S HE SAT IN her bed at the Seelie palace, an empty
plate next to her, watching Maddock absorb everything she had told him.

"You can't be...I would have known..." He paced
back and forth, battling with himself and the new knowledge she had just laid upon him.

"Oh, but I am."

"How did I not notice?"

"Well, I'm not your average half Fae. I mean, I'm
probably the most human one you will ever meet, considering I only found out I'm half Fae several months ago and
hadn't noticed any changes in myself until I turned seven-
teen only around half a year ago," she explained.

"But, you're not just any half Fae—you're royal. There
are signs," Maddock pointed out.

"Oh, well, there are ways to hide those things." Maddock's head snapped toward her face and his eyes narrowed, studying her closely. "Like, um, contacts. We have these things called colored contacts so you can change your eye color if you want," she continued.

"Show me."

"Did you see a little plastic case in my backpack? I'll need that before I can show you."

"Fine." He snatched her plate off the bed. "I shall return shortly," he stated simply before turning and leaving the room.

She was still trying to gauge his reaction to her news. It was obvious he doubted the honesty of her words, but she had told him the truth, as unbelievable as that truth may be. She hoped he returned with the contact case quickly. Her eyes were starting to get a little irritated and she had left contact solution in the case to help her clean the contacts for just such occasion. Perhaps he'd bring her whole backpack with him when he returned.

Her hope was dashed the instant he opened the door. He had the plastic case in his left hand, but her bag was nowhere in sight. "Here. Show me." He thrust the case toward her.

"Oh, I thought you might have the whole bag with you…" She couldn't hide the disappointment in her voice.

He rolled his eyes at her assumption. "You thought wrong. Now, show me."

"Okay, okay. Geez, pushy, just give me a moment." She shook the case gently, hoping the liquid inside hadn't spilled or leaked, and then carefully unscrewed the cap for the left contact.

"I'm not pushy, I just want to see for myself that you are indeed who you say you are, *Lady Ianthe*." His voice oozed doubt as he spoke her name.

She bent her head as she carefully removed one contact at a time, placing them delicately in the case with solution. She felt relief at having them out, but also extremely nervous. They were her shield—a slightly uncomfortable shield, sure, but they kept the Fae from automatically knowing who she was, so not having them on in the middle of the Seelie palace left her feeling slightly naked. She blinked several times before lifting her head to look at Maddock.

The instant their eyes met, he staggered back a step, grabbing hold of the chair next to him to steady himself. She heard his sharp intake of breath and the whispered curse on his exhale. "You weren't lying."

"I told you I wasn't."

"I know. It just makes everything that much more complicated."

"You're telling me," she mumbled.

"Do you understand the position you've put me in? To not report to the king right now and tell him who you are could be considered an act of treason."

She gulped. "I know, but I don't have any other options. I only came here to rescue my friend Callie, who is being returned as I speak. It's not like I wanted to return to Fae, especially to the Seelie palace. I had no other choice. I couldn't leave her here knowing it was my fault. I know I can be used as a tool to start a war. I can be tortured and kept in the Seelie dungeons until your king finds the right use for me. I'm aware that if you return me to my father, it's likely that the Unseelie will demand my execution for violating the terms of my exile. I also know if you took that walk through my head and found out who I really was without me explaining it to you, you would not have hesitated to unveil my identity, but I am asking you—no, *begging* you to help me. Please, Maddock, I don't have any other choice, and if you want to avoid a war with the Unseelie, the best bet is for us to figure out a way for me to get out of here without anyone being the wiser, if you get what I'm saying."

He released a long pent-up sigh, as well as another curse. "First, you have to stay away from Angus."

"Angus?"

"The redhead who was with me when we found you."

"Oh, the Lampir. Yeah, I figured if he got one taste of me, he'd know what I'm hiding. At the very least, he'd know I'm not completely human."

"He'll also turn you over the second he figures things out. He has been aiming to work his way up the chain of command, and he will see this as an opportunity to prove himself worthy to the king."

"Yeah. I wasn't planning on being anywhere near him, given that he gives me the creeps, so I don't see that as a problem."

"I will talk to Torin and we'll figure this out. I'm going to find him now. Stay in your room. If you try to get out, Angus will be there to greet you, I guarantee it."

"I'll be here." When he seemed appeased, he left the room. She felt a little relieved knowing she had two allies within the palace. She was still in quite the predicament, but at least she wasn't the only one working to get her home.

# CHAPTER 31

*Conall*

CONALL RODE RIGHT up to the gates of the Seelie palace where the guard was standing. "Greetings, I've come to pay my respects to Torin," he called out as he approached.

"Sir Conall, I didn't expect to see you again so soon. Did your king send you with a rebuttal to our last agreement?" the curious guard inquired.

"No. As I've said, I'm here on my own accord today. I wasn't able to properly offer my condolences to Torin on my last visit as business got in the way."

"Don't you think that will be a little odd coming from you? It was your crowned prince who slaughtered Reid, after all."

This was exactly what Conall had been afraid of. He'd hoped to get by without so much questioning, but he was at the mercy of the guard to even be allowed in the palace.

"Yes, well, that's why it's even more important that I'm here, to show that not all Unseelie are like Casimir. I have known both Torin and Reid for many years and have the utmost respect for both of them. The loss of Reid's life was a great one."

The guard snorted but allowed Conall to pass. "He'll most likely be in the company of the king, and if you think I am a little cautious, just wait until you run into Lachlan. Recent events have led him to be more paranoid than usual."

"I wouldn't expect less, thank you," Conall replied, dismounting his steed and handing the reins to the stable boy who came over after a shout from the guard.

The first guard whistled and another approached to escort Conall inside. He led him to a room to wait. "I will notify the king you are here, sir."

"Actually, I'm here to see Torin." The guard looked slightly taken aback, so Conall continued, "Of course, you're welcome to notify King Lachlan that I am here, but not for business. It's a personal matter."

"Of course, then I will see if Sir Torin is available."

Conall was left alone, sitting in the waiting room. Knowing Ianthe was in the same building was driving him nuts. He yearned to search for her. His leg bounced as he tried to dispel some part of his nervous energy. Each minute he sat there waiting felt like twenty, and he was surprised he hadn't broken into a sweat yet. He didn't want to pace the room in case someone wandered in, but the sitting and waiting was killing him. Just when he thought he couldn't take it any longer, a door opened and in stepped Torin.

"Conall," he greeted as he closed the door firmly behind him. Torin's voice dropped to a whisper as he approaced. "Did everything go as planned?"

"Yes. Evin returned home, and when I explained the situation, he was in agreement with our plan. He seemed to be very repentant of his actions. He regrets the choices he has made."

"He damn well should. I know his heart was in the right place, but I can't imagine what's going on in that boy's head."

"He blames himself for Reid's death—that much is clear. I think he was trying to set things right, to avenge Reid the only way he knew how—by going after Casimir through Ianthe. Unfortunately, he didn't stop to think about why Casimir would be so interested in the girl in the first place, or why a girl like her would need Unseelie guards. Perhaps he thought they were placed there by Casimir, or he was simply too blinded by his need for revenge."

Torin sighed. "Well, at least he has started to make things right. It gives us a little more time to figure out how to get Ianthe released without anyone figuring out who she really is or why they can't locate Evin."

"Do you think Lachlan will let her go without questioning Evin?"

"It's possible. I'm certainly working on it, but he hasn't really mentioned her after the initial inquisition. He does feel she's hiding something, that she wasn't being completely honest during her questioning, so he may take more coaxing than normal."

"Maybe we can convince him she's just a stupid human girl who was incredibly nervous the first time she was questioned and that's what made her seem like she was hiding something, or she was trying to protect Evin and that's what he picked up on."

"Perhaps… I guess it depends on how gracious or merciful he is feeling at the moment."

The door opened and the subject of their conversation stepped through. "Torin, could you—" The king paused, glancing curiously at Conall. "Ah, I wasn't aware you were here, Conall. Did your king send you with a rebuttal?"

Conall bowed his head slightly, showing respect. "No, sir. I came on my own time to pay my respects to Torin. Reid was a well-respected soldier."

"Interesting. Does your king know you are here?"

Conall debated about lying for a moment or two, but decided it best to seek an ally in King Lachlan. He licked his lips nervously, hoping this was the right choice. "Um, not exactly, sir. I merely asked for some time away to attend to a personal matter, and he did not deem it worthy to question what the matter was."

"Even more interesting, although I suppose if Torin asked for the same thing, I would not care to question his personal matter either. Well then, even though you are not here on official business, you are still welcome to your room here for the duration of your stay if you would like."

"That is most generous of you. Thank you, Your Majesty." He bowed again.

"I find it very honorable of you to take personal time to deliver your condolences to my first in command, and as such, I would like for you to dine with us this evening."

"Of course. You are an ever-gracious host. I thank you."

"Think nothing of it." King Lachlan waved his hand dismissively before returning his attention to his first in command. "Torin, will you have Maddock prepare our little female visitor to dine with us as well? Lady Bronwen has some dresses that should fit her. Perhaps the little bird will sing for her supper."

"Of course, sire," Torin said with a bow. The king turned and strode out the door without further acknowledgement.

"Was he talking about Ianthe?" Conall asked, his heart pounding against his chest.

"Yes, I'm afraid so."

"Torin, what did he mean by 'the little bird will sing for her supper'?"

"I'm not exactly sure, to be honest. Either he thinks she will be entertaining to have at the table, or he's planning a different technique to uncover whatever she's hiding. Either way I hope your princess is quite the actress. Who knows—maybe she can charm him into releasing her after dinner, but I wouldn't hold my breath. I'm quite positive this evening will test us all." Conall studied Torin while he spoke, noting that the poor man seemed to have aged several years in the last week.

"If anyone can pull it off, it's her. Is there any way for you to get a message to her?" Conall asked.

"I think I can manage that."

"If she's already pretending to be a clueless human, remind her not to let her training show. We spent countless hours this summer working on proper etiquette and table manners with the Unseelie court, but I'm afraid if she shows that knowledge tonight, the king will become even more suspicious."

"Of course. Good thinking, Conall. I'll see what I can do. It'd be wise for you to use the time to freshen up before dinner. She's being held in the same wing as your room, but there will be a guard or two posted at her door at all times. Now would be a good time for you to investigate how we might be able to sneak her away."

"All right then, I'll see you at dinner." Conall paused as Torin walked toward the door. "Oh, and Torin"—he turned and faced Conall once again, his eyes that of a weary soul—"I am truly sorry for your loss. I meant everything I said about Reid. He was a great soldier and I had looked forward to working with him more. I know you were grooming him to take your place."

Torin's eyes warmed. "Thank you, Conall. Your words mean a lot to me. I know Evin is foolish and rash, but he's all I have left. If you can help me save him and save our people from an unnecessary war, I would find that your respects have been paid tenfold."

Conall nodded his head in acknowledgement just before Torin left the room. He plucked his satchel off of the floor and exited the room, only to find the same guard there that had escorted him earlier. *Did he overhear any of our conversation?* He didn't think so, but the possibility still made him nervous.

"Your room is ready at the king's request. It is the same one you used last time you were here, so I take it you can find it fine on your own."

"Of course, thank you," Conall replied before walking away.

"Oh, and Sir Conall," the guard called out to his retreating form. Conall halted and turned. "Just because you no longer have an escort while you are here does not mean we won't be watching you. There are guards on every hall, and even though we have been ordered to treat you as our guest, if you show any unfriendly behavior, we won't hesitate to correct it."

Conall nodded in acknowledgement of the guard's

thinly veiled threat. While their king may have trusted him for the time being, the other Seelies did not. Of course, he was well aware of that from all of his previous dealings. They would always see him as an Unseelie, as the enemy, first and foremost, and he was used to that by now. What worried him was that the guards' extra attention was going to make it that much harder to communicate with Ianthe, let alone help her escape. They were all walking on a tightrope, and the slightest wobble could send everyone plummeting over the edge.

# CHAPTER 32

*Ianthe*

I T HAD PROBABLY been about an hour since Maddock had left her room. The minute he left, she put her
contacts back in, not wanting to let anyone else in on
her secret. As it was there were two—no, make that three
Seelies who could turn her over at a moment's notice if
they felt so inclined. It's a terrifying thing to trust someone
who's supposed to be your enemy, but she really had no
other choice. She was getting a little stir crazy being in the
same room for so long, but she didn't want to risk running
into Angus the Lampir in the hallway, so she did the only
other thing she could think of: she lay down on the bed and
closed her eyes.

*She imagined the school courtyard where she ate lunch*

with Callie every day the weather allowed. She could almost picture the last time they had eaten lunch there, discussing the possibility of the double date with "Reid" and Kyle. Callie had been so happy, the air full of promise and excited chatter. Now everything was eerily silent and still. It was bizarre and almost creepy to be in a place so familiar, but empty of any other people. A strange chill raced down her spine as if someone was watching her, and it wasn't Callie. She hoped this meant Callie was already back home or on her way there, but if Callie wasn't there, who was? Because someone else was most definitely there, creeping around the edges of her dream.

She shifted her focus, hoping to shake the spectator, and envisioned herself by the familiar tall oak tree at the edge of the woods at her great-aunt's house. She remembered the first time she met Conall there and the violet flower she found after he left. She looked down at her left hand, almost surprised to see she had conjured an exact replica of the flower. She wasn't sure exactly when she noticed she wasn't alone again, but there was a slight shift in the air.

"Conall?" she called out, hopeful he'd appear since she had been focusing her energy on him.

A shadowed man stepped forward from the woods to her right. "Afraid not, my love." The first thing she recognized was his voice, which was like oil on her skin. The second was his pale blue eyes glowing against the darkening evening sky.

"Casimir," she whispered, horrified. What did I do to bring him here? She had been so sure her focus was clear, and it definitely hadn't been on him. "But—how?"

"Seems some part of you must have been thinking about me. Do you miss me, little one?"

*"No! Of course not,"* she retorted, but her mind wondered. Is there some small part that wanted to see him, part of me that was thinking about him? No, the only ones I was thinking about were Callie and Conall, and a slight mention of Kyle and Evin, but definitely not Casimir.

*"How did you find your way in? You're not a Mara."*

*"I told you, little one,"* he said, stopping just in front of her face. *"You must have been thinking about me. Did my little Unseelie princess miss her prince?"* He pouted his lips forward and blinked his eyes up at her like a little puppy dog, but the look was just strange on him.

*"Don't be ridiculous, Casimir. I wasn't thinking about you, and I certainly don't miss you."*

He pressed a finger against her lips to stop her from talking. *"Shhhh...no need to deny your true feelings."*

Wow. He's taking creeper to a whole new level.

*"I know exactly what you crave."* His finger slid down from her lips to her throat, where his sharp nail pressed roughly into her skin.

*"Get your hands off of me, Casimir, or I will make sure you regret it,"* she growled.

*"But I could never regret touching you."* She swallowed hard against his finger, and although she tried not to let it, her pulse raced under his touch, not because she enjoyed it, but because she was scared of what he might do. His nail cut into her skin and she hissed, automatically reaching for his hand to remove it. She wasn't sure how he did it, but before she could blink he had both of her hands pinned above her against the tree with his left hand. How did he get so freakishly strong? And fast? Damn, I really need to hone my Fae powers soon.

His voice pulled her back to the present. *"And if I re-*

*member correctly, you like things a little rough."*

*He dug his fingernail against her neck again until a trickle of blood dripped down. She squirmed against him, trying to break free. He bent his head toward her and slowly licked up the path of blood on her neck. She gagged.*

*"I will make you regret this, Casimir," she threatened.*

*"Oh I sure do hope so, little one, but what are you going to do about it right now?"*

*She tried to knee him in the balls, but he moved to block her. Chuckling, he bent his lips toward her neck again and sucked hard. "I do love them with a little fight," he commented, finishing his blood fest with a hard bite against her neck. Ianthe began to panic. She needed to get out of this situation and regain control—fast.*

*"What the hell? You're not a Lampir—why would you even do that?" she tried to reason.*

*"Oh, you have no idea what I am, little one. No idea."*

*The words struck her, ringing with truth. She never had discovered what type of Fae Casimir really was. It wasn't like it had come up in everyday conversation while she was at the Unseelie palace, and the last few times she had spoken to Conall and Alfie, they'd had bigger problems on their minds. She knew for a fact he wasn't a Lampir, but could he be something similar...something worse?*

*Whatever. She didn't have time to debate it at the moment. She had to figure out how to get herself out of this predicament. With her hands pinned, she was at a disadvantage. She tried once more to knee him in the nads, but he dodged her attempt.*

*"Tsk, tsk, such a feisty little thing." He leaned in toward her neck again, inhaling deeply near her ear, and she snapped. She turned her head and bit his cheek as hard as*

she could. Her teeth had sharpened at some point and sank into his flesh. She made sure she had a good hold on him so when he tried to pull away, his skin tore further. He hissed and released her, raising his hand to cover the wound she had inflicted on him. Part of her—the part she had tried so hard to ignore—was thrilled at the sight of the spilled blood. Her darker half was there just below the surface, like a beast waiting to be unleashed.

"There's my little Unseelie." He smiled as blood ran down his shoulder from the wound. "I knew I could get her to come out and play."

She spat his blood from her mouth and instantly imagined a knife in her hand. If she wanted any chance to get away from him, she needed a weapon. "You're wrong, Casimir. She's not here. It's just me."

"Ah, but she is." He pointed at her eyes. "I can see her in the way your eyes swirled from violet to deep plum. You think you can control her, don't you? You think she won't eventually take over completely, but you're wrong. I'm just waiting for you to come to your senses. You can't hide what you are, Ianthe, and she is part of you, whether you like it or not."

She didn't like how he referred to her Unseelie desires as a person separate from herself. She knew what she was, but she wasn't fully Unseelie. She was half human, and that was the part that mattered the most.

"I'm well aware of who I am Casimir." She circled him with the knife in front of her, ready to lunge at a moment's notice. "It's you who is mistaken, because I was never yours and never will be. No part of me will ever want what you have to offer."

He growled and lunged, and in that second she made the choice that mattered most. While her Unseelie blood *boiled, demanding she use the knife, her human logic kicked in and she did what made the most sense: she woke herself up.*

She sat up straight, panting, and placed her palm on her chest, trying to calm her racing her heart. She swiped her hand across her aching neck and sighed in relief when it came back clean, no blood in sight. Shakily, she stood and walked the length of the room, trying to calm herself down. In doing so, she glanced in the mirror and grimaced at the pointed teeth that gleamed back at her. "Shit," she said breathlessly, covering them with her hand. Worse than the teeth, though, was that she could tell her eyes were glowing underneath the blue contacts. She had to get herself under control or she was going to be discovered. She sat in the chair, avoiding the bed and any chance of slipping back into that nightmare with Casimir.

There was a knock at the door and she turned away before it opened, just in case she still wasn't in complete control. "Callie, your presence is required at dinner this evening, as ordered by King Lachlan." Maddock did not seem happy as he issued the very formal declaration. He shut the door behind him and she heard the rustling of fabric. "Did you hear me? You're expected to have dinner with the king tonight."

She turned to face him. The minute he saw her face, the bundle of blue fabric slipped from his hands and his jaw dropped. *Okay, obviously still not in control of things.*

"I know, I know. I'm trying to get things back to normal, I swear."

"What the hell? How did that even happen? How is

this even possible? You can just hide your Fae features?" He looked astounded.

"Yes—well, no…I don't know. I'm not quite sure how it works, I only know this is a recent development and has been getting a little worse since I arrived back in Fae, like my time here is changing me somehow…if that even makes sense. I just had a particularly nasty run-in with someone in my dreams that seems to have heightened my looks somehow." It was the best explanation she could offer him, because to be honest, she really had no clue.

"Well, you'd better get it under control fast because the king is expecting you for dinner in fifteen minutes and you cannot go down there looking like that."

"I'm trying, okay?" She took a few deep breaths and rubbed Conall's leather band around her wrist, remembering his comforting touch and all the things that made her human. She thought about her dad, who was probably sitting at home eating takeout since she wasn't there to cook for him, spending his night working or watching TV alone. The thought made her sad. Maybe he was worried about her; after all, her note hadn't really given him much information or reassurance. Then she thought about Aunt Grace, who was probably beside herself with worry. She would definitely have to pay her a visit soon, and perhaps she could even attempt to check in on her dad via her powers. She thought about Callie getting home and being greeted by her family, only to sit there and not sleep all night because she would be worrying about her. She sighed and took another deep breath. She had to get home, and soon.

After a few minutes of sitting there and thinking about everything she loved about her life in the human realm, she ran her tongue across her teeth. They felt like they always did, definitely not as sharp as they had been earlier. She smiled up at Maddock, showing her teeth.

He sighed in relief. "Good. Now we have to get you dressed."

She looked down at her outfit. "I am dressed."

"Yes, but not for dinner." He lifted the pale blue garment off of the floor and held it up. It was a stunning dress, the sheer fabric placed artfully over metallic gold lace. The bodice had a sweetheart neckline with silver, blue, and gold appliques and beadwork starting at the point of the neckline then angling out underneath the bust, stopping at the waist in the front. The small cap sleeves also had the same applique, whereas the material covering the bust was a ruched pale blue over the golden lace. It was magnificent. She wasn't sure if she could do the dress justice.

"Whose dress is that?" she asked curiously, approaching him for closer inspection.

"It belongs to Lady Bronwen, but don't worry, I have a feeling it will look much better on you." Maddock winked flirtatiously and she blushed, plucking the dress delicately from his fingers. He also held a pair of shimmery gold heels.

She dreaded heels, but didn't really have a choice. She took them as well.

"Do you need any help getting into the dress?" he asked, waggling his eyebrows suggestively.

"Nope, pretty sure I can handle that just fine, thank you." She rolled her eyes at him, and he smiled in return.

He turned to leave the room but stopped before he reached the door. "I'll be just outside—oh, I was also supposed to deliver a message for you. Torin said you are to keep the act up, so don't let any of your good manners slip through. Apparently you had training at the Unseelie palace, but we still want the king to see you as a ditzy human girl, and believe me, you will be under close inspection during the meal. Don't mess this up. If you do, I'm not sure how much I can help you, and I will not put myself at risk for you. Do you understand?"

*Oh, I understand. While I might consider Maddock an ally, he'll look out for himself first.* "I wouldn't expect anything less," she replied, acknowledging his declaration. She held the dress up against her chest and admired it in the mirror until she heard the door close behind him.

When she was fully dressed, she was a little taken aback by the super high slit over the left leg and thigh. The sheer blue fabric was split until the applique at the waistline, but luckily the metallic gold lace was only split up to mid-thigh. The dress hugged her body tightly, almost as if it were a second skin, but the sheer blue fabric in the skirt flowed outward. She looked beautiful and ethereal. She wasn't sure what do with her hair but did manage to find a brush in the room. She hummed the tune she had learned from Alvina during her stay in the Unseelie palace and when she was done, her hair looked shiny and fell in perfect, slightly curly waves. She loved it, but she knew she couldn't go down looking that polished, so in the end she tipped her head upside down and shook her hair out with her fingers. When she flipped back over, it had slightly more volume and a not quite as finished look to it. Unfortunately, there were no makeup brushes in sight, so they would have to make do with her face as it was.

She squeezed her toes into the slightly small sparkling gold heels and grimaced, knowing the price she would pay later for wearing them. Finally, she opened the door and found Maddock with his fist poised to knock. His eyes widened as he took her in from head to toe and he licked his lips.

"You look stunning, Ia—Callie." Ianthe's eyes widened slightly at his near slip, but luckily she didn't see any other guards lingering nearby. "I think I picked the perfect dress," he went on. "Now remember who you are supposed to be, and don't slip up."

"You too there, Casanova," she remarked, placing her hand on his arm so he could escort her down to dinner. "Do you know why the king insists I join him for dinner?"

"I do not, although I have my suspicions," he replied, and she motioned with her hand for him to explain further while they walked. "I have a feeling he may be bored and looking for entertainment for the evening, and he found you slightly amusing earlier. That, or he suspects you are not who you say you are and will be putting you under close inspection. It could be a mix of the two. Just make sure you stick to your character this evening, *Callie*. Be as honest as you can, and try to play off anything else as silly human notions or nerves," he whispered, pausing the conversation any time they came near someone who might overhear them.

They approached a large door, and she tried to steady the rapid beating of her heart. "All right, time to use your best acting skills," he murmured in her ear before reaching in front of her to open the door. She blinked rapidly, remembering that from that point on she was Callie, the clueless human. Her awe at the magnificence of the room on the other side of the door wasn't fake. The dining hall was classic and regal, like a ballroom Elizabeth Bennet might have danced in in *Pride and Prejudice*. There was a large table set with a magnificent feast, and at the head sat King Lachlan. To his right was an older Fae with dark brown hair and dark blue eyes. More interesting was the lady to the older Fae's right. She had gorgeous, rich chocolate ringlets and stunning turquoise eyes. The woman's eyes widened slightly as Maddock led Ianthe to a seat directly across from her.

Maddock held Ianthe's hand on his arm. "Your Majesty, I present Callie."

The king smiled. "Ah yes, our human guest. Glad you could join us, my dear." She could tell his words weren't genuine. He acted as if he was humoring her by having her there when really he was the one who had requested her presence.

"Thank you, sire," she said, falling into a deep curtsy like one might see in the movies. The stunning chocolate-haired girl giggled. Ianthe rose. "I'm so honored you are allowing me to eat with you. You're such a gracious host, and your home is magnificent." The king smiled widely, soaking up her overly sweet flattery. "I feel like I've woken up in some sort of movie." She placed her hand on her chest as if to show her disbelief at this whole situation being real. She imagined most humans would think they were dreaming if they ended up there.

"I imagine it would feel surreal to you," he replied. "You may be seated." She sat down on the chair Maddock had pulled out for her, and Maddock sat to her right, leaving the chair to her left empty.

She looked around, taking in her surroundings. She could see two more places had been set at the table. There was one to her left between her and King Lachlan, and one to the other side of the model-esque Fae across from her. Before she had time to consider who might be sitting at those two seats, the doors swung open. In walked Torin, and she worked hard to stifle the gasp that escaped her lips because following right behind him was someone who was so achingly familiar that every bone in her body screamed for her to run toward him. She felt fingers roughly squeeze her right thigh and glanced down to see Maddock's hand there. She turned her attention to him for a second and could read the warning in his eyes for her to not give herself away.

She flicked her gaze back toward Conall, who didn't seem surprised at all to see her sitting there. *Interesting.* He took a seat next to the gorgeous woman, who smiled at him flirtatiously.

"Good evening, Sir Conall. What an honor to have you here again so soon." She seemed very familiar with him—*too* familiar—and before Ianthe could mask it, her face tugged down in a frown.

Maddock tightly squeezed her thigh again, sending the signal for her to get it together.

"Everything okay, Callie?" Lachlan's voice cut through the air. *Shit, he noticed.*

"Um, yes, sir. I, um—I just realized how beautiful all of you are—I must look awful in comparison." It was the first thing that came to her mind, and it seemed to work.

"Ah, yes. Well, what did you expect being around Fae, my dear? Isn't your Evin good looking?" he inquired slyly.

"He most definitely is. Before coming here, I had never seen anyone quite like him. He was so striking and breathtaking." Out of the corner of her eye, she could have sworn she saw Conall scowl, but thought she was just imagining it. "It's just I've never been around so many gorgeous people in the same room before. It's a little overwhelming."

King Lachlan chuckled and the chocolate-haired girl smiled at her with a look of pity in her eyes. *Damn this naïve girl act. If that curly-haired model looks at me one more time with a "poor little human" look, I might just scream*, she thought. She dared to sneak a glance at Conall, who stared at her quizzically. Just as she was about to make direct eye contact with him, that little minx drew his attention away. The girl placed a delicate hand on Conall's forearm, which was resting on the table, and whispered something into his ear. Ianthe withheld the growl and the sudden animalistic urge to jump across the table and forcibly remove the girl's hand. Even worse was the sinking suspicion that the two knew each other in more than just a friendly sense. They seemed almost intimately acquainted, and she wondered briefly if the beauty was one of Conall's exes. She knew there were probably tons of girls chasing after him; he was quite a catch. She quietly watched the girl's hand snake below the table. Conall jumped slightly and inched away from her. Ianthe's eyes narrowed.

Maddock's large fingers tightened their grip on her thigh painfully and dragged her away from jealous, vengeful thoughts. She shook her head and turned toward him. Maddock's lips were set in a tight line as he nodded his head slightly toward the king.

"I'm sorry, Your Majesty. What did you say?" She hoped he wasn't like the Unseelie king who was easily enraged by not being the center of everyone's attention.

"A coin for your thoughts, my dear." He quirked an eyebrow and his eyes twinkled with amusement.

*Think, Ianthe, think.* "Oh...I...um...was just wondering where Evin is. Being around all of you is making me miss him terribly."

"Ah yes, your elusive boyfriend. We have yet to locate him. Doesn't seem like very honorable behavior for your lover to run off and leave you here all alone, unprotected, and at the mercy of some who might take advantage of you." King Lachlan tsked several times and shook his head in dismay. "I think you're probably better off forgetting all about him. He obviously doesn't care as much for you as any of us thought."

"Yes, well, that's kind of hard to do when you're holding me hostage." Ianthe thought she had just mumbled the words, but the sudden silence that filled the room led her to believe everyone must have overheard her. All eyes were glued to the king, waiting for his reaction. She bashfully stared at her plate while Maddock's fingers dug painfully into her leg.

King Lachlan's lips quirked up before he tipped his head back and released a loud, booming belly laugh that filled the room. Once everyone realized he was laughing in merriment, most of the guests joined in. She glanced up and saw Conall silently laughing and shaking his head. *Is he embarrassed by me? Worried I'll dig my own grave?* Her cheeks flamed at her slip of the tongue.

"Oh my, Callie, you are quite a treat. I now see exactly what Evin saw in you," the king mused before calling for dinner to be served.

She attempted to discretely reach down and pry Maddock's fingers off of her thigh, and he turned his head in her direction. "You're hurting me," she hissed.

His eyes widened slightly and his grip relaxed, but he didn't remove his hand. He spoke through the corner of his mouth while refocusing his gaze on the king. "Well, if you would stop trying to get yourself killed, I wouldn't have to remind you."

"I'm doing the best I can." She ground out each word, reining in her anger.

"Try harder," he growled in return.

She sighed and turned away from him, accepting the fact that he would not remove his hand no matter how much she protested. A plate of the most delicious smelling food was placed in front of her. Another Fae came around and filled her goblet. Once the food was served, the guests waited for the king before digging in.

King Lachlan raised his goblet and called out, "A toast! To old friends"—the king motioned his head toward the brunette and the older man—"and to new ones." He moved his glass toward Ianthe and then toward Conall. "May our future meals always be this pleasant." Everyone raised their goblets toward the center of the table in a saluting manner before drinking heartily to the king's toast. Ianthe had no choice but to follow along, although she only took a small sip from her goblet. The rich, floral, and fruity tones of the Fae wine tickled her tongue and throat on the way down. She made a mental note to remember its effect on humans and not take much unless she wanted to be a sloppy drunk.

The table around her fell into comfortable chatter as they ate. The king focused his attention more on the man sitting to his right, occasionally engaging Maddock and Torin in conversation. For the most part he ignored both Ianthe and Conall, but that didn't seem to bother Conall in the least bit. The brunette next to him seemed rather content to be the center of his attention, constantly drawing him back to her when his mind seemed to wander.

"Are you trying to murder your venison? Because I'm quite confident it's already dead," Maddock's playful teasing interrupted the vengeful thoughts running though her mind involving a Mara visit to the model-esque beauty across the table. She hadn't realized her thoughts were causing her to unconsciously lacerate the meat on her plate.

"Oh, you're a funny one," she commented sarcastically before setting her fork and knife down and glancing in his direction.

His eyes widened. "Shit," he hissed under his breath. "Keep your head down, and whatever you were thinking about while you were slaughtering your meal, stop—immediately. Your eyes are glowing through your contacts."

Her heart pounded and she instantly glued her eyes to her plate and froze. *What should I do?*

"Pick up your fork and continue eating. Act like nothing is wrong," Maddock's voice commanded in her ear. She nodded her head and picked her fork back up, stabbing a piece of venison and bringing it to her lips. She had grown used to the taste of wild game while staying at the Unseelie palace, but still wasn't a huge fan. After she chewed her bite, she took a deep breath and released it, hoping to bring things back to normal, but it must have come off as a sigh of contentment.

"Do you like your meal, Lady Callie?" King Lachlan inquired as she took another bite.

She almost choked on the food in her mouth at his respectful term, and the brunette across from her deemed it an appropriate time to comment. "I doubt that one could ever be a lady," she sneered quietly.

Maddock's low growl echoed across the room, or was she hearing two growls? Conall didn't look pleased with the girl's remark either. The older man looked slightly aghast that she would have the gall to utter such words in the presence of the king, and Ianthe immediately turned her attention toward him. His eyes were slightly narrowed on the girl.

"Lord Aedan, I would expect better manners from your offspring," Lachlan snapped.

"I apologize, sire—" Lord Aedan began, but the king cut him off with a cold stare before focusing the power of his deadly glare on the brunette.

"I would think all of my people would know it is up to me who has titles around here. They are mine to give and mine to take away, *Lady* Bronwen. I suggest if you want to keep yours, you learn to hold your tongue and show a little more class. In other words, act like a lady." Bronwen paled, looking properly admonished, and Ianthe couldn't help the smug smile that graced her lips. King Lachlan then turned his head back toward her. "So, Lady Callie, what do you think of your meal?"

"Oh, it's delicious. Thank you, sir. I don't think I've ever tasted anything as wonderful as this in my entire life." *Okay, that might have been laying it on a little thick*, she thought, but she kept smiling.

"I'm glad to hear that. I hope you don't think us barbarians. I know I may have been a little short with you before and a little harsh to punish you for Evin's mistakes. It's been a while since I've been in the presence of a human. I've forgotten how refreshing they can be." He seemed nice, but she had the feeling there was more to his politeness and sudden respect for her. *Has he figured out who I am somehow?* "Maddock, don't you find her refreshing?"

Maddock hesitated, unsure of how to respond or what would be the correct response. "I suppose so, sire."

"So, Callie, tell us about your life in the human realm," King Lachlan implored.

"Oh, um, it's not very exciting. I go to school, study, and hang out with my friends."

"Was that what you were doing when you met Evin? Studying or hanging out with friends?"

*Crap.* Her mind frantically searched for what she had told him the first time. Was she studying at the coffee shop? She couldn't remember. "Oh, um…" She grabbed her goblet and took a sip to stall for time. "Mm, this wine is delicious."

The king didn't take the bait. He still stared at her, waiting for her to answer his question. "I was writing…in my, um…journal at a coffee shop when I first met Evin."

"And how did that go?" The king seemed a little too interested in her story, so she suspected he was trying to catch her in a lie. It would make sense to make her feel comfortable, feed her, get her drunk, and then watch her self-sabotage, but she wasn't drunk. *One of the benefits of being a half Fae—it takes more than a few sips of Fae wine to get me drunk.*

She tried to put a dreamy look on her face and closed her eyes as if remembering what happened. "Well, I was just writing in my journal when he came over to my table. He sat down across from me and asked what I was writing. Of course, since it was my journal, I didn't want to say, but then we started talking. He was so considerate and sweet. He seemed to be amused at every little thing I did. It was nice to have someone be that attentive…" She trailed off. She wasn't sure when her thoughts had turned from a fabrication to her own wishes and desires. As much as she didn't want to admit it, the months of radio silence from Conall had taken their toll, and while their dream visit had been close to how she'd envisioned their reunion going, she was obviously still battling some residual abandonment issues.

Lachlan chuckled. "I can see where he could charm a girl like you. In fact, it would be easy for any Fae to charm a human. I'm sorry he didn't turn out to be your knight in shining armor. How long were you two seeing each other before he brought you to our land?"

Ianthe fought the urge to roll her eyes and reminded herself that she needed to be a naïve little human. "It was maybe two weeks, but it felt like so much longer. We had been out a couple of times before and he said he wanted to bring me somewhere new—somewhere *special*." She continued to eat her meal, hoping that would stall the conversation or redirect the king's attention.

The king seemed to contemplate her response. Maddock's hand hadn't tightened during the conversation, and the other table guests remained silent. It seemed Bronwen was regretting her slip of the tongue after all, and Conall... who knew what was going on in his head. She certainly didn't.

"I hope in the future you will take more care with who you trust," Lachlan advised.

"Most certainly, sire," she replied meekly.

Thankfully, Torin drew the king into conversation before he could interrogate her further, and Maddock leaned over to say, "You're doing great. Keep it up." She smiled at the praise, feeling slightly relieved to be out from underneath the microscope.

"So, Conall, how long do you plan to be with us?" The king's voice echoed across the table. Ianthe placed her utensils on her plate to show she was full, and sure enough, a servant appeared within a moment to take away her plate.

"Not very long, sir. King Corydon only gave me a few days' leave."

"Yes, well, that doesn't surprise me. However, what does surprise me is that you are here of your own free will. I find it hard to believe you merely came to pay your respects. You are an Unseelie, after all, and the king's first in command at that. I wonder what your king would think if he knew you were here. Perhaps he sent you for another purpose." Lachlan's veiled accusation irked Ianthe. She hadn't even realized she had opened her mouth to defend

Conall until Maddock's fingers constricted around her thigh. She closed her mouth, trying to pass off her gaping as a yawn. To the surprise of everyone at the table, it wasn't Conall who jumped into defense, but Torin.

"If I may, milord..." He paused, waiting until Lachlan motioned for him to continue. "While Conall may have been born an Unseelie, he does not operate as one. He has never once encouraged bloodshed. In fact, if it weren't for him, I have a feeling we would be dealing with more deaths between our people. I know you have your suspicions, but everything Conall has said rings with truth and genuine compassion. He's not like the rest of them. He's... better." Torin's words rang throughout the hall as everyone held their breaths to see the king's response.

"That may be, but I still don't believe those are his only intentions."

"All I can say, sir, is that I came of my own free will. My king has no knowledge I am here, and I mean you and your court no harm." It was a brave thing for Conall to admit that Corydon didn't know he was there. If someone were to report it back to the Unseelie king, it could be seen as an act of treason, and the consequences of that accusation were not lost on anyone there. They all took his admission as a statement of truth, and even the Seelie king appeared appeased. They continued to eat and produce chatter around the table. Bronwen mistook Conall's admission as an invitation for more affection as she rubbed his arm and leaned in close, pressing her breasts against his side. Ianthe felt Maddock's burrowing fingers once again, and she closed her eyes, hoping nothing was going to give her away. She ran her tongue across her teeth, this time noticing that the jealousy had brought them to points. She knew it would be a great time to exit, so she stood quickly and intentionally swayed off balance.

"If you would excuse me, Your Majesty…" She fumbled to curtsy drunkenly. "I think I may have had a bit too much wine." She even managed to throw in a good hiccup to add to her drunken appearance. "I'd like to go back to my room now."

The king smiled indulgently. "Of course, my dear. I forget how our food and drink can affect you humans so quickly. Maddock, please escort Lady Callie back to her room. It was a pleasure dining with you."

She waved her fingers sloppily to the king and the rest of the table as Maddock rose and grasped her shoulders, turning her toward the door. She made a point of stumbling so he had no choice but to hold her up slightly as they walked away. Lady Bronwen giggled and commented under her breath about drunken trash. Had Ianthe not been half Fae, she may not have heard, but she couldn't resist flipping the girl off as they walked by, discreetly of course—or at least she thought so until she heard the king's chuckle accompanied with the words, "Refreshing indeed."

Maddock pushed her a little more forcefully toward the doorway. Once they made it through, she tried to shake off his grip. "I can handle myself, thank you. I'm not actually drunk."

"Ah, but you forget the halls have eyes, and even though you don't see them, that doesn't mean the guards don't see you."

"Fair enough, although I'm getting tired of stumbling like a drunkard."

"Would you prefer that I carry you?"

"Perhaps that would be best. I can act as if I passed out, and no one would be able to question or scrutinize me along the way." She thought on it for a moment. "Okay, ready? 3, 2, 1…" She swooned backward into him, and he swung her into his arms with ease then carried her back toward her room.

# CHAPTER 33

*Conall*

**I**T TOOK ALL of Conall's self-control not to challenge Maddock right there or at least insist that he remove his dirty paws from Ianthe. He longed to follow them but knew that would only draw unwanted attention. He ground his teeth together and withheld the primal growl that begged to be released. He was surprised he didn't break the arms of his chair when he glimpsed Maddock swinging Ianthe into his arms, but he came rather close. He had to get her out of there soon. It was bad enough that the king was questioning both of them at dinner, and it would only be a matter of time until their covers were blown.

Bronwen's hand landing on his arm for the umpteenth time that evening pulled him out of his thoughts. He'd told her during his last visit that he was taken, but she obviously didn't understand what that meant. He'd have to have that discussion again because he'd hate for her to do anything to make Ianthe jealous or uncomfortable. He still hadn't worked out how he was going to get Ianthe out of the palace without anyone noticing, because if they were discovered, it wouldn't be her heritage that caused a war, it would be his actions, and none of them could afford that.

He plucked Bronwen's hand off of his skin and dropped it none too lightly on the table. Instead of engaging her in front of the others, he ignored her inquiring gaze and focused on the king's conversation, although he knew he wouldn't be able to glean anything important because Lachlan was not a fool and would not discuss Seelie business in front of him.

"Torin, would you like my aid in searching for Evin?" Conall asked, knowing this could be the perfect excuse to extend his stay in the Seelie territory.

Torin caught on quickly to his intentions. "That would be wonderful, Sir Conall. Your reputation as a tracker proceeds you."

"I thought you said you needed to return to your king," Lachlan interjected.

"I do, but I still have a few days," Conall replied. He decided to take a little gamble and see if it would pay off. "What do you plan to do with the human?"

Torin jumped in before the king could respond, perhaps sensing he could help steer the conversation. "We were hoping her detainment would encourage Evin to return for her. Unfortunately, that does not seem to be the case."

"Yes, well, when you bet on matters of the heart, you don't always win," Lachlan commented. "I find her rather entertaining, but eventually she will have her memory wiped before we return her to her home."

That didn't help him determine how long the king planned to keep her. He wasn't sure who would be the one to alter her memory, but if that were to happen, they would figure out who she was, and Conall wasn't sure what Lachlan would do if he knew he had his nemesis' daughter in his possession.

Eventually everyone seemed to have had their fill of the meal, and their evening was drawn to a close. When Lord Aedan and Lady Bronwen rose to take their leave, Conall took a moment to help her out of her chair, as was the proper and honorable thing to do. He leaned forward as he pulled her chair back. "Meet me in the garden at ten," he whispered in her ear. She gave him a flirty wink before sauntering away, and he could barely contain his eye roll. He didn't think she was going to take the conversation well, but he had to make sure she knew he wasn't interested at all. Before he excused himself from the hall, he realized Maddock had never returned to dinner after escorting Ianthe to her room. He was quickly discovering that jealousy was not an emotion he cared to experience, but it churned through his gut nonetheless. He'd have to visit her in her dreams that night to figure out what was going on and come up with a way to get her home, but first he had to meet Lady Bronwen in the garden. On his way back to his quarters, he scanned the hall where he knew Ianthe's room to be, and to his dismay, the guard posted outside was not one he could approach. He sighed and opened his own door, hoping to kill some time before ten and deduce a solution to their dilemma.

# CHAPTER 34

*Ianthe*

**M**ADDOCK LEFT IANTHE in her room shortly after he carried her there. He was going to attempt to talk to King Lachlan about his plans for "Callie" and how long they would detain her if they couldn't locate Evin. She sighed. She had repeatedly tried to reach Conall in her dreams, but he was a no-show. Perhaps he wasn't asleep yet or was still at dinner, or maybe he was plotting with Torin. She was frustrated and tired of waiting for someone to save her. She flung the covers off of her bed and silently crept toward her door. She was amazed to find it unlocked, and even more surprised to not see a guard posted outside.

She quickly crept back into her room and arranged pillows in the bed to look like a human form sleeping under the covers, a trick she had learned from her party days. Thankful that Maddock had at least returned her regular clothes to her, she put them on quickly and crept to the door again.

Just like before, she opened it silently and was thankful there was still no guard. She couldn't pass up this opportunity, so she tiptoed out of her room. She debated what to do and where to go. She couldn't just wander around inside the palace hoping she wouldn't stumble into a guard. Maddock had warned her they were stationed throughout the halls and would be especially vigilant around Conall's room, although she wasn't sure where Conall was staying, so that didn't help either.

She spotted large glass double doors at the end of the hallway to her right. She knew she was on the second floor, so perhaps those led to a balcony, and she could check to see if there was a way to climb down from there. She took stock of her surroundings before making a quiet dash for it. She tried to move quickly but lightly, hoping she didn't sound like a herd of elephants that would instantly send a guard to investigate. She almost cheered when she discovered that the double doors were also unlocked, and she slipped outside. Scooting away from the glass, she leaned against the brick wall and placed her hands on her knees, trying to catch her breath and calm her racing heart as her body hummed with adrenaline. It suddenly dawned on her that there could be a guard on the balcony so she whipped her head up, scanning her surroundings. Thankfully, the area appeared to be empty. She released a sigh of relief before creeping toward the railing. The full moon lit the night, making it easy for her to see. She gazed at the most amazing garden below her, filled with flowers and trees, and even a small hedge maze in the distance. She realized how much she missed being outside after being trapped in that room for so long. She found a large potted tree near the corner of the balcony she could hide behind and take in what was below. There didn't appear to be any immediate way to climb down, but she knew from experience that where there was a will, there was a way.

She crouched behind the potted tree and peered around the edge. Thankfully there were no guards in sight, but what she did see was far worse. There, below her on a bench in the garden sat Conall, but that wasn't what made the bile rise in her throat; it was the familiar brunette whose long legs were straddling his lap. Ianthe sank to her haunches behind the tree and stifled a sob with her hand. *Surely it must be a mistake. Conall would never...*

Convinced her eyes were playing tricks on her, she peered around the tree again, only to be sucker-punched in the gut. Conall and Lady Bronwen were clearly enjoying each other's company. His hands roamed to her backside as he kissed her passionately. She could even hear Bronwen moan. She pinched her arm, sure it must be a dream, but felt the sting of the pinch instead. She rubbed her eyes, hoping the hallucination would go away, but it didn't. It only vanished when Conall picked Bronwen up, her legs wrapping around his waist, and without removing his lips from hers, carried her toward the hedge maze and disappeared under the cover of night.

Ianthe thought she was going to be sick. She felt as if her heart had just been ripped from her chest. She no longer cared who could hear her or discover her. She sank to the floor, pulling her knees toward her and wrapping her arms around them to hold herself together. Only then did she shatter into an ugly, sobbing mess. She wasn't sure how long she sat there bawling, alternating between shock and betrayal, heartbreak and rage. She realized that at some point someone had come out onto the balcony from another set of doors and stood watching her curiously.

"We often forget what a fragile thing a heart can be," Lachlan's voice mused above her. She glanced up at him, not even caring if he knew exactly why she was so upset. "We give our hearts away so easily to those who do not deserve them. Such a precious gift love can be, and yet such a curse."

She sniffled and nodded, knowing exactly what he meant. She wondered what had happened to him, why there was no Seelie queen. If she hadn't been so self-centered lately, she might have bothered to ask Maddock, but all she could think about was herself and how she would get out of this mess and return to Conall's arms.

The last thought had her crying anew, and the Seelie king bent down to offer her a hand. "Come, my dear, let us get you back to bed." His eyes were soft with compassion. She let the tears silently fall and placed her hand in his, allowing him to help her up. He walked her back to her room, never once chastising her for being out on the balcony.

Maddock was pacing madly in front of her door, gripping his hands into the longer part of his golden hair. He was radiating with anger, but the minute he caught sight of her state and the fact that the king was escorting her, his face filled with concern. "You found her!" he exclaimed.

"I wasn't aware she was lost."

"Yes, well…I was just going to check a few places before notifying you," Maddock lied.

The king smiled and shook his head slightly, his voice laced with disbelief. "I'm sure you were."

"What happened?"

"That I cannot tell you. I found her like this, and she hasn't spoken, although I suspect finding out your knight has no intention of rescuing you is enough to break any girl's heart." The king gave her a sad smile before handing her off to Maddock. "I would like you to take her home tonight. Erase her memory of Evin and of her time here, but leave behind the heartbreak. She'll learn from it and become stronger, hopefully avoiding our kind in the future. Gather her things. I do not wish to keep her further." Maddock disappeared down the hall, and the king turned her toward him once more, tipping her chin up with his finger until their eyes met. "My dear, it has been refreshing to have you here. You remind many of us of the things we forget to experience as Fae. I wish you much happiness in the future. Do not let this heartbreak destroy you, but rather take the pain and use it. Let it guide you to be a little more cautious with your heart." He kissed her cheek, much as her own father used to, and walked away. *The Seelie king is full of surprises.*

Maddock appeared beside her with her bag. "I'm not sure what just happened, but let's get you home." She nodded and followed Maddock out of the palace toward the stables. He saddled the same horse he had brought her into the palace on then hoisted her up into the saddle. "Can you hold your bag? I'm going to have you sit in front of me this time."

She nodded again, afraid that if she spoke, she wouldn't be able to hold back the sobs. She could read the worry in his eyes as he passed the backpack toward her, and she clutched it in her hands while he swung himself onto the horse behind her. He took the reins in one hand and wrapped his other arm around her waist then they set off for the portal to the human realm.

They rode in silence for about an hour, during which she cried on and off. Each time he could feel her shaking from her weeping, he pulled her closer to him, offering her what comfort he could. Now that he had the king's permission to take her back, they rode at a relaxed trot. He was afraid she was going to collapse at any moment and fall off the horse, which was why he had placed her in front of him this time. Finally, he could take it no longer.

"Ianthe, what happened?" She didn't respond. "Please tell me. I'd like to help."

"You can't help," she finally murmured. "Unless you can mend a broken heart."

"I don't understand."

She took a deep breath and recounted her humiliation to him. "I went out on the balcony to see if there was a way I could escape, but when I got out there, I saw—I saw—I—" Her breaths were heaving, and he pulled the horse to a stop then dropped the reins, rubbing his hands down her arms to soothe her.

"Shhhh, it's okay."

"But it's not. It's not okay, and it never will be! How could he do this? I thought he loved me." Her voice broke with desperation on the last word.

"What are you talking about?"

"I saw Conall with Lady Bronwen in the garden. They were—they were—" She couldn't get the words past her lips, but she didn't need to.

"Oh, sweetheart, I'm so sorry. I had heard the whispers from servants before, but I was sure it was over."

Her eyes widened and she turned to face him. "You knew? You KNEW?! You should have told me. I told you *everything*."

"It wasn't my place to tell you, and besides, they were castle rumors. I wasn't sure they had been involved, and if they had, I assumed it was over."

"Yeah, well you know what they say about when you assume…"

"What do they say?"

She forgot that sometimes things like expressions and slang that were popular in the human realm didn't always make it over to Fae. She sighed. "Never mind. It's not important. Can you just take me home, please?"

"Of course. For what it's worth, he's an absolute idiot to pick her over you," he added quietly, reaching around her to pick up the reins. She thought she felt his lips press briefly on her hair, but she figured she must have been mistaken.

They rode in silence until they had passed through the portal and reached the cabin. She hadn't noticed the small horse stable by the cabin before, but they dismounted and he settled the horse inside it. Part of her wanted to keep riding, but she knew riding into the middle of town on a horse would definitely have been too conspicuous. Maddock flicked his wrist and used magic to unlock the door to the cabin. She half expected to find Evin there, but it would make sense for him not to be. It was probably one of the first places the king had searched (after Evin's house, of course).

He led her through the house toward the garage. When they entered, she was a little surprised to see a large black SUV parked inside.

Maddock snickered at her inspection. "What, did you think we just ride our horses into town?" She hadn't really given it much thought, but he was right. They couldn't just ride horses around her realm, so it made sense that the Fae had access to cars. She climbed in the passenger seat and tried not to act surprised when he expertly exited the garage and drove her toward town. Of course, she had to give him directions on how to get to her home from there.

They pulled up in front of her father's home—well, her human father's home—and she was surprised to see a light on in the living room. The clock on the dashboard showed it was past two in the morning.

Maddock parked the car and moved to exit, but she placed a hand on his arm, holding him in place. "I think I can take it from here, but I want to thank you, Maddock. You aren't who I thought you were initially. I'm glad we got to know each other, and that I can call you my friend."

He took her hand from his arm and squeezed it. "If you ever need anything, you know where to find me, although I do hope for both of our sakes you don't find yourself in that position." He smiled and squeezed again before releasing his grip.

She unbuckled her seatbelt and hugged him as best as she could within the confines of the vehicle. "Thank you for everything." She released him and grabbed her bag off of the floor before exiting the SUV.

She plucked her keys out of her bag. Only when she was walking up the driveway did the fact that her car was sitting there register. She briefly wondered who had returned it to her home and how, but she also knew there was no telling if Fae were involved.

She unlocked the front door and stepped inside, closing and locking it behind her. When she turned back, her father was standing in the hallway, staring at her as if she were a ghost.

"Lola?" he asked, his voice filled with disbelief. While the use of her middle name would have annoyed her a few weeks before, it was now a welcome reminder of her father and who she was.

"Hi, Dad." She waved awkwardly, hoping he wasn't about to yell at her. She didn't think she could take it, but he didn't do that at all. The minute she spoke, he rushed toward her and gathered her into his arms, hugging her tightly before he started to cry.

"Oh, honey, I thought I'd never see you again. The police couldn't find any clue to where you had gone, and while Aunt Grace was positive you were okay, I just couldn't believe it. I was so worried." *What happened to the cold, heartless man that is my father?* He released her from his bear hug and held her out in front of him, his hand gently resting on her shoulders. "Where have you been?" She opened her mouth to reply, but he didn't let her. "You know what, it doesn't matter. What matters is you're here now and you're okay."

He pulled her in for another hug, and his unexpected words and affection broke what was left of her calm. She dissolved into sobs in his arms.

"It's okay, Lola. It will all be okay," he soothed, running a hand down her hair. She cried a little harder, because she had desperately been yearning for a moment to connect with her father for so long, and now here it was.

After her tears stopped flowing, he led her upstairs, had her change into pajamas, and tucked her into bed, something he hadn't done since the night of her mom's funeral. "I love you, Lola. I'm so happy you're home. You don't have to tell me what happened, but if you want to, I'm here for you."

"Thanks, Dad. Tomorrow?" she asked, hoping he wouldn't press the issue.

"Of course, sweetheart." He kissed her forehead and bid her good night before exiting her room.

Ianthe curled into her familiar, comforting bed. She tried not to think about everything that had happened that evening, instead taking comfort in the fact that she was home and her father was happy to have her there. She was so exhausted and emotionally drained that she fell into a dreamless sleep.

# CHAPTER 35

*Conall*

CONALL AWOKE TO sunlight streaming through his window and the faint sounds of the servants preparing for the day. His head slightly ached, and he wasn't sure why. He hadn't consumed anything out of the normal the previous day. In fact, he'd had less ambrosia than he normally did. He stretched and stood, and that was when he remembered that he had said he would meet Lady Bronwen in the garden the night before. He grimaced knowing she would hold it against him today. *And where is Ianthe? Why didn't she show up in my dreams last night?* He couldn't even remember if he had dreamed, but he would have remembered a visit from her. He got himself dressed and headed down to the hall, hoping to find Torin to figure out a plan for her extraction.

The first thing he noticed as strange was the lack of guards around Ianthe's room. *Maybe she's down at breakfast*, he thought, but when he entered the dining hall, no one was there. He walked toward the kitchen then over-heard voices coming from the hallway.

"What do you mean, he just asked you to take her home?" Torin grumbled.

"Exactly that. She was really upset. He said he didn't want to torture her further and ordered me to escort her home immediately, so I did," Maddock replied. "I wasn't about to look a gift horse in the mouth. This really was the best solution we could hope for. She's back home, Callie's home, and her true identity can remain a secret."

"You're forgetting one thing—" Torin started.

As if on cue, Conall stepped into the hall and cleared his throat. "Care to explain what is going on?"

"Actually, I don't," Maddock sneered. "You don't de-serve to know." He shoved his shoulder into Conall as he walked by, intentionally knocking him off balance.

"What the hell, Maddock?" Conall yelled.

Maddock froze, clenched his fists at his sides, and spun around, barely containing the rage that burned within his eyes. "You have some nerve. I can't believe you would treat her that way. Well, I guess it really shouldn't be that much of a surprise—you are *Unseelie* after all." He spat the word like it was a derogatory term.

"What are you talking about?"

"I'm talking about *you*, Conall—you and your de-spicable behavior." He lowered his voice, realizing they could be easily overheard in the hallway. "She saw you last night. She saw you with Lady Bronwen in the garden, you moron."

Conall looked taken aback. *Ianthe saw me with Lady Bronwen in the garden? But I never made it to the gar-den...* He searched his mind for any scrap of memory but came up empty. All he could recall was going back to his room and thinking he would just rest for a few minutes. After lying down on the bed, the next thing he could remember was waking up.

Seeing no sign of remorse on Conall's face, Maddock stomped away before he did something he would regret.

"Torin, I didn't go to the garden last night. I went to my room and fell asleep. How could she have seen me in a place where I wasn't?"

"Are you sure, Conall? I mean, we've all heard the rumors about you and Lady Bronwen."

"Of course I am sure. I planned to meet Bronwen last night to clarify that I was serious the last time I told her I was taken and there would never be anything between us, but I fell asleep instead. I would *never* do anything to hurt Ianthe—*never*. She is everything to me. I just...I don't understand how this could have happened."

"I guess you'll have to ask Lady Bronwen what happened. Maybe she can shed some light on this situation, and while you do that, I'll convince Maddock not to murder you. The good news is that your lady love has been returned to her home in the human realm. Both girls are safely back where they belong."

Conall nodded. "Thank you, Torin. Do you know where I might find Bronwen?"

Torin heaved a loud sigh. "She's in the garden." *Of course she is.*

Conall marched over and found Lady Bronwen sitting on a bench. "Ah, Conall. Care for a repeat of last night?" she asked with a suggestive wink.

"I don't know what you're talking about."

"Come now, no one is around. There's no reason to

pretend to be a gentleman—you certainly weren't one last night." She smiled lewdly and licked her lips, practically assaulting him with her eyes.

"Stop. You must be mistaken. I was in my room all night, and I came to apologize for missing our rendezvous time," he countered.

"Whatever helps you sleep at night, sweetheart, but you and I both know exactly where you were last night, and *what* you were doing." She waggled her eyebrows for emphasis, frustrating him to no end.

"I'm serious, Bronwen. I wasn't here, but obviously someone was."

Bronwen laughed. "Conall, it was you. I'm fairly certain I would remember who I slept with. I met you out here just like you asked. We kissed passionately for a while on this bench and when things started getting a little more heated, you carried me off to the hedge maze."

*What the hell is she talking about? We may have had a tryst or two in the past, but that was before Ianthe. I would never to touch another woman in that manner now. "Bronwen, have any of our previous trysts been in public, where we could have been discovered?"*

She quirked her eyebrow, puzzled. "Well, no."

"And what did I tell you the last time I was here?"

"That you are seeing someone." Her face fell. "But I thought maybe you had a change of heart and that was why you couldn't keep your hands off of me."

"Listen to me: I don't know who you were with last night, but it wasn't me." He stared into her eyes so she would see his sincerity.

"But that's just not possible. I swear to gods it was you, Conall."

He paced back and forth, running through all the possibilities before landing on the only one that made sense, the option that made is gut clench. "Are there any Seelie Changelings you know of?"

Bronwen gasped. "A Changeling? That's such a rare thing these days. I only know of Hamish, but he's still a little thing, only 11 years old."

"Could there be another that you don't know about?"

"I don't think so."

"Then I'm convinced whoever was with you last night was an Unseelie Changeling, because it most definitely wasn't me."

She paled, knowing she had been with someone she didn't even know. "Oh my gods! I think I'm going to be sick. Do you know who?"

Conall grimaced. "I have a feeling, but I'm not at liberty to say. I'm so sorry that your involvement with me led to this. I don't know what I can do to make this right, but be assured I'll do everything within my power to make him pay. I wish you happiness in your future, Bronwen, but know one thing is certain—my heart belongs fully to someone else, and she will hold it for as long as I breathe."

Bronwen bowed her head, most likely to hide her shame or tears. "I understand, Conall."

He left her sitting there and sought out Torin to explain. He was walking through the doors when he almost ran right into Maddock instead. If looks could kill, Conall would probably have dropped dead in that moment.

Have fun getting your story straight with your *girl-friend?*" Maddock snapped.

Conall sighed. He knew he'd have a hard time convincing Maddock what had actually happened, but it would help to have a few allies.

"I know what you think of me, but could you help me find Torin so we can get this all straightened out?"

Maddock snorted loudly but stepped around him and led him to the stable. Torin was there getting Rain ready for Conall. He'd already tied Conall's pack on and saddled the horse.

Torin shrugged, leading Conall's white stallion outside. "I figured you'd be needing him."

"Indeed, I will, but I'd like to explain the situation to both of you before I go."

Torin motioned with the dismissive flick of his hand, indicating that he need not explain a thing, while Maddock crossed his arms and stared at him expectantly.

Conall continued, "I may've been involved with Bronwen in the past, but during my last visit I told her I'm in a relationship with someone and my heart fully belongs to that person." He could see Maddock's mouth open to say something, but he pressed on, not allowing him the chance to speak. "I have information to share with you that is considered top secret, information that, if released, would be considered treason and guarantee my execution, but it explains what happened last night and why I must leave you immediately to protect Lady Ianthe."

"Protect her? You're the one who destroyed her!" Maddock fumed. "You didn't see her like I did. She was shattered. There was no fire in her eyes—it was like she was an empty shell of a person."

Each confession was an arrow through Conall's heart. There were a million things he wished he could do, ways things could have gone differently, but what mattered the most right then was that he reached her as fast as he could.

"Look, you can choose to believe me or not, but the fact of the matter is I spent last night asleep in my room. I never met Lady Bronwen, but someone else did—a Changeling."

Maddock snorted again. "Yeah right, and I just adopted a pet pegasus."

"This is the part that could result in my death, so listen closely. You cannot repeat this information to anyone, and I am trusting you since you have both been determined to keep the peace between our peoples, and you care about Ianthe as well." He paused so the gravity of what he was to say next would truly sink in. "Casimir is a Changeling." He paused again before continuing. "It's the best kept secret of the Unseelie court. In fact, many Unseelie do not even know what he is, since he is lucky enough to have aspects from both of his parents. Casimir also uses his powers very sparingly and discreetly, but if you think about it, this all started with him. He's the reason Evin kidnapped Callie, the reason Ianthe came back to Fae. He's been obsessed with her since before she ever learned she was Fae, let alone the Unseelie princess. He's been single-minded in his obsession, and I was sent to track him before I caught Ianthe's trail and headed here. Who knows how long he was at your palace or who he pretended to be, but I can assure you that he was the one with Lady Bronwen last night. He pretended to be me in order to break Ianthe's heart. Now, if I am right, I am also certain he has no intention of leaving her alone to wallow in her misery. He has plans that involve her, and I cannot allow him to carry them out, so I must leave at once."

Both men seemed to seriously consider Conall's words. Maddock still looked slightly skeptical but was no longer shooting death glares in Conall's direction. They stepped away to discuss what Conall had just told them, and while they were talking, he mounted his steed.

"I'm coming with you," Maddock stated, getting his own horse from a stall.

"I'll tell King Lachlan I sent you both to track Evin."

They all nodded in agreement as Maddock mounted his horse. "Oh, and Maddock," Torin called out. "Make sure you do bring Evin back with you to appease the king."

# CHAPTER 36

*Ianthe*

**T**HE NEXT MORNING greeted her too soon for her liking. She woke to sunlight filling her room, and the aroma of crispy bacon drew her out of bed. It took her a moment to get her bearings and recall exactly where she was then she lumbered downstairs to an unusual sight: her father standing in the kitchen in his pajamas, flipping pancakes. She couldn't remember the last time he cooked for her, let alone made her pancakes. It had to have been before her mother died.

"Dad?" she asked, rubbing her eyes to make sure she wasn't seeing things.

"Good morning, Lola. I hope you're hungry."

"I…why…why aren't you at work?" She was so confused. He plated up their meal and carried it to the table in the kitchen nook.

"I took a few days off."

Her jaw dropped at the notion of her workaholic father voluntarily taking vacation days. He usually went into work sick because he said he didn't like to miss even one day. *What is going on?*

He smiled at her reassuringly. "Have a seat, honey. I think it's time you and I finally had a talk."

*Who is this person and what has he done with my father?* She felt like she was in the movie with Pod People. She sat at the table across from him, eyeing him suspiciously.

"Eat, please," he implored. She picked up her fork and took a bite. It was delicious. After a few moments in which they both chewed silently, her dad cleared his throat. "Look, I know I haven't been the greatest father to you these last few years." She could have quipped a snarky response but clamped her lips shut, eager to hear where this conversation was going. "But your letter and disappearance were a rude awakening for me. The truth of the matter is that I already lost your mother, and it destroyed me. You... You're just like her, and I guess I wasn't very good at hiding the fact that you remind me of the best parts of her. Sometimes just the sight of you broke my heart over and over again. I know I didn't handle things well—at all—with her death and with you, and I'm sorry. I tried to do the best I could. I honestly did, it was just so hard..."

Her eyes began to water. She had yearned to hear those exact words for so long. She reached across the table and placed her hand on top of his. "It's okay, Dad. I understand."

"I don't think you do, honey. It's just..." It was like she knew exactly where this conversation was headed. It was something he should have told her ages ago, but perhaps he had been doing her a kindness by not saying anything.

She smiled weakly. "Dad, I know. I know more than you probably think. I—" She struggled with how to word her thoughts. "I know I'm not really yours." The last part came out as a whisper as she stared down at her plate, unable to look her father in the eyes.

"I'm so sorry," he replied, his voice cracking as he began to weep. She squeezed his hand, offering him comfort through her touch. Through his tears, he continued his confession. "I was going to tell you, but I was sure if I did, I would lose you forever, and I couldn't say goodbye to you—to the last bit of your mother in my life. I knew I had done things the wrong way and if you discovered the truth, you wouldn't have a reason left to tie yourself to me. H-How did you find out?"

"First, Dad, it's not your fault. I've come to understand that a bit better now, though I didn't used to. I was angry that no matter how hard I tried, I couldn't make you love me, couldn't make you happy."

"Honey, I always loved you." His voice broke, guilt and regret etching every line and wrinkle in his face.

"I want you to remember that when I tell you the next part..." And so she began. There across the kitchen table, the day after her heart had been decimated, she told her father the truth. She told him what had really happened the night at the party when she ended up in the hospital. She told him about her summer at Aunt Grace's house, meeting Conall, and discovering who she really was. She was amazed at how quietly and actively he listened. While his expression showed some surprise, he wasn't staring at her like you would when entertaining a person who was clearly off their rocker, and for that she was extremely grateful. She described her time at the Unseelie palace, her eventual arrest and escape, how she'd returned to find Callie. She told him about Casimir and how she was afraid he would never leave her alone, and lastly she described the previous night, how Conall had betrayed her and broken her heart.

At some point in their conversation, she found herself sitting on his lap and crying into his shirt like she used to when she was a little girl. He held her until all her words were gone and her tears had dried. Then he kissed the top of her head and merely responded with, "Well, that certainly explains a lot." Of course he had many questions for her, but what mattered most was that he didn't doubt her. He believed every word she said and held her as if finding out his non-biological child was half supernatural monster had no effect on him. He could read the question on her face and reassured her. "Your genetics don't decide what kind of person you are. They don't make up who are you are inside, and finding out you're different doesn't change who I know you to be. You are still every bit my little girl."

God, how she needed to hear those words. Ever since Casimir first accused her of enjoying torturing him, she'd needed someone to remind her that there was always a choice, that we all have the capability to choose who we want to be. "Thank you, Dad."

He hugged her tightly before letting her go. "Now, let's get this kitchen cleaned up so you can call Callie and let her know you are home. She came by every day this week to reassure me you were okay and planned to come home but circumstances were keeping you away, and she made me promise I would have you call her when you got home."

After cleaning up the kitchen with her dad, an odd but meaningful moment of bonding, she grabbed her cellphone and hesitantly called Callie. Her bestie squealed into the receiver when she discovered Ianthe was home and they made plans to meet up at Starbucks in a couple hours so they could grab some coffee and head over to the park to catch up. With that phone call down, she called Aunt

Grace next. She told her everything that had happened and broke down crying again when she recounted the previous night's events.

"Oh, darling. I'm so sorry. Are you sure it was him who you saw?"

"Oh it was definitely him. I was sure of that." She sighed.

"Perhaps this is for the best. I know you cared for him, but what you really need is a nice human boy."

Ianthe brushed off her aunt's words. She knew they were coming from the right place, but she wasn't ready to hear them yet. She used meeting up with Callie as an excuse to end the conversation and hung up the phone. While she still felt like there were gaping wounds in her heart, she was starting to become angry—angry at herself for trusting Conall to begin with and, of course, angry at him for betraying her. Asking for fidelity was really not asking for too much.

She took a nice, long, hot shower and got ready to meet Callie. By the time she managed to pull herself together and look somewhat decent, it was time to go.

She found her dad working in his home office. "Dad, I'm going to Starbucks to meet Callie." His brow furrowed in concern, but she smiled reassuringly. "Don't worry, I won't be out long, and I'll have my phone with me if you need anything." It was weird to have him paying so much attention to her, let alone showing concern for where she was going—weird, but comforting. It was nice to know things were out in the open between them, and they were both eager to rebuild their relationship.

"All right sweetie. Try to have fun," he replied. She started for the front door then she heard him call out behind her, "I love you!" His words made her miss a step.

She placed a hand over her heart, feeling it skip a beat, and smiled. "Love you too." Every ounce of heartbreak she was experiencing right then over Conall, she would gladly experience a thousand times more just to hear those three little words from her father.

When she pulled up at Starbucks, she glanced at the clock on her dash and noticed she was 10 minutes early. *No worries, I'll just go inside, grab my drink, and wait.* Once she had a chai latte in hand, she sat down at a table and started scrolling through all the social media posts she had missed, wondering what people had done to catch up on each other's lives before social media.

After a few minutes, a male voice interrupted her musings. "Hey there." She raised her eyes from her phone to see the golden-haired Greek Adonis, Kyle, pulling out the chair across from her. *That's very presumptuous of him.* "I haven't seen you around in a while."

"Oh yeah, I was…um…out of town…visiting a friend."

"A friend, huh?" He quirked his eyebrow.

She nodded her head slowly. "Yep, a friend."

"Well I'm glad you weren't gone too long. In fact, after no one was home when I came by your house for our date, I've been back here several times hoping to run into you again."

*Noooo. That doesn't sound creepy at all,* her inner voice said, oozing with sarcasm. She didn't want to be rude, but she had no patience for him. "Look, Kyle, I'm sure you're a great guy and all, but I just got out of a relationship and I'm not looking to jump into another one." She tapped her fingers against her cup, hoping he would take the hint and leave.

She noticed a slight curve up in his lip and a twinkle

in his eye, almost as if he were pleased by her response, which was very odd and contradictory to his words. "I'm sorry to hear that. Can I at least get you a refill before I go?"

She glanced down at her drink, realizing she had indeed finished most of it. "Sure, why not." Who was she to pass up free Starbucks? It wasn't like she was leading him on; she'd told him she wasn't interested. He eagerly jumped up from the table and walked over to the counter.

After several minutes, he returned with a steaming hot chai latte. She graciously accepted the cup and took a sip to show her gratitude. He smiled widely before resuming his place across from her. She fought not to roll her eyes and prayed Callie would hurry up and arrive so she could leave. She smiled tightly. "Thanks, Kyle."

He didn't respond, just watched her closely as she sipped her latte, and for lack of desire to make conversation, she kept sipping, hoping the absence of stimulating conversation might encourage him to leave.

She placed her cup down on the table when a wave of dizziness washed over her. "I'm sorry, Kyle, I'm not feeling very well. I should go." Deciding it might be best to go home and just have Callie meet her there, she rose from the table only to sway on her feet. Before she could blink, Kyle was there to help her.

"Are you okay? Do you want me to help you to your car?" he asked. People were beginning to stare at the spectacle she was making, so she quickly accepted his assistance.

"Thanks again, Kyle," she said as they reached the door of her car. She leaned against it for support, her vision fraying around the edges. There was no way for her to get home; she couldn't drive like this. She prayed Callie would be there shortly or she could at least send a text before she passed out. She fumbled with her purse, pulling out her keys and searching for her phone. She closed her eyes, knowing fainting was imminent, and then she felt Kyle pluck the keys from her hand. She opened her mouth, but her tongue felt heavy and thick in her mouth. She glanced up at Kyle to see him smiling at her smugly just before everything went black.

# CHAPTER 37

*Ianthe*

**H**ER DREAMS WERE *fragmented, like reflections from twisted fun house mirrors that kept shifting and changing. The scenes jumped and shifted, people blurred, dizziness and nausea assaulting her time and time again. A flash of Callie and she reached out to grab her, only to realize it had already dissolved. She tried to focus on just one moment, one memory, but using her powers felt like moving through quicksand and she was afraid it would pull her under for good. What was wrong with her? She licked her lips. They tasted faintly of chai. Chai? Chai! That was it—she had been at Starbucks with Kyle when she started feeling dizzy out of the blue, right after she'd had quite a bit of the latte he brought her.*

*Her mind slowly came into focus. She tried to center her thoughts on one person, but anyone she wanted to reach was most likely not asleep. She tried Callie, Aunt Grace, Alfie, Maddock, even Conall. As a last resort, she pictured her own bedroom and focused on her dad. The memory of breakfast was fresh in her mind, and her emotions associated with it were running high. She opened her eyes and was happy to see her vision had stopped blurring. Things swayed every once in a while, but she could at least focus on them. It was no longer as if the room was spinning around her.*

*"Dad!" she called out loudly. No one answered. "DAD!" she yelled. She heard loud footsteps approach her door then it swung open and her dad stood in the doorway. Relief washed over her by the bucketful.*

*He seemed unsure as he stepped inside. "I don't understand. I was just in my office working, and I closed my eyes for just a second..." he muttered.*

*She didn't know how much time she had so she cut to the chase. "Dad, I know this is probably a little confusing right now, but you have to listen to me. I need your help. I was at Starbucks waiting for Callie when I ran into this new guy from our street, Kyle. I-I think he put something in my drink. He offered to get me a refill and after drinking some of it, I started to feel dizzy so he walked me to my car. I tried to get into it, but I think I passed out. I don't know what happened. I don't even know where I am right now. I can't seem to wake myself up." She was starting to panic.*

*Her father grabbed her hand. "Okay, Lola. Calm down, honey. We'll figure this out. Can you tell me what this boy looks like?"*

*"He's—" A sharp pain across her face whipped her head to the side, and she hissed in a breath. She raised her hand to her cheek. It was hot.*

*"What the hell?" her father's voice boomed. She glanced past him to the mirror on her wall, which revealed the blooming red handprint now visible on her cheek.*

*"Dad, help me...please..." she managed to croak out before another violent slap pulled her out of her sleep.*

Ianthe gasped and bolted upright.

"There we go, little one."

*Oh, what fresh level of hell is this?* That voice, that moniker, and the fingers gripping her shoulders made her blood run cold. She dreaded opening her eyes to her new reality but knew she must. Of course, when she did, she was greeted with unwelcomingly familiar blue eyes.

"Casimir," she sneered.

"Oh, my sweet, how I love my name coming off of your lips." He plucked her bottom lip with his thumb then stuck it into his mouth as if tasting her. She went to smack his hand away, but her hand wouldn't rise. Each wrist and ankle were bound with rope to the arms and legs of a rather uncomfortable wooden dining chair like a generic kidnapping in a low-budget movie. She tugged hard, but only succeeded in earning herself rope burns on both wrists.

She snarled at Casimir. "Then I'll make sure not to use it in the future. So, douchecanoe, where am I?"

He chuckled, as if amused by a naughty child. "There's my Unseelie princess."

This time she did not hold back her eye roll, and he snickered again. "Are you going to answer my question or not, dickshitter?" She used her inventive vocabulary to stall for time and keep her panic at bay.

"We're at my house." It wasn't what she'd been expecting, but she took a moment to look around her. It looked as if she were in the middle of the living room of a rather empty, large, modern house, very similar to her own if all the furniture and décor had been removed. At least that meant she wasn't back in Fae.

She raised her right eyebrow. "*Your* house?"

"Yes, my house." He smiled at her as if this knowledge would please her.

"Okay, twatwaffle, what gives? Why do you have a house in the human realm? And how the hell did I get here?"

He chuckled again. "While I do love your very colorful nicknames, I think I would prefer my own name." She stared daggers at him, indicating that his request would not be honored. He continued, "And to answer your question, yes, I have a house here. How else would I be able to keep an eye on my fiancée?"

*Oh sweet baby Jesus, not this crap again.* "For the last time, asshole, I am. NOT. Your. Fiancée. And I never will be." She attempted to accent each word with a stomp but couldn't get her a foot loose enough. She was pretty much at his mercy, and that didn't sit well with her—not at all.

He tsked. "It's only a matter of time, little one. I'm the only one who will be able to truly make you happy. After all, you didn't look so happy in the coffee shop. What did Conall do to break your pretty heart?"

Shock echoed through her body. "How do you know about that?"

"Oh, I have my ways. Haven't you ever wondered what my powers are? What kind of Fae I am? I know Alfie gave you some tutoring, so let's see if you can guess." He stood across from her with a knowing smirk on his face.

*Ah, hell, why haven't I researched what type of Fae he is? Probably because I was trying to avoid him at all costs, including thinking about him and his abilities.* She should have been studying her enemy for a way to defeat him, although, to be fair, initially she'd thought she had defeated him in her Mara visit the night he almost killed Conall, but obviously she was wrong. She racked her brain for any indication of his powers but couldn't come up with answer. "I never gave you a second thought, so why would I spend time trying to figure out what kind of Fae you are? I have no interest in you, dipshit," she spat with false bravado.

"I suppose you're right. I think if you had, you may have been a little more careful than to trust anyone." His skin glimmered and sparkled, his features morphing, until it wasn't Casimir who stood in front of her, but Kyle!

*She gasped. She was so bewildered she couldn't speak, and she stared at him, eyes wide. Why didn't I know he could do that? You would think Conall or Alfie would have mentioned that my stalker could shape-shift.*

"I take it by your silence you haven't done much research on Changelings. It appears Alfie is slacking on his duties."

"I...I don't understand. I thought Changelings were Fae babies who switched places with human babies." She did at least remember that from one of her mom's folklore books.

"Ah, humans are seriously misinformed—well, that, and we do tend to keep this sort of power a secret. Just think about what I could do with it. I could easily sneak into the Seelie palace under the guise of a guard or maid." With each new suggestion, he shimmered and shifted until the very person he described was standing right in front of her—a guard she had once seen outside her door, the maid who served her dinner last night. It was extremely unnerving. "I could be your best friend"—watching him changed

into Callie was enough to disturb her for years to come—
"or even your boyfriend." She had to mentally remind herself it was not Conall standing in front her. Casimir caressed the cheek he had previously slapped and stared at
her through Conall's eyes. A cold shiver raced down her
spine, which Casimir felt and mistook for something else.
He leaned in and pressed his lips forcefully against hers.
She fought against her bindings, feeling them dig deeper
into her skin. Her skin felt raw and sore, but she would
never stop fighting. He pried her mouth open with his and
when she felt his tongue, she did the only she could: she
bit down—hard.

"Shit!" He drew back, his appearance back to normal
with the exception of blood trickling from the corner of
his mouth. He bent over and held a hand over it for several
minutes, quietly cursing to himself. She spat his foul blood
from her mouth onto the floor. He narrowed his icy blue
eyes before smiling widely, his sharp teeth stained with
blood. He reached his thumb to her face and wiped some
of his blood away then licked his finger clean.

"Mm, I thoo luf a good challenge. I've thold you this
before and I'll thell you again: you and I are not thath different." Hearing his lisp from the injury she gave him almost
made her laugh, but the urge faded quickly. It would've
been humorous if she were not helplessly tied to a chair. He
ran his hand down her arm, causing her to thrash against
her restraints. "I can feel your Unseelie blood boiling under your skin. Even now, your eyes are glowing, and judg-
ing by how you almost bit my tongue off, I would guess
that your teeth are also very sharp. Lucky for me, changing identities speeds up my healing rate." She discreetly
ran her tongue against her teeth, absorbing the truth in his
statement. "You and I are going to have lots of fun, little
one. I will enjoy every moment it takes to make you mine."

Ianthe spat again, this time in his direction. "I will never be yours—NEVER!" She screamed as the front door flew open and in stepped Maddock followed by Conall, Evin, and a familiar fierce redhead.

Maddock and Conall both had their swords drawn and were quickly advancing on Casimir while Evin held Callie back as she frantically tried to get past him. Ianthe wasn't sure if Callie's intentions were to attack Casimir or rush to her aid, and knowing her bestie, it could have been either.

"Let me go, dammit! She needs me!" Callie yelled at Evin. He assessed the situation in the living room, noticing that Casimir was under control, and then stepped aside. Callie rushed toward her. "Oh, Thee! I'm so glad we found you." She quickly went to work untying the ropes that bound Ianthe in place. Once her arms were free, Callie hugged her tightly before continuing on to release her feet.

Ianthe tried to stand, wobbling from the residual drugs in her system and her injuries, and Callie was quick to support her. Evin gathered the rope from her chair and tossed it to Maddock, who used it to bind Casimir's hands behind his back then shoved him into the chair Ianthe had previously occupied. Conall held the tip of his sword at Casimir's throat.

"Conall, consider the consequences," Evin warned. "Trust me, I know firsthand the need to hurt that son of a bitch, but some things are not worth the consequences. Think about others who would be affected." He motioned toward all of them, because if one of them killed Casimir right then, there would be serious consequences, and King Corydon would make sure they all paid—even his own daughter.

Conall still held his sword in the same place, but most of the fire faded from his eyes. "Is she okay?" he asked.

Maddock searched her over from head to toe. "A little bruised and scraped, but otherwise unharmed."

"Whose blood is on the floor?" he growled, pressing the tip of the sword into Casimir's skin.

Casimir cleared his throat. "Ah, that would be mine."

Conall's eyes narrowed, clearly not believing Casimir's admission until Ianthe spoke. "It's the truth. He kissed me so I bit his tongue—hard."

"You go, girl." Callie held her hand up for a fist bump, which Ianthe returned. Conall didn't seem as amused, or perhaps he was focusing on the fact that Casimir had kissed Ianthe, because he pressed the sword a little farther, drawing a droplet of blood that ran down Casimir's neck.

Maddock patted Conall's shoulder, drawing Conall's sword arm back slightly so the blade was no longer digging into Casimir's skin. "Conall, if you'll allow me…"

Conall drew his sword back but kept it pointed threateningly while Maddock squatted down in front of Casimir. He put both of his hands on either side of Casimir's head. Casimir clearly knew what was going to happen next because he fought against his bindings, whipping his head back and forth to shake Maddock's grip until Conall brought the sword closer to his neck. Maddock's eyes glowed a brilliant orange before he closed them then Ianthe watched in surprise as Casimir's eyes rolled back into his head and he slumped back into the chair, unconscious.

After a good five minutes or so, Maddock drew his hands back and stood. Casimir remained unconscious. "It's done," Maddock stated as he wiped his hands on his pants and stepped away from Casimir.

Callie voiced what Ianthe was thinking: "What's done?"

"I altered his memories. I took away some involving you, Lady Ianthe, and modified others. He should stay away from you for now on, or at least not have that disturbing obsession with you," Maddock explained as he approached the two girls.

"Wicked Vulcan mind meld," Callie whispered, easing the tension in the room.

Ianthe heaved a sigh of relief. "Thank you, Maddock. You have no idea—that means so much to me." She sniffled, throwing her arms around him and hugging him fiercely. It took a moment before he awkwardly returned her embrace.

Before she pulled away, he whispered in her ear. "Give Conall a chance to explain—you owe it to both of you." Then he winked and released her.

Her gaze flicked over Maddock's shoulder to Conall, who was no longer looking at Casimir but instead staring at her with a stricken expression.

"All right, Evin, our work here is done. Let's get Casimir into the car so Conall can take him back to his king," Maddock stated.

Evin turned and looked at Callie. "Well, I guess this is goodbye. Take care of yourself, okay?" He moved to hug her, but Callie folded her arms across her chest and stepped back, arching one eyebrow in a challenge. Evin's lips pressed into a line before he dropped his arms and stepped back then approached Ianthe. He leaned in close and whispered, "Please look after her for me. She may put on a brave face, but she'll need some help to work through everything." Then he leaned back and raised his voice back to normal volume. "I truly am sorry for my part in all that took place and hope that someday you both can forgive me."

He stuck his hand out for her to shake, and she took it; he had come in her rescue party, after all. She could see pain and longing in his eyes, and he glanced once more at Callie before walking over to Maddock. The two men approached Casimir from behind, placed a hand underneath an armpit, hoisted him up, and carried him out the door.

Now it was just the three of them: Callie, Ianthe, and Conall. "Wait, boys! We need to check his pockets for Thee's keys!" Callie yelled before running out the door and chasing after them.

*And then there were two.* She wasn't sure what to say, so she just stood there, awkwardly staring at Conall's feet, which stepped closer toward her.

"Maddock told me what you saw," he started, his tone indicating that there was more to what she'd seen than she'd realized. "Will you let me explain?"

"What is there to explain, Conall? I saw you with my own eyes! It's something I wish I could un-see, but every time I close my eyes, it plays on repeat." Her voice bordered somewhere between fury and tears.

"Please, my flower, it wasn't me."

She rolled her eyes at his cliché denial, and for a moment she could hear Shaggy's "It Wasn't Me" running through her head.

Conall gently grabbed her face and forced her to stare into his eyes. "I swear on my life, Ianthe. I should've told you about Casimir a while ago, but you never asked and it was such a well-guarded secret, something few of us know and never speak of. I'm sorry I didn't tell you because it may have saved you some heartbreak. Casimir is a Changeling."

"Yeah, I know."

"You know?"

"He was pretending to be Kyle, this guy who lived down the street from me. He showed me. It was…it was actually quite jarring."

"So you've seen what he can do." His voice was laced with relief. "Then you should know how it is possible that the person you saw with Lady Bronwen wasn't me."

Suddenly it all clicked. She flashed back to when Casimir shifted into Conall, how he showed her exactly who he pretended to be at the Seelie palace to watch her. That sadistic fucker had pretended to be Conall, hoping she would see him, and it would lead her back home into Kyle's arms. She smacked her forehead lightly. "How could I have been so stupid? Of course it was him."

His relief filled the room, his emotions projecting through his power. "I'm sorry for any of my actions that may have led to you believe that lie. I'll be honest with you: I was involved with Lady Bronwen in the past, but the last time I saw her, I told her my heart belongs to someone else." He took her hands in his own. "Ianthe, my beautiful flower, I love you. I have since the moment you unknowingly invaded my dreams. I could not possibly give my heart to anyone else because it's no longer mine to give. It's yours."

Her breath caught in her throat. His words were music to her ears, the best declaration of love she could have imagined. Even if she hadn't heard it, she definitely felt it; his love washed over her in waves and made her knees week.

"I love you too, Conall," she said breathlessly before he covered her mouth with his own. She wasn't sure how long they kissed before someone cleared their throat, interrupting them. She turned toward the door to see Callie standing there with a huge grin on her face.

"While that was way hot and I'm a little sad to miss wherever that was going to lead to, the boys are waiting outside for you, Conall. Maddock said to hurry because he isn't sure how long Casimir will stay knocked out."

He sighed. "I'm sorry, my love, but I must leave you again. I have to return Casimir to King Corydon, but I promise I'll be back as soon as I can. I have a plan that ends with us in the same place for quite some time." He winked at her before placing a brief kiss on her lips and releasing her hands.

"You better not make me wait long, Spock," she said with a smile.

He gathered her into his arms once more, hugging her tightly and pressing another quick kiss on her lips that might have been longer had they not overheard Callie giggle. He stared adoringly into her violet eyes. "I love you, Ianthe."

"I love you too, Conall. Be safe and hurry back."

He released her with a short squeeze and walked to the door then turned once more, soaking in the sight of her before passing by Callie. He stopped and said something to her, but he was whispering so low that Ianthe couldn't hear. Then he patted Callie on the shoulder and left.

Ianthe sighed, missing him already. As if she'd summoned him with her thoughts, he raced back into the living room. "I forgot one thing." He held up a familiar leather strap, its brown shade now a deep bronze. "The guys found this in Casimir's pocket." He ran over and tied it on her wrist before kissing her cheek and running back out the door.

Ianthe hadn't even realized it was missing. Casimir

must have removed it at some point before tying her to the chair. Whatever magic he placed in it this time filled her with comfort and love, taking away all the soreness from her wrists and ankles. She glanced down at the leather bracelet tied around her wrist and noticed that not only was the pain gone, the rope burns were gone too. There was still some slight bruising, but for the most part, they were healed.

"Ready, chica?" Callie asked, dangling Ianthe's keys from her fingers. "Your car is in the garage." She led the way, and they both piled into the car. Callie had offered to drive, and Ianthe wasn't one to argue. They didn't have to drive very far because the house was just down the street. He had been holding her in the corner house at the bottom of the hill, to be exact.

"How did you guys find me?"

"Oh, well, when you weren't at the coffee shop, I called your dad. He was freaking out about a dream he had with you in it, so I called Evin, and he met us at your dad's house with Conall and Maddock in tow. I'm not sure how they all met up."

*Ianthe's eyes went wide. My dad met full-blooded Fae—I hope he wasn't traumatized.*

"Anyway, your dad was totally freaking out. Oh, and apparently he has a tracking app on your phone, but don't be pissed because it totally saved you today. Thank God dumbass Casimir didn't leave your phone at Starbucks or we would have been up a creek without a paddle. We saw that you were down the street, and the boys rushed off to save you. I, of course, wasn't about to sit at your house with your dad and insisted I go too. After all, I have some mad skills they could have used."

Ianthe laughed, happy to see Callie back to her normal

self, and turned to notice her purse with her phone was on the back seat. The second they pulled up to her house, her dad sprinted toward the car. "Thanks, Cal. You're the best-est friend I could have ever asked for." She reached over and squeezed Callie's hand.

"And don't you forget that!" Callie added, giving her hand another squeeze. Ianthe's door was yanked open by her dad, who pulled her into his arms.

"You're okay! Thank goodness you're okay. I swear I must have aged ten years in these last few weeks. I don't think I can take much more of this." He exhaled heavily as he released her.

"We can all rest a little easier now—I don't think Casimir will be bothering me anymore," she replied, hoping Maddock's memory wipe had done the trick.

"Come on in girls. I ordered some pizza while I waited for you."

"YES! I love me some pizza," Callie cheered. Ianthe walked in sandwiched between them, surprised at how the turn of events had brought her right there, to that moment with them. She was happy to be home. Of course the only thing that would have made the moment perfect was if Conall were there for good, but she was willing to wait for him. She knew he would fight for her to the ends of the earth, and now it was her time to fight for him by being patient and having faith in him.

# CHAPTER 38

*Conall*

**C**ONALL HAD NEVER felt more relieved in his life than when Ianthe accepted his explanation, but to hear her return his feelings—there were no words to describe the amount of joy that filled him. He must have looked like a grinning fool when he climbed in the car with Maddock and Evin, and Maddock raised an eyebrow at his expression. "I take it everything went okay."

"Yeah, um, I guess Casimir got a little full of himself and decided to show off for her, so after seeing firsthand what he could do, she believed it was him and not me. I'll have to get the full story on that conversation and experience later, though."

The boys waited for Ianthe's car to pull out of the garage and followed her home. They watched as she was practically tackled in a bear hug by her father and both girls were safely escorted inside. Conall smiled, knowing she was well on her way to mending her relationship with her dad. He knew how strained their relationship had previously been, but the man she had described didn't seem like the same one he had met earlier. Maybe the prospect of losing her had woken him up. He hoped so, as it would be nice to see some good come out of this mess.

Luckily, Casimir remained unconscious for all of the drive and the transfer to Conall's horse. Conall bid farewell to Maddock and Evin, and even though it was Evin's actions that had gotten them into the mess that could have potentially ended badly for all them, he worried what the Seelie king's punishment for Evin might be. He hoped it wasn't too severe. Any idiot could see the regret in his eyes, and the way he observed Callie's every move. It was the same way Conall watched Ianthe, and Maddock—who would have thought he'd have an ally in Maddock? Certainly not Conall. That was a most welcome surprise, but he supposed Ianthe had that effect on people—she made them care about her without even trying. Oddly enough, he trusted those men with his life and hoped with time they would prove worthy of his trust by not breathing a word about the Unseelie Changeling.

Conall mounted Rain behind the prone Casimir and rode off into the night toward the gateway, heading back to Unseelie territory. Eventually Casimir awoke and complained loudly about being tied up, but Conall wasn't about to risk his escape. Casimir made no mention of Ianthe, which led him to believe Maddock's Skepseis powers had worked. At the first Unseelie town they came to, he acquired a horse for Casimir and tied it to his own. When they got close to their village, he untied Casimir's hands but kept the two horses roped together.

King Corydon was in a fine state when they arrived at the palace. Conall had never seen him so stressed. Usually he had his cold façade in place, but this time it was slipping, allowing Conall to glimpse beyond the mask. Casimir's return only removed a small part of the king's anxiety, which was even more cause for concern. Once Casimir retired to his room, Conall held his breath and approached the king, hoping he wasn't overstepping his boundaries. He could never tell how King Corydon would take things; sometimes he would act as if Conall were his closest confidant, and others it was like he was no more than a servant.

"Your Majesty, is there anything I can do for you?"

The king chewed on his nail anxiously and sighed. "I never thought I would feel this way. I thought I was done with these stupid human emotions."

"What do you mean?"

"Well, it seems I may have a soft spot where my daughter is concerned."

Conall's eyes softened at the king's honest admission. "That's to be expected, sire. She is your child. Parents are supposed to worry and desire the best for their children."

"Yes, but I'm the Unseelie king, and emotions are a weakness I cannot afford," he countered.

"They are only considered a weakness because you consider them a weakness, Your Majesty. You're the one who makes the rules—the others merely follow your example."

The king considered Conall's words for several minutes. "Wise words for such a young man."

Conall took a gamble, guessing at what was troubling the king. "Lady Ianthe was returned safely to her home last night." The king looked sharply at him, assessing him carefully, but Conall could feel the king's relief; it was almost palpable. He held his breath, hoping the huge risk he was about to take would reap a great reward. "I have a confession to make, sire."

"Your feelings for my daughter are no secret, Conall. Any man who has been in love before would recognize it in another."

Conall smiled. "While I won't deny my feelings, that was not what I was going to confess." He took a deep breath. This was one hell of a risk and it could very well end in his own execution, but he was hoping with the king's current mood, it would pay off, so he confessed. He told Corydon how Casimir had attacked Ianthe at a party long before he had discovered her, and how Casimir had been stalking her. He explained how he found out that Ianthe had gone to Seelie territory to rescue her friend. He confessed to following her trail instead of Casimir's once he discovered it and how it led him to the Seelie palace. He reassured the king that only three Seelies knew exactly who she was and were all devoted to keeping her secret in order to maintain balance and protect her. He described how they found her kidnapped by Casimir, and finally he confessed to allowing a Seelie soldier alter Casimir's memories. The last bit was the part that many would consider treason and cause for execution. He studied the king the whole time he talked, watching the emotions play over his features, for once completely unmasked, and then he held his breath, waiting for Corydon's reply.

It was several agonizing minutes before the Unseelie king uttered a word.

"I understand."

Conall wasn't sure how to take those words, didn't know if they were a pardon or a death sentence.

Finally, the king spoke again. "Casimir's obsession with Ianthe needed to end. While I may not be happy with how you handled things, I understand. Once he ascends to the throne, she could be used against him. She would be his greatest weakness—hell, she already is mine. I have been worried sick about her since her guards notified me that she gave them the slip. She definitely has her mother's rebellious spirit." He chuckled.

Conall smirked at Corydon's admission. "Actually, I'm pretty sure she gets that from you, sire."

The king smirked. "True, true. I never was one to do as I was told, even as a small child. I guess what I'm trying to say is that I understand why you did what you did. However, I would've preferred you leave that decision in my hands and certainly not let a Seelie wander through Casimir's mind." The king's eyes flashed and Conall waited to see if an explosion would follow, but Corydon merely sighed. "I guess my word wasn't enough to keep her safe, especially after I had her exiled to protect her." Conall had had a niggling suspicion that the king had done what he thought was best for his daughter. "I'm considering reassigning you to a different position. It would mean a demotion, of course, and you'd have to let me give anyone who asked about you whatever explanation I care to offer. It will not look favorably for you and may make some doubt your honor, which I know you value greatly, but…"

The king paused. Conall's heart pounded in his chest. He'd do anything if it meant he could be with Ianthe. He was even considering getting himself exiled at that point.

"I would like to reassign you to guard my daughter. It would mean you'll be spending most of your time in the human realm. I will, of course, expect frequent updates and want to be notified immediately of any changes or concerns involving her."

Conall's jaw dropped. It was as if the most unexpected

present had just landed on his lap. "Yes, sir. I would do anything to protect her. I would give my own life for hers if necessary."

The king smiled affectionately, a strange expression to see on his face. "I expect nothing less from you, Conall, which is why I won't worry about her if I know you're the one there protecting her. Do you accept your new position?"

"Yes!"

"Even if it means I have to tell others you were demoted because you were no longer fit to be my first in command?"

He sighed, his heart soaring. "Even then. There's nothing that would keep me from this opportunity."

"Excellent. Then I suggest you gather what you need from your home and leave in the morning. I will do my part. In her human town, there is a stable where you can house Rain. I've already taken care of all the arrangements, and I will see that the deed to the house Casimir purchased on her street is transferred over to you."

"Thank you, Your Majesty. I won't let you down."

Conall turned and walked out of the palace with his head held high. His gamble had paid off in the best possible way. It was almost too good to be true, but he wasn't about to question it. He mounted Rain and raced off to his house to start packing.

# CHAPTER 39

*Ianthe*

**T**HINGS WERE FINALLY starting to get back to normal. Her dad had taken care of the school days she and Callie had missed by getting a client to write doctor's notes for both of them saying they had a severe and highly contagious case of the flu. Of course, there would be lots of work to make up, but she would gladly take it to get back to her old life—actually, her new and improved life. Her dad had been making an effort to be home for dinner every night, and they talked more. He even watched a few episodes of *Supernatural* with her, although he didn't seem to appreciate it as much as Aunt Grace did. She visited Aunt Grace the night she came home using her Mara ability, and they talked for hours. Grace was thrilled to hear Casimir wouldn't be bothering Ianthe anymore, but she seemed a little hesitant to believe Conall bore no blame in the events that drove them apart. Ianthe thought

Aunt Grace was still hoping she would forget about her handsome half Fae and find a human boy instead.

Callie stayed over for the first few days Ianthe was home, and they filled each other in on everything. While Callie seemed not to be affected by what had happened with Evin, there were moments when Ianthe would catch her lost in her own thoughts, which were filled with sorrow. She could understand. Callie had truly liked Evin before the whole mess began. It was natural she'd be sad after finding out he betrayed her. She could relate to those feelings, so she made sure to supply Callie with plenty of Ben & Jerry's and took her out for some retail therapy.

The doorbell interrupted her thoughts. It was late afternoon, so it was too early for her father to be home. She walked downstairs and peered into the peephole on the front door. In excitement she threw the door open and launched herself into his arms. Conall spun her around before kissing her thoroughly then a crazy thought dawned on her and she pulled back. "Wait a minute, how do I know it's really you and not Casimir in disguise?"

"Ask me something only I would know," he suggested.

"Okay, what was the first nickname I gave you?" She couldn't recall using that one anywhere Casimir could have overheard it.

He grinned widely. "You called me Spock because of the pointed ears," he replied, tapping his ears, and then he held up his hand in the 'live long and prosper' sign like she had done to him that first night. She squealed and threw herself back into his arms.

"So, how long do I get to keep you?" she asked.

"Well, funny thing about that…" he began before tugging her inside. "Let's go sit. I've got a great story to tell you." He told her everything that had happened when he brought Casimir back to the king, including his reassignment and the fact that he would now be living just down the street from her.

"But…why would he do that?" Her biological father's actions were contradictory to everything she knew about him—but then she remembered that her mother was a kind, smart, and compassionate woman. In order for her to have fallen in love with Corydon, there had to have once been some good in him. He had to have been capable of love. She longed to discover what kind of man he used to be, and if it were possible for him to become that man again.

"Because he loves you, my flower. Your father loves you. He was worried sick about you when you escaped your guard. You should have seen him—I've never seen him so distraught in all my years of service, and I don't blame him. I mean, look at Torin, Maddock, and Evin— shoot, you even got the Seelie king to let you go because he cared about you. You have that effect on people. You inspire their love and devotion."

She smiled. "I suppose you're right. I am pretty awesome."

He snickered. "That you are, that you are." He leaned over and kissed her on the forehead.

"So, you're going to be living just down the street. What will you do during the day when I'm at school?"

"I was thinking I'd enroll at your school too."

His response made her double over with laughter. She laughed so hard she cried, and then she thought of Callie's expression if he showed up at their school and laughed all over again.

"Does that mean you'll go with me wherever I go? To my aunt's house to visit? To college?"

"If you'll have me. Otherwise I can just watch you from a distance."

She punched him lightly on his arm. "Of course I'll have you, you goof. I love you."

"I love you too," he said before kissing her senseless until they heard her father come home.

Ianthe was amazed at how everything seemed to be falling into place. She knew her future would still be full of obstacles with her developing powers and Unseelie heritage, but she felt ready to face whatever came her way with her friends and family by her side. It was truly more than she could've hoped for. Her once lonely and empty life was now filled with love.

# ACKNOWLEDGEMENTS

I originally wrote Ianthe and Conall's story as a stand-alone. It wasn't until one of my dear friends and beta readers, Callie Vestal, told me she hated the ending because she wanted more that I wrote more. So, Callie—thank you. Thank you for seeing what I did not, that this world I have built has more stories to tell. (Oh, and those pretty purple pigs are most definitely flying.)

Next I'd like to thank my husband, Hassan Shahriary. Your support and encouragement have helped me achieve more than I thought possible. I'm a better person because of you. Thank you for pushing me and being my number one fan.

My other betas: Tonya Shaw, Haley Wolf, and Kristann Monaghan—thank you for being my sounding board and helping me mold Exile into the best version it could be.

My Book Swap girls (and Cody)—you are my tribe. Your support, encouragement, and advice always amazes me. I am so honored to be a part of such a caring group of assholes. Love you all!

M.E. Carter, Sara Ney, Rachel Schneider, Andee Michelle, Teagan Hunter, Shirl Rickman, Dawn Chiletz, Stacey Grice, and my minxes—you brilliant authors. Thank you for welcoming me to the club with open arms. You guys have been incredibly helpful with all things book and promotion related. Seriously, many days you are my sanity in this crazy world.

Murphy Rae—your creativity is always appreciated. You design one mean cover, my friend (and by mean I mean gorgeous, of course).

Caitlin—you're the best editor a girl could ask for! Thank you for helping to make Exile the best it could be.

Alyssa at Uplifting Designs—thank you for making the interior of my books just as gorgeous at the exterior.

To my dear family and friends (including Momma Peggy and my school staff, past and present)—thank you for all of your love and support. Knowing so many people have faith in me is a powerful thing.

To my students—always keep reading!

And finally, to you, my readers—thank you. Thank you for picking up my books and giving me a chance. Thank you for your sweet notes, comments, and support. This is definitely not the end, so stay tuned for more in the Fae Realm series.

# ABOUT THE AUTHOR

Cathlin Shahriary lives in North Texas with her husband, cats and dog. By day she is an elementary school teacher, nurturing future book nerds and writers. By night (and weekends and summers), she is an avid reader, cat fosterer, and writer. You can also find her fangirling over books, authors, and TV shows (like *Supernatural, Dr. Who*, and *The Walking Dead*, to name a few). She still believes in the existence of magic and the power of love.

*Turn to the next page to see a sneak preview of the next book in the Fae Realm series.*

# SACRIFICE

The following is an excerpt from Sacrifice, a prequel to Fate, Cathlin Shahriary's next book in the Fae Realm series.

# PROLOGUE

AYANNA RESTED HER hand over her belly, knowing she wouldn't be able to hide the truth much longer. Either a slightly protruding baby bump or someone's Fae magic would reveal the secret she was hiding, and she had to escape now before it was too late.

As much as she loved Corydon, she didn't love the man he had become since assuming his father's seat on the Unseelie throne. The power, responsibility, and need to be the uncontested Unseelie king were all changing him. He was no longer the man she had first met and fallen in love with two years ago. Had it really been so long? It felt like she had only been there a couple months, but she sighed knowing a few months could equal a year back home. She knew her birthday had mostly likely come and gone in the time she'd stayed; she could very well have been nineteen already and not even known it. Nineteen and soon to be a mother—too young. She focused her thoughts on her baby, using her love and protectiveness to fuel her determination.

She rubbed her hand against her flat stomach. "Don't worry, my precious baby, your mommy will protect you. I will do whatever I have to do to keep you safe. I'm sorry you will never know your true father, but trust me, this is for the best."

She dressed quickly and started braiding her golden blonde hair. She was glad now, more than ever, that Alvina had listened when she insisted she didn't need anyone to help her dress anymore. If that woman ever found out... She shuddered to think of it. Alvina would probably insist it would be better if the baby were raised by a pure Unseelie like herself, and Ayanna couldn't let that happen. She would die before she let anyone take her baby away. She slipped the knife she had smuggled from the kitchen into her right boot then plucked her necklace off the vanity, the midnight blue one he had first given her. She carefully put it on, tucking it underneath her tunic. It made it easier to leave knowing she still had a piece of him with her, something that might help protect her. She checked her pack to make sure she had all the necessities and quietly closed the door. Tiptoeing her way through the castle, she hoped her plan would work and she and her baby would soon be free.

Made in the USA
Columbia, SC
05 August 2024

39476958R00181